MORE PRAISE FOR ELAINE BARBIERI!

TO MEET AGAIN

"Elaine Barbieri certainly knows how to capture the reader's attention. Utterly delightful characters, tender romance, and plenty of harrowing adventures make for a splendid Western."

—*Romantic Times*

NIGHT RAVEN

"A fast-paced page-turner, *Night Raven* will keep you up all night until you get to the satisfying end."

—*Romantic Times*

EAGLE

"The situation is explosive! Ms. Barbieri knows how to pull you through an emotional knothole. Her characters are terrific!"

—*The Belles and Beaux of Romance*

WISHES ON THE WIND

"…Skillful…vivifying…!"

—*Publishers Weekly*

WINGS OF A DOVE

"…Will bring out every hope and dream you could have…run to the nearest bookstore and find this five-star book!"

—*Bell, Book and Candle*

IRON HAWK

"Is that why you gave yourself to me, Eden . . . so I'd let you go and you could return to your son?"

"No, I—"

"—because you thought I wouldn't be able to refuse you anything once I had held you in my arms again?"

"Let me go, Kyle."

"Tell me some of your beautiful lies, Eden." Kyle clutched her tighter. "I want to hear them. Tell me that you loved me once, and could love me again. Tell me you want to forget the past as if it never happened. Tell me your sighs were sincere when I sank myself inside you, and that you want me now, more than you ever did before. Tell me, Eden . . . tell me what you think I want to hear."

"Kyle, please . . . let me go."

"It might've worked, you know, but you made one mistake." His eyes holding her, he whispered, "You see, you were depending on *Kyle* to believe you . . . but Kyle's dead. He died in chains, a long time ago. The man who holds you now is Iron Hawk. *Iron Hawk*, Eden! Say it!"

HAWK

Elaine Barbieri

LEISURE BOOKS   NEW YORK CITY

To Holly, Siobhan, and Mike.
I love you, my darlings.

A LEISURE BOOK ®

January 2005

Published by

Dorchester Publishing Co., Inc.
200 Madison Avenue
New York, NY 10016

ISBN 0-8439-4646-6

Visit us on the web at www.dorchesterpub.com.

Chapter One

1845

"I love you, Kyle."

Eden's unsteady whisper reverberated in the silence.

A warm breeze rustled the wooded copse, stirring the heavy spring air. Sunlight filtering through the leafy cover overhead danced against Kyle's sober expression as his dark eyes perused her face. He made no reply.

Eden stared at Kyle's mouth. Moments earlier, those lips had moved passionately against hers. They had tormented her with loving worship, uttering ragged endearments as Kyle clutched her close.

Now his lips were tight.

"Kyle . . ."

Golden shafts of light glinted on the raven sheen of Kyle's hair, flickering against taut, sun-darkened skin and chiseled features. Eden had somehow known the moment she first saw him that she would love him, but the courage to speak the words had come slowly.

The silence stretched unmercifully long.

"This wasn't supposed to happen, you know that, don't you, Eden?"

Startled at Kyle's response, Eden drew back from him. "I don't know what you mean."

"Yes, you do."

Eden's cheeks flushed hot. "What are you tryin' to tell me—that you're sorry we ever met?"

"No."

"What are you sayin', then?"

"I'm saying that you weren't supposed to love me."

"Kyle . . ."

"And I wasn't supposed to love you."

Abruptly crushing her close, Kyle covered her mouth with his. His body was tight and strong, supporting her, and Eden surrendered to the myriad sensations assailing her as his kiss deepened. She hadn't believed it was possible to love anyone the way she loved Kyle. She didn't care what anyone said about her youth, about the differences between them, about any of the meaningless obstacles others sought to raise between them.

Kyle groaned softly as he tore his mouth from hers. The sound was imbued with bittersweet pain, with a shuddering yearning she shared.

Kyle stroked her cheek, her shoulder. He brushed the line of her jaw with his lips. Finding the hollow at the base of her throat, he explored it with gentle kisses, with a tenderness that set her heart pounding. His mouth found the rise of sweet flesh beneath, and he—

"Let go of her, you bastard!"

The furious shout shattered the moment, turning Eden toward the sound of her father's voice. She gasped at the rage that darkened Tom Richards's face, her eyes widening at the sight of his drawn gun as he ordered, "Get away from him, Eden!"

"No!"

"Do what your father says, Eden."

Protesting when Kyle attempted to put distance between them, Eden turned back toward her father with growing panic. "Put the gun down, Pa!"

"I told you to get away from him!"

"I won't!" Stubbornly clinging to Kyle, Eden rasped, "What's the matter with you, Pa? Kyle hasn't done anythin' wrong."

Richards addressed Kyle with chilling coldness. "Get away from my daughter now, or I'll shoot you dead where you stand."

Slipping in front of Kyle, Eden shielded him with her body, responding, "If you shoot him, you'll have to shoot me, too!"

Richards's face twisted with fury. "If that's the way you want it."

"Pa!"

His gaze scathing, her father hissed, "How can you stand to let him to touch you, Eden? He's an *Injun!*"

The heat of Tom Richards's hatred scorched Kyle. He had seen that same hatred on too many faces since stepping down from the train onto Texas soil months earlier, but he had never seen it glare with such deadly intent.

Outraged, Kyle responded, "That's right, I'm an Indian. I know you'll be surprised to hear me say that I'm proud to be one."

"Mongrel coward! Hiding behind a woman's skirts—that's all you're good for!"

"I'm not a coward, Mr. Richards, and I'm a *full-blooded* Kiowa."

"Bastard! You're goin' to be a *dead* Kiowa!"

Eden shuddered and Kyle grated, "Move away from me, Eden."

Holding onto him with all her strength, Eden rasped, "No, I won't! He'll kill you if I do!"

"Get away from him, Eden!"

Pushing Eden aside unexpectedly, Kyle leaped at her father.

A gunshot barked!

Thrust backwards by the impact of the bullet that struck him, Kyle hit the ground with jarring force.

"Kyle!"

Strangely numbed, Kyle struggled to steady the reeling world around him. Darkness rose and fell in alternating waves, allowing only brief glimpses of Eden's tear-streaked face as she leaned over him.

Voices echoed in his ears as if from a distance.

"Kyle . . . Kyle, are you all right? Please answer me!"

"Get away from him, Eden!"

"You shot him!"

"He's only grazed."

"He needs a doctor!"

"We're goin' home."

"I can't leave him. He'll die!"

"No, he won't. Redskins know how to take care of themselves."

Contempt filled Eden's tone. "Get away from me, Pa!"

"Let's go!"

"I won't leave him!"

"You'll leave him, all right, or I'll put a bullet through his head right now!"

"You wouldn't!"

"You think I won't?"

"Pa, please . . ."

"No redskin's goin' to make a squaw out of my daughter!"

Kyle glimpsed a gun barrel close to his face.

"No, Pa, don't! I'll go with you." The sound of a sob. "Kyle, please . . . please forgive me."

Footsteps retreating.

I love you, Kyle.

The darkness pounded with pain.

Please forgive me.

The throbbing would not cease.

Kyle raised an unsteady hand to his head. He

groaned, his hand coming away from his temple wet with blood. The ground was hard underneath him and night sounds surrounded him. An occasional firefly lit a darkness relieved only by pale rays of moonlight filtering through the undulating leaves above.

Yes, he remembered.

No redskin's goin' to make a squaw *out of my daughter!*

Gradually pulling himself to a sitting position, Kyle fought to hold himself erect. The events of that afternoon whirled in his mind, but one fact emerged with full clarity. The bullet that grazed him had not been intended to miss.

On his feet at last, Kyle walked unsteadily toward the tree where his horse was tied. He mounted.

Uncertain of the passage of time, Kyle struggled to remain in the saddle as his mount moved steadily forward. He did not see the Kiowa village when it came into view. He did not hear the horses approaching, nor did he see the tight expressions of the men who took his mount's reins. He felt only the strong hands that handed him down to the softness of a sleeping bench before he knew no more.

"Let me out of here, Pa!"

Eden pounded at the locked door of her room. Hoarse from hours of fruitless entreaty, she pleaded again, "Please . . . please let me out!"

14

No response.

Desperate, Eden was suddenly silent. She hadn't had a choice when she'd left Kyle lying unconscious and bleeding where he had fallen. In the time since, she had tried to reason with her father. She had attempted to explain that Kyle wasn't like the Indians who killed her mother, that he was no more of a savage than she was, but he wouldn't listen!

Eden stared at the moonlight slanting through the wooden slats her father had ordered nailed across her window. She had watched with incredulity as the boards were added, one by one, making her prisoner in her own home. She had implored her father to relent, but he remained deaf to her entreaties.

While Kyle lay wounded and alone.

That thought snapped the last thread of her control, and Eden ran to the window in a new frenzy. A sob escaped her throat as she picked up a chair and smashed it against the pane. Paying no heed to the glass that shattered around her, she swung the chair against the wooden bars again and again.

Breathless, Eden turned at the sound of the door opening behind her. The frigid contempt in her father's gaze halted her, holding her immobile for a long moment before he pulled the door closed again without speaking a word.

Eden swallowed as the key turned in the lock. She looked at the broken chair in her hands and at the wooden bars still fixed unyieldingly in place.

Suddenly sobbing in earnest, Eden sank to her knees.

A dog barking . . . a voice chanting in guttural tones . . . the pungent scent of herbs . . .

Kyle awakened gradually to a rhythmic rattling near his ear and the vibration of ritual steps pounding the earth beside him. He glimpsed White Horn's lined face through the smoky mist as the aged shaman turned slowly toward him. He waited, his eyes drifting briefly closed as the man brought his healing song to an end and came to crouch beside him.

White Horn addressed Kyle softly in their native tongue.

"I have driven out the evil spirits of the white man's bullet, Young Hawk. You will soon be well."

Young Hawk. Shadowed images of his childhood flashed again through Kyle's mind at the sound of his Kiowa name spoken in a language he had not heard during the many years he was away. The language had returned with surprising ease to his tongue, stirring memories that rapidly eliminated his initial strangeness upon returning, memories that revived a pride in the ways of his people that was as instinctive as each breath he breathed.

Kyle struggled to focus as White Horn spoke again.

"The mark of the white man's bullet will remain, and that is good. It is a lesson well learned, now that you have returned. It will remind you of the white man's hatred of your Kiowa blood, and the deception he practices."

Kyle studied White Horn's figure as it loomed over him. He saw an old man with sun-darkened, leathery skin, with strong features deeply ridged by time, and gray hair adorned with a single eagle feather hanging limply against narrow, rounded shoulders. He saw an old man who was physically weak, but who was nonetheless powerful.

White Horn's harsh words stirred a familiar uneasiness. Kyle remembered that Asa and Henrietta Webster's skin had been pale and their voices softly cultured. He remembered that when those two good people rescued him from the soldiers—a wounded Kiowa boy of eleven who was orphaned and near death—they brought him back East and raised him as their own. Their love remained constant, and when they died within months of each other, they left him all they owned.

Responding hoarsely to White Horn, Kyle rasped, "How did I get here?"

"You were delivered by a destiny that would not be denied."

Kyle's foggy mind considered that cryptic reply. Of course—his Indian pony had returned to camp.

White Horn scrutinized Kyle closely.

"You do not fully accept the path your Kiowa heart seeks, Young Hawk! You clothe yourself as a white man. You speak as a white man. You *think* as a white man—but you are Kiowa!" His gaze grew intense. "You have learned little from your close encounter with death. You refuse to accept that the white woman will not be yours."

"The white woman?"

"I have seen her in the smoke. Her hair shines like the sun and her eyes are light. Her arms cling to you and your heart answers, but she will not be yours."

Suddenly angry, Kyle rasped, "You're wrong!"

White Horn stood up abruptly. "Wisdom is silent when anger speaks."

Watching as the shaman left the tepee, Kyle cursed his lapse. White Horn had suffered much and his memories were bitter. Kyle could not fault the aged shaman for his beliefs, especially now, when he lay wounded from Tom Richards's bullet.

The woman will not be yours.

White Horn said he had seen Eden in the smoke. Kyle did not doubt that was true. Years spent in the white man's culture had not affected his belief in the powers of his people's shamans—but this time, he would prove White Horn mistaken.

The pounding in his head returned with new vengeance, forcing his eyes closed. In the uneasy darkness he saw himself disembarking from the train the first day he saw Eden. Somehow, he had not anticipated the hostility his appearance would raise when he stepped down onto Texas soil dressed in the well-tailored, Eastern clothing he was accustomed to wearing as the adopted son of Asa and Henrietta Webster. Nor had he expected the jeers he would hear as he walked down the main street of town.

Hell, looks like that Injun thinks he's a white man!

Where'd you steal them clothes, Injun?

Got a haircut, did you? Well, you still don't look like a white man!

Then a voice that snarled with true hatred.

Tryin' to look like a white man ain't goin' to make you live any longer, Injun.

The threat in that last statement had snapped his head toward a man with graying red hair who stood in a doorway a few feet away. He saw Eden then. She was standing beside her father, frowning her disapproval of his comment. He had known the moment her gaze met his that he would one day hold her in his arms.

The sound of a gunshot reverberated in his mind.

Kyle . . . are you all right? Answer me!

He had not been able to respond.

Forgive me, Kyle . . . please, please forgive me.

Eden's sobs . . . her footsteps retreating.

I love you, Kyle.

Agitation prickled up Kyle's spine. Eden's father couldn't see past his hatred. There was no telling what the man would do. Kyle needed to get back to Eden, to make sure she was all right. He needed to tell her he loved her, that he would protect her with his life, and that no one would ever separate them again.

Kyle forced his eyes open. He shrugged off

the dizziness that set the world reeling as he struggled to sit. He ignored the nausea that filled his throat with bile when he stood up. He took one step . . . then another.

Kyle's third step never touched the ground that opened up suddenly to swallow him.

Chapter Two

Eden awoke slowly to the bright sunlight of morning. Disoriented, she looked around her. She was fully clothed, lying on the floor of her room. Shattered glass littered the space around her.

Reality returned abruptly, and Eden gasped aloud. It was morning. She had fallen asleep!

Kyle . . .

Desperate, Eden scanned the room. Her gaze stopped at the tray lying on the floor beside the door. Someone had brought her food while she slept. Did her father intend to continue keeping her a prisoner?

Jumping to her feet, Eden ran to the door and turned the knob.

Locked.

Oh, God!

"Eden."

Eden turned toward the sound of a deep voice at her window.

"Eden, are you all right?"

"Witt, is that you?"

Eden raced to the window and squinted out through the wooden slats. Relieved when familiar brown eyes looked back at her, she pleaded, "Witt, get me out of here, please!"

"You know I can't do that, Eden." The fair-haired wrangler's gaze was sober. "I ain't never seen your pa so mad. If he knew I was talkin' to you now, he'd run me off this spread for good."

"Please, Witt. I have to get out!"

"I can't help you, Eden."

"Witt, please . . ." Reaching through the narrow slit, Eden wound her fingers around Witt's where he rested his hand against the wood. He made no attempt to withdraw from her touch as she pleaded, "I need your help. *Kyle* needs your help."

Witt snatched back his hand. "I ain't helpin' no Injun!"

Eden took a ragged breath. Her father's hatred had even infected Witt—who was her friend and who never refused anything she asked.

Eden studied Witt's expression anxiously. His lips were tight. She knew that look. He'd leave in a minute, and her only chance would go with him.

Witt's lips twitched. "I just wanted to see if there was anythin' you needed."

"I need to get out of here, Witt."

"No."

"Where's my father?"

"Him and the rest of the boys rode out to the north section this mornin' to do some brandin'. He left me here to look after things."

"To see that I didn't get out, you mean!" Eden frowned, then asked, "Why did he pick you to stay behind?"

"Because my horse went lame."

"Buster went lame?"

Witt averted his gaze. "Temporarily . . . with a little help."

Eden gave a choked laugh that snapped Witt's eyes back toward her. Her voice was tremulous. "Please, unlock the door, Witt."

"Don't keep beggin' me to let you out! Hell, you know there ain't nothin' I wouldn't do for you—except this."

"Please."

"Damn it, Eden, what's the matter with you? That Injun dresses like a white man and talks like a white man, but he ain't a white man—and his name ain't Kyle! His name's Young Hawk. For all his education and big talk about where he's been and what he wants to do, he's just an Injun like the rest of them savages. The first thing he did when he came back here was to ride out to find that damned Injun camp. Nobody knew where it was, but he found it. And when he did, they welcomed him with open arms. He's a Kiowa and he'll always be a

Kiowa—one of them same Injuns who killed
your ma."

"Kyle didn't kill my mother."

"No, but his *pa* probably did!"

"Don't say that, Witt!"

"Why? It's the truth."

"Even if it was the truth, that still wouldn't
give my father the right to shoot Kyle."

"Nobody around here gives a damn that he
shot that Injun!"

"I do."

Eden was unaware of the tear that slipped
down her cheek until Witt rasped, "Don't cry,
Eden. I don't want to see you cry."

Eden responded hoarsely, "You know my father, Witt. He won't let anythin' that happened
between him and me affect the workday on this
ranch. He won't be back until sundown. We
have more than enough time to look for Kyle
without my father ever knowin'. I just need to
be sure Kyle's all right—that he's not still lyin'
where he fell. I promise . . . I promise that if you
help me, I'll come right back here and let you
lock me up again so my pa won't ever know."

"He'd know."

"No, he won't! Doc Bitters will help us if we
need him, and he won't tell Pa. He knows how
things are. He's been livin' with a squaw for ten
years."

"Your pa hates Doc Bitters."

"That's all the better, isn't it?"

Witt shook his head doubtfully. "Somebody's
bound to find out."

"Nobody will. Please, Witt." Pausing when her throat choked tight, Eden continued hoarsely, "I won't be able to live with myself if anything happens to Kyle because of me. I won't be able to live with my pa, either. I'd have to go away somewhere . . . do somethin' . . ."

"Don't talk crazy."

"I mean it!" Eden's voice cracked. "I never meant anythin' more."

"Eden . . ."

"Please."

Witt's gold brows knit in a frown. She held her breath.

"Do you give me your word you'll let me lock you up again before your pa gets back?"

"Yes."

"I'm trustin' you, Eden."

"I promise."

Eden turned toward the door when Witt disappeared from sight. Her heart started pounding at the sound of heavy footsteps approaching in the hallway. The key turned in the lock and she sobbed aloud.

Rushing forward when the door opened, Eden threw her arms around Witt and hugged him tight. She was hardly conscious of his arms closing around her in return when she drew back and said, "Let's go."

Kyle closed his eyes against the bright morning light streaming into the tepee. He touched his forehead. The wound was still seeping blood.

25

"Only a fool would risk his life for a white woman!"

Kyle's eyes flew open at the sound of the familiar deep voice. Lone Bear stood beside the sleeping bench, his face dark with condemnation.

His thoughts still unclear, Kyle stared at his father's brother for silent moments. Strangely, he had recognized his uncle the moment he saw him, despite the many years he had been away. The raven black color of Lone Bear's hair was streaked with gray and his strong features had thickened with age, but the nobility of brow that Lone Bear and his father shared had not been altered by time. Nor had the proud set of his shoulders changed, nor the powerful muscular tone that set him apart from other warriors. As a child Kyle had wanted nothing more than to earn the respect of those two great warriors and to be like Gray Hawk and Lone Bear in every way. Despite the years he had spent apart from them, those feelings had not changed.

Lone Bear crouched beside him unexpectedly. His anger apparent, he hissed, "The white man sheds your blood as he shed your father's. His bullet did not reach its mark and you were spared, but you have learned little. You cast White Horn's words aside. You refuse to accept the wisdom he would share."

"I respect White Horn's visions." Struggling to contain the throbbing in his head, Kyle continued gruffly, "But I don't share the malice he feels toward all white men."

Lone Bear's expression tightened. "Yet you lie wounded by a white man's bullet."

"A white man who couldn't control his hatred!"

"One of many! Peace with the white man can come only with victory!" Lone Bear's expression turned to fury. "Your father was a brave warrior. Gray Hawk knew no fear in battle, and his judgment was sound when leading his people. I was proud that his blood flowed in me as well, and when that blood was shed, I mourned his loss. When our village was burned by the soldiers and you were taken, I mourned your loss with even greater grief, because I believed I had lost my brother forever."

Lone Bear continued with great emotion, "Then you came back to us, and my joy was unmatched. So similar was your appearance to that of Gray Hawk, even the white man's clothes you wore could not disguise it. You spoke with your father's voice. You walked with your father's step. You rode with your father's ease. And in your eyes I saw reflected your father's keen mind—a mind that could lead the Kiowa to triumph over the white man at last."

Lone Bear's lips twisted into a sneer. "But what do I see before me now? The strength inherited from your father has been sapped by the white man's bullet, and the keenness of mind which was Gray Hawk's legacy to you is clouded with thoughts of a woman who can never be yours."

"Eden *will* be mine."

"Young Hawk is a fool as his father never was!"

The contempt in Lone Bear's gaze slashed deeply. Kyle responded to it softly, "It's not my intention to anger you, Lone Bear. My respect for you and for White Horn is great, but I've lived among the white man for many years. I've attended the white man's school in Washington, where the Great White Father speaks and his people listen."

"The Great White Father speaks, but his people *here* do not listen."

"I could help change that."

"A *dead* man can do nothing!"

"My wound is slight. I'll soon be well."

"Hear my words." Lone Bear's tone deepened with warning. "I know this man, Thomas Richards. He will not give up his daughter to one of our people. Rather than see her in the arms of a Kiowa, he would put a bullet through her heart."

"I won't let that happen!"

"There is only one way you could stop him. In doing so, you would put all in jeopardy . . . *for a woman.*"

Allowing the silence that followed to speak his contempt more eloquently than words, Lone Bear then turned and left the tepee as abruptly as he had come.

* * *

Her heart pounding as the familiar wooded copse came into view on the horizon, Eden forced her laboring mount to a faster pace. She glanced at Witt Bradley, who rode beside her. The wrangler's hat was pulled low on his forehead, accenting the boyish profile that drew so many teasing comments from the other hands. But Eden had never been misled by his youthful appearance. Witt was older than she and mature beyond his years. He had proved his friendship to her in countless ways in the past, but he had never proved it more positively than he did at that moment.

Her throat tight, Eden clung to her rapidly waning composure as they reached the bank of trees. She reined up, hearing Witt's step behind her as she dismounted and ran into the clearing where she had left Kyle. She halted abruptly. The clearing was empty.

"This is where he fell, but he's gone." Crouching down, Eden ran her hand over the ground. She drew back with a gasp when her hand touched a spot still sticky with blood. She turned toward Witt in sudden panic. "We have to find him!"

"Your pa said he only grazed him. That means he's probably back in town right now, leanin' up against the bar in the Silver Dollar, regrettin' the day he first saw you and your pa."

"Kyle wouldn't do that!"

Anger flashed in Witt's sober eyes. "Maybe you're givin' that Injun more credit than he deserves."

29

"Witt, please." Her gaze frantic, Eden glanced around the clearing. "He was bleedin'. He might've gotten up and wandered off. He could be lyin' somewhere, helpless."

"Where was his horse tied?"

On her feet in a moment, Eden ran into the dense undergrowth nearby. She turned at the sound of Witt's step behind her. "His horse is gone."

"Doesn't that tell you somethin', Eden?"

Suddenly angry, Eden rasped, "No, it doesn't!"

Staring at her for silent moments, Witt grated, "All right. I'll help you look for him."

Struggling against tears, Eden turned away. Again in control, she replied, "Thank you, Witt," then waded into the brush.

Afternoon was waning.

Kyle stared up at the bright patch of sky visible through the tepee's smoke hole. That particular patch of sky had become all too familiar to him as the morning hours waned and he slipped in and out of consciousness. The dizziness and pain would not relent. It galled him that he was so effectively incapacitated, and that each attempt he made to overcome his debility resulted in a greater disaster than the last.

Kyle's anxiety deepened.

Rather than see his daughter in the arms of a Kiowa, he would put a bullet through her heart.

Eden was Richards's only child. He wouldn't hurt her.

If you shoot him, Pa, you'll have to shoot me, too.

If that's the way you want it.

No!

Kyle closed his eyes against the nausea assaulting him. He needed to remain calm. Agitation increased his physical distress. He would be on his feet tomorrow and he'd go to Eden then. He would tell her that he'd been wrong when he said she wasn't supposed to love him, and he wasn't supposed to love her.

Their love was right.

And it was forever.

He'd tell Eden that . . . tomorrow.

The twilight shadows deepened.

Eden looked out through the barred window of her room. She stared at the stars just beginning to twinkle in the darkening sky, her heart a dead weight within. Witt and she had searched every inch of the area surrounding the spot where her father and she had left Kyle. They found a blood-smeared branch that Kyle had evidently used for support when he hoisted himself up onto his mount, but they were unable to follow his horse's tracks on the hard-packed ground.

A fruitless search of the surrounding area had followed. Doc Bitters hadn't seen him. Witt's cautious inquiries at nearby ranches had turned up nothing. No one in town had seen him. When afternoon waned and there was nowhere left to search, Eden had attempted to convince herself that Kyle had found a safe haven where he was recuperating from his wound.

She had prayed it was the truth, and had then turned back to the ranch to keep her promise to Witt.

Despondent, she had gone immediately to her room. When she turned around to see Witt standing in the doorway behind her with the key in his hand, his expression as downcast as her own, she had walked into his arms and given full vent to her tears.

Holding her until she was again in control of her emotions, Witt had then locked the door behind him and left to settle the horses in the barn. Within the hour, her father and the ranch hands had appeared in the distance.

Her father had not spoken a word to her when he unlocked the door of her room upon his return. She had remained as silent as he when he stood briefly in the opening, and she had then watched as he drew the door closed behind him. The click of the lock had said it all.

Tom Richards's heavy footsteps in the hallway beyond her bedroom door interrupted Eden's thoughts. His footsteps faded and the outer door of the house banged shut. Eden was not surprised that her father made no attempt to talk to her. He had made it plain that the shedding of Kyle's blood meant nothing to him at all. She had made it just as plain that if anything happened to Kyle, she would never forgive him.

Eden stifled the rise of tears. Kyle was all

right. She would know, somehow, if he wasn't. She would wait. When he was able, he would come to her.

Eden closed her eyes. Oh, God . . . he had to.

"What're you doin', Witt?"

Halting the brush in mid-stroke on his horse's back, Witt turned toward the sound of Tom Richards's voice behind him. The barn stall held the same peculiar tension between Richards and himself that he had sensed since the older man's return.

Witt studied his employer cautiously before replying. Tom Richards was a hard man, but it had been a difficult day for him. Witt knew that however harshly Richards had treated Eden, the rancher loved his daughter and was not as unaffected by her distress as he would have everyone believe. But he also knew that Richards's love for Eden was rivaled only by his hatred of the Indians—and that sooner or later, something would have to give.

Witt's jaw hardened as he silently acknowledged that it had been a difficult day for himself, too. He had ridden beside Eden for endless miles while they had searched for that damned redskin. He had recognized the chance he was taking by helping her, but he had also known he couldn't stand by while she was suffering.

Still, Eden's misery had infected him with a misery of his own. Hating that Injun bastard more with every mile they covered, he had spent the day alternating between wanting to shake Eden to within an inch of her life, and wanting to console her with all the love in his heart.

Yes, he loved Eden. Hell, he had loved her forever! He had loved her as the boss's gangling young daughter with the impish grin, and he loved her as the beautiful woman she had grown to be. When he told her that there was nothing he wouldn't do for her, he meant every word—which included helping her find the man she loved instead of him.

He was a fool for Eden Richards. He knew it and accepted it, but her pa was waiting for his reply and he couldn't help wondering what the man was thinking.

Responding with affected ease to Richards's question, Witt shrugged. "What am I doin'? I'm just makin' sure Buster will be all right to ride out tomorrow. It wasn't nothin' but a bad shoe that had him limpin'. I fixed it, and he's as good as new."

Richards's answering laugh crawled up Witt's spine. The older man walked closer, his gaze knowing.

"You ain't foolin' nobody, you know."

"What're you talkin' about, boss?"

"You know what I'm talkin' about. There was nothin' wrong with your horse this mornin', and there's nothin' wrong with him now." Richards advanced another step. "You let Eden out of her room while me and the boys were gone, didn't you? And you took her out to look for that Injun, too."

Silent for a long moment, Witt responded, "That's right, I did."

"I knew you would."

"You knew—"

"That's right. Hell, I ain't blind! Every man on this ranch knows how you feel about Eden, even if she don't!"

Not bothering with a denial, Witt snapped back, "If you knew I was goin' to let her out, why did you leave me behind to watch her?"

"Because I knew you wouldn't be able to turn her down."

"You wanted me to take her out to look for that Injun?"

"That's right." Richards's jaw twitched. "You think I don't know my daughter? Eden's so damned stubborn that there's no way she'd let up until she satisfied herself that the bastard wasn't lyin' dead where we left him."

"You took a pretty big chance, didn't you? What if he *was* dead when we got there?"

"I wasn't about to let that happen."

"Meanin'?"

"Meanin' me and the boys went back there this mornin' . . . before you and Eden did."

"What did you do with him?"

"I didn't do nothin'. The bastard wasn't there."

"Wasn't there?" Witt frowned. "So that means he's all right."

"Maybe."

"What do you mean, maybe? Eden and me couldn't find him nowhere."

"My shot hit him hard. There's no way he just got up and rode off."

"He got up on his horse, all right. That much Eden and me did figure out."

"He might've gotten on that horse, but he didn't get far. He's out there, all right, lyin' under some brush somewhere with the flies makin' a banquet out of him right now."

"Damn it, boss!"

"Damn *him*, you mean!" Richards shuddered with sudden fury. "If you think I'm one bit sorry I shot him, you're wrong. There's no way I'd let Eden hook up with a redskin like the one that killed her mother—not while there's a breath in my body!"

Drawing back as he struggled for control, Richards continued more slowly, "But Eden's my daughter, even if she is behavin' like a damned fool. I don't like seein' her suffer, and I figured with her trustin' you the way she does and you feelin' the way you do, you were the right person to leave her with. You got a common bond between you two now. She's goin' to wait for the Injun to come for her, and when he never shows, it seems to me she just might turn in your direction."

Witt didn't respond.

"Don't make like that wouldn't suit you fine!"

Witt bristled. "I want to make somethin' clear. I don't like that Injun bastard no more than you do, but boss or not, I'm not goin' to let

36

you use me a second time like you did today."

"You're not, huh?"

"That's right!"

"I suppose you're goin' to tell Eden everythin'."

"No. I ain't."

"Smart fella."

"That's right, I'm smart . . . too smart to have Eden thinkin' that maybe I had a hand in your scheme, after all, and to have her lookin' at me the way she's lookin' at you now. And I'm tellin' you somethin' else, too."

"Yeah? What's that?"

"I'm goin' to do whatever I can to turn Eden around and make her look my way—if that redskin's dead *or* alive. I'm goin' to do that because I *want* to, for *myself* and for Eden, because I think I can make her happy."

"I think you can make her happy, too."

"Don't do me no favors!"

"You mean that?"

"I do!"

"All right. That's fine with me. Just forget we had this conversation."

Witt's jaw locked tight. "I wish to hell I could."

His jaw just as hard, Richards grated, "But before you do, I got somethin' else to tell you that you can forget or not, whatever way you want it—and it's this. I'll never let that Injun bastard have Eden."

"What're you sayin'?"

A steely-eyed glance his only response, Richards turned and strode from the stall.

Chapter Three

Three days.

Unmindful of the glorious red and gold sunset spreading across the sky, Eden walked slowly toward the barn.

Three days.

The two words drummed in her mind as she entered the shadowed interior and walked toward her horse in the rear stall. The animal whinnied at her approach, and she smiled briefly. She had awakened the morning after the futile search for Kyle and discovered that the door to her room was unlocked. She did not hesitate to contemplate her father's reason for relenting. Nor did she stop or even look his way when she strode past a breakfast table that went suddenly silent at her appearance. Instead, she went directly to the barn, where she then saddled her horse and rode out to search for Kyle.

Eden unconsciously sighed. She had done the same thing that morning, making sure to return home to eat when she would not be forced into the company of her father or the men loyal to him. Witt was the one exception. Despite his disapproval of Kyle, Witt had become her confidant because she knew he would never betray her. He had won a special place in her heart—a heart that was presently breaking.

Calico whinnied again as Eden neared the stall and reached into her pocket for the treat the mare awaited. It was the least she could do for the animal who had carried her over countless, endless miles without a trace of Kyle.

Eden fought tears. Where was Kyle? Had he found a doctor to treat his wound, or was he lying somewhere, helpless and alone?

"Eden."

Turning to Witt's concerned expression, Eden spoke the words still drumming in the back of her mind.

"It's been three days. Where is he, Witt?"

"Don't upset yourself, Eden." Walking closer, Witt attempted a smile. "You ain't been able to find him, but between you and me, your pa don't know no more than you do about where he is—which is good. If that bullet had caused real damage, somebody would've found him by now."

"If Kyle was all right, he would've contacted me somehow."

"Maybe not."

"What are you sayin'?"

"I'm sayin' that maybe he went back to his tribe."

"His tribe . . ." Eden's lips twitched. "Kyle has a loyalty to the Kiowa, but he isn't really a part of the *tribe* anymore."

"Did he say that?"

"No, he wouldn't."

"So why are *you* sayin' it?"

"Because it's true!"

"Because it's true—or because you *want* it to be true?"

Suddenly angry, Eden spat, "I thought you were my friend!"

"Why can't you get it through your head that there ain't no such man as Kyle Webster, Eden? That fella don't exist. The man you're lookin' for is Young Hawk. Your pa may hate the Injuns, but part of what he said is right. Young Hawk is a Kiowa and he'll always be a Kiowa. I'm thinkin' there's no other place he can be than at that Injun camp."

"Do you think it would bother me if he was?" Eden took a shuddering breath. "I just want him to be all right so he can come back for me!"

"And what would you do if he did?"

"What do you mean?"

"If he came back for you—would you go off and live with the Injuns and turn your back on your pa and everythin' and everybody you've ever known?"

"Kyle wouldn't want that!"

"No . . . but Young Hawk might."

Eden's throat tightened. "Why are you sayin' these things, Witt?"

"I'm tryin' to talk some sense into you."

"Some sense? What sense did my pa use when he shot Kyle? What sense is everybody on this ranch usin' when they act like nothin' happened? What sense am I supposed to use when I look at the father I loved all my life and see the person who shot the man *I* love? There's no sense to be made in any of it!"

"Yes, there is."

"Is there? How?"

"Forget that Injun! Forget him and everythin' that happened."

"Witt . . ." Eden struggled against the pain his words evoked. "You don't really think I could do that, do you? Please, tell me you don't think so little of me that you believe I could."

Witt's expression twitched. "It's because I think so much of you that I *want* you to forget him, Eden. Oh, hell, can't you see this whole thing just wasn't meant to work out? You're your pa's whole life—everythin' he's worked for! Then this Injun comes along and—"

"His name's Kyle!"

"His name ain't Kyle to your pa!"

"That's my pa's fault!"

"No, it ain't. It's the fault of all them Kiowa that butchered innocent people—includin' your ma. And it's the fault of them Kiowa who're goin' to do even more killin' before everythin' out here is settled at last."

Eden opened her mouth to reply, but the

words would not come. What was the use? She was too tired to argue anymore.

"Eden, honey . . ."

Closing the distance between them in a few steps, Witt slipped his arms comfortingly around her. The warmth of Witt's embrace choked Eden's throat even tighter as she whispered, "All I care about right now is knowin' that Kyle's all right. I'd be glad if he was with the Kiowa, as long as he was safe. I'd go to him, too . . . if I knew he was there . . . if I knew where the camp was."

"Now you're talkin' foolishness, and you know it." Witt's voice was gruff as he stroked her hair. "Even if you found the camp and he was there, there's no guarantee you'd either get in or out alive."

"They didn't hurt Kyle any of the times he went there."

"He's one of them."

"No, he isn't—not like you mean."

"He's an Injun. His blood don't change."

Angry again, Eden jerked back from Witt's embrace. "You don't give up, do you? You're like everybody else here! You don't want to see any good in Kyle!"

"I don't give a damn about *Kyle*! I told you, it's *you* I care about!"

"Well, you can stop carin' if it's going to make you talk like that!" Shaking, Eden rasped, "I've had enough of this. I don't want to talk anymore."

Eden strode toward the doorway.

"Eden, wait!"

Ignoring Witt's plea, Eden started back toward the house.

No, she wouldn't wait. There was only one man she'd wait for, and that man was Kyle.

Now he'd done it!

Witt stared at the barn's entrance where Eden has slipped from sight. Suddenly punching the stall with all his might, he ignored the mare's frightened snort and the pain that shot through his knuckles. He muttered a soft string of curses born of pure frustration.

He should've known better than to try to reason with Eden now. She was stubborn. She wouldn't back down. Not that he could really blame her for being upset, with her worrying the way she was, and with her pa and the rest of the men acting like nothing had happened at all. It was just that he couldn't think clearly when Eden was in his arms.

Hell.

Witt ran a hand through his sandy-colored hair, his spirits sinking. Eden had opened her heart to him—telling him about *the man she loved*. Couldn't she see what that did to him? How could anybody as smart as Eden be so dumb?

Witt sighed. It had felt so good to hold her in his arms, even for a little while. She had leaned against him, and it had been all he could do to stop his arms from tightening around her, from turning her face up to his and telling her flat out to forget that damned Injun and concentrate on the man who was holding her. He wanted to tell her that he could show her what it was like to really be loved, by a man who wanted to marry her and raise his children with her, who wanted to cherish her and grow old with her—by a man who could think of no more fitting end to his life than to have her face be the last one he saw before he closed his eyes forever.

He wanted her with all his heart. How could she not see how he felt?

Witt's frown tightened at the unavoidable answer to that question. Eden refused to see what she didn't *want* to see.

Yeah, he was a fool, all right.

But even a fool could see that Eden liked him . . . a lot. And she trusted him. Trust was important. He'd build on that, and when the time came, she'd turn to him.

The trouble was, he was more like Eden's pa than he wanted to admit—because, like her pa, he'd never let that Injun have her.

Another long night.

Eden twisted and turned, unable to sleep. Her angry exchange with Witt had added to her distress. Witt was her only friend—as dear to her as a brother. She hated arguing with him, but she could not seem to make him see Kyle as the man he really was.

Eden glanced at the window of her room where bright moonlight streamed through the new pane. She had returned from searching for

Kyle the previous afternoon and found the broken window fixed and the wooden bars removed. Her father had made no mention of it and neither had she. She wondered if her father considered the repaired window an overture toward reconciliation. If he did, he was wrong.

Eden's throat thickened. It would be so easy if she didn't love her father, and if she wasn't sure he loved her. Yet, he had shot Kyle, and in doing so had taken a step beyond forgiveness. She didn't know what the future held but she did know that—

Eden's thoughts halted abruptly at a sound outside her window. She caught her breath as a shadow moved across the glass. She was unable to breathe as the pane was slowly raised and a male figure slipped through the opening into her room.

Uncertain if she was dreaming, Eden sat up. The figure's broad stretch of shoulder was familiar, as were the fluid strides she recognized despite their stealth.

A silver shaft of light briefly illuminated the man's face, and Eden reached toward Kyle with a sob of pure joy.

Eden, in his arms at last!

Covering her lips with his, Kyle crushed Eden close. Savoring her warmth, he pressed his kiss deeper. Her scent, her taste, soothed the aching hunger that had gone too long unassuaged.

His emotions ragged, Kyle drew back abruptly. The brilliant blue of Eden's eyes was moist. Her cheeks were streaked with tears. Her lips quivered as she rasped his name. He whispered, "We're together again. Everything's going to be all right now, Eden."

"Kyle, I was so afraid!" Eden's trembling fingers touched the fresh scar at his temple. "I went back for you as soon as I could, but you weren't there. I didn't know what had happened to you. I couldn't find you anywhere!"

"I managed to get on my horse and it brought me back to the Kiowa village. They took care of me there until I was on my feet again."

Eden's smile was tremulous. "Witt was right."

"Witt?"

"Witt Bradley. He was the only one who helped me search for you. He said there was nowhere else you could be."

Kyle remembered Bradley—and the way Bradley looked at Eden. Kyle replied stiffly, "What else did he say?"

Eden's pause in responding revealed more than she intended before she replied, "Wouldn't you rather know what *I* said to him?" Not waiting for an answer, she continued earnestly, "I told him I didn't care where you were, just as long as you were safe, because I knew you'd come for me when you could."

Kyle held her gaze. "Are you ready to leave with me now?"

"Yes."

Elation pounded through Kyle. He had spent three tortuous days waiting to hear Eden speak that single word. He rasped, "Get dressed. Let's get out of here."

Moving to the window as Eden slipped into the shadows to dress, Kyle surveyed the yard. It was empty . . . silent. A few minutes more and he would have Eden safely away.

The taut planes of Kyle's face hardened. But this time it would be different. He had returned to the land of his birth to discover that however benign his intentions, he was the enemy to those who saw only his Kiowa heritage. And among his own people, the white man's hatred was reciprocated.

Kyle glanced back as Eden emerged from the shadows and started toward him. From the pained confusion of the past three days, hard truths had emerged. He had almost lost his life by thinking he could combat violence with reason. He could not afford to make the same mistake again. Nor would he risk losing Eden to those on either side who were unwilling to see past their hatred.

Eden reached his side and Kyle clasped her hand in his. Whatever the cost, he would not lose Eden. That was his solemn vow.

The air in the darkened bunkhouse was heavy and still.

Witt turned toward the breeze coming through the small window at the far corner of the rough dwelling, knowing it would have little effect on his discomfort. He grimaced. He didn't like to think how many years he had slept on this same cot in the company of the snoring wranglers who called the Diamond R home.

Witt surveyed the shadows surrounding him. He saw narrow bunks lining the walls, a pot-bellied stove that was the sole source of heat during the winter, a table and chairs that had seen better days, and an assortment of accoutrements piled haphazardly in the corners. He had been too cold in the winter, too hot in the summer, and damned uncomfortable during the seasons in between, all for the sake of a dream that dimmed more with each passing day.

A series of choking snorts turned Witt toward the bunk beside him. He stared at Joey Booth as the wrangler shifted in his sleep without missing a beat. The steady, even snores around him continued and Witt muttered a low curse. Nobody else seemed to have any trouble sleeping.

He needed some fresh air!

Standing up, Witt pulled on his clothes and strode toward the doorway. Grateful for the cooling breeze that met him when he stepped outside, he pulled the door closed behind him and breathed deeply.

Eden followed Kyle's lead as he drew her through the darkness toward the border of trees. She scanned the yard behind them, grateful to see no sign of movement when he halted beside two Indian ponies almost indiscernible in the shifting shadows.

His hands encircling her waist, Kyle lifted her effortlessly onto one of the animals, then mounted the other. The moon slipped from behind a cloud, briefly illuminating his face. Her heart skipped a beat when his gaze linked briefly with hers before he spurred his mount into motion.

Standing silently outside the bunkhouse, Witt inhaled the heavy night air. The breath caught in his throat as his gaze came to rest at the border of trees in the distance. The moon broke briefly through the overcast sky, and Witt stared harder. He strained to hear above the hum of night sounds as he searched the undulating shadows with his gaze.

No, it couldn't be.

Witt raced across the yard. He halted breathlessly beside Eden's open bedroom window, then lifted himself inside and strode toward the bed.

Empty!

He strode back to the window to see two mounted figures riding into the distance. The long blond hair streaming out behind the second figure was unmistakable.

A lingering incredulity held Witt immobile. The Injun bastard had come for Eden, just as she'd said he would! Fool that she was, she had actually run off with him! Didn't she realize what would happen when her pa found out? He'd go after her, and he'd shoot the first Injun he saw. Then he'd shoot every Injun he saw after that, until he finally shot the Injun he was looking for. By that time there'd be a full-fledged war, and Eden would be in the middle of it!

He couldn't let that happen!

Out in the yard again, Witt headed for the barn at a run. Eden was living in a dream world. That Injun didn't love her. If he did, he wouldn't put her life at risk when her father had already proved he was willing to use his gun to keep them apart.

He'd find them, damn it! He'd bring Eden back before her pa found out, and if that Kiowa bastard had touched her . . .

The semidarkness was eerily still as Kyle drew back on the reins, signaling a halt to their steady pace of the past hour. Grateful for a respite from their seemingly endless flight, Eden remained motionless as Kyle urged his horse a few feet ahead to a spot that allowed him a clearer view of the trail behind them.

The dim light of a crescent moon revealed a landscape that was silent and clear.

Eden breathed a relieved breath and nudged her mount to Kyle's side to say, "There's nobody followin' us. That means nobody saw us and no one will even realize I'm gone until mornin'."

Kyle made no comment.

"Where're we goin', Kyle?" When he maintained his silence, Eden urged, "Are we goin' to the Kiowa camp?"

His chiseled features sober, Kyle whispered,

"Not directly. We're heading south. The camp's to the west, near Sweet Water. I want to be certain no one's following us before we go there." Pausing, he continued more softly, "I have to go back to talk to Lone Bear before I do anything. I owe him that."

Cupping her cheek unexpectedly with his palm, Kyle leaned toward her and pressed his mouth to hers. The contact assuaged Eden's brief uncertainty. It raised a yearning so swift and deep that Eden muttered a soft protest when he drew back.

Somehow, no further explanation was necessary when Kyle turned his mount back onto the trail and spurred him forward.

He had lost them!

Witt paused to scan the shadows surrounding him. He had had no difficulty following Eden's tracks at first. Then the clouds had thickened, allowing no more than meager slivers of moonlight to illuminate a trail that had gradually disappeared on the hard-packed ground.

Witt hissed a frustrated curse. Not only had he lost the trail, he had also lost his bearings! The truth was, he had been wandering for the past half hour, so uncertain of his heading that, for all he knew, Eden and the Injun bastard were traveling in the opposite direction.

Witt rubbed his throbbing temple. In a few hours it would be morning. He had to find Eden before her pa discovered she was gone. He didn't want to consider what could happen if

Richards found them before he did, especially if that Injun decided to make a fight of it.

Witt looked up at the starless sky above him, his jaw tight. It was so damned dark! He'd never be able to pick up the trail now. He'd have to wait until morning.

With a sense of utter despair, Witt closed his eyes.

Eden's mount stumbled in the darkness, and she gasped aloud. Kyle glanced back at her as the mare righted herself, but he did not slacken his steady pace. Her mount stumbled again, and Eden was about to speak when she saw the outline of a cabin through the trees.

Dismounting beside Kyle, Eden watched as he lit the lantern hanging outside the structure with easy familiarity. She followed cautiously as he entered, seeing an interior that was primitive and sparsely furnished, but free of webs and debris.

"I found this place just after I came back to Texas," Kyle said at last. "I used it as a base while I refamiliarized myself with the area. No one knows it's here. We can rest for a few hours and go on at first light."

Eden did not respond as Kyle hung the lantern on a hook and turned toward her. The shadows flickered against the sharp contours of his face, lending an unexpected menace to his features that momentarily stole her breath. In the semilight, subtle alterations in his appearance struck her for the first time. When had he abandoned his short haircut, letting his hair grow until it hung past his ears in black, gleaming strands? When had he exchanged his Eastern clothing for the buckskin Indian garments he presently wore? When had the look in his eyes changed from keen observance to one of almost ominous intent? She was uncertain, but the result was a raw masculinity that was stunning . . . almost feral.

He's a Kiowa, and he'll always be a Kiowa.

Yes . . . that truth was suddenly clear!

As if sensing her thoughts, Kyle took a spontaneous step toward her. His dark-eyed gaze searched hers, and in that moment Eden's heart responded with another truth that was just as clear.

It made no difference whoever or whatever Kyle was. She loved him.

"Eden . . ."

Whispering her name in a tormented rasp, Kyle wrapped his arms around Eden and crushed her close. The true import of the previous few moments did not escape him. He had seen a flash of fear in Eden's eyes, then uncertainty. However briefly, she had looked at him through the eyes of a stranger. In a night of grave danger, he had tasted true fear only in those few tense moments when he thought he might lose her.

Holding her tighter still, Kyle covered her mouth with his. There were so many things he wanted to say to her now. He wanted to tell her that he had been driven by an uncertain force to return to the land of his birth, and that he had somehow sensed the first time he saw her that she was a part of himself which he had returned to seek. He wanted her to understand that he had recognized the danger and attempted to deny his feelings, but that all denial ended the moment he took her into his arms. He wanted her to know that only in her eyes was he now able to see a future which was otherwise unclear, that hope remained as long as they were together, and for that reason he wouldn't let anyone separate them again. But Eden responded to his kiss with a soft sound that echoed the aching tribulation Kyle felt deep inside, and all coherent thought was swept away.

Kyle pressed his kiss deeper. Eden's need trembled through her, reflecting his own, and he could wait no longer. Tearing his mouth from hers, he scooped her up into his arms. A shaft of moonlight illuminated Eden's face as he placed her on the bunk, and his hunger for her soared. Lying down beside her, he whispered the only words his ardent surfeit of emotion would allow.

"I love you, Eden."

Catching her hand with his as Eden's unintelligible response quavered on her lips, Kyle pressed his mouth to her palm, then slid her arm around his neck to gather her intimately close. Mouth to mouth they indulged their joy. Heat to heat they savored emotions rising ever higher. Stripping away the loose cotton shirtwaist Eden wore, Kyle tasted her sweet flesh at last. It was honey to his lips as he suckled her breasts. It was joy to his heart as Eden clutched him closer.

Kyle abandoned the warm mounds to cover Eden's mouth with his once more. He worshiped her fluttering eyelids with growing ardor, the rise of her cheek, the curve of her ear. He covered her quivering lips with his, swallowing her gasping words of bliss with his kiss. He slid his hand down her body, stroking her, reveling in the play of emotion on her faultless features. Halting only when a driving need within could no longer be restrained, he slid himself down to taste her intimately. He cupped her buttocks with his palms, exulting as she surrendered fully to his sensuous assault.

Intoxicated by the ecstatic look that transfused Eden's face, Kyle drew on her with loving fervor. His heart thundered with true glory when her slender body convulsed to full fruition beneath his lips.

Stripping away his clothes, he lay back down to position himself atop her. He strained for control at the meeting of their flesh, echoing Eden's rapturous gasp as he slid himself inside her at last. Her female warmth closed around him, and Kyle held himself immobile at the sheer splendor of the moment.

Eden was his.

"Kyle . . ."

Enraptured, Eden held her breath. Kyle was

inside her, filling her, making them one at last. She closed her eyes as his powerful body moved against hers and the rhythm of love began. She clasped him closer as the cadence increased.

She loved him. She needed him. She wanted him more than she had ever believed herself capable of wanting.

Love . . . need . . . want.

The words pounded through Eden, driving her to meet each forceful thrust. Kyle's strong body shuddered, bringing their escalating passion to a sudden, mutual climax that left them ecstatic . . . breathless . . . shaken in each other's arms.

Raising himself above her in the silent aftermath, Kyle cupped her cheek with his. His voice was hoarse with emotion as he repeated, "I love you, Eden."

I love you, Kyle.

The words rose to Eden's lips but they went unspoken as Kyle absorbed them with his kiss, sealing them within.

Kyle awakened with a start to the gray light of dawn. He glanced beside him where Eden lay curled at his side in the silence of the cabin. Her small features relaxed in profile, her lips slightly parted, her lashes lying in thick crescents against her cheeks, she was beautiful beyond belief.

And she was his.

As Eden moved in her sleep, the coverlet shifted, slipping down to reveal a small, rounded breast. The erect pink crest beckoned his kiss, as did the delicate skin of Eden's throat as she turned, and her warm lips as she emitted a soft sigh.

Conscious of his body's responsive hardening, Kyle clamped his teeth tight with determination. No, they had no time. They needed to be on their way before it was fully light.

"Eden . . ."

Eden's eyelids fluttered, and Kyle was unable to resist any longer. Covering her mouth with his, he kissed her gently, then with deepening ardor. His emotions heating, he drew back abruptly, urging, "Eden, wake up."

The incredible blue of Eden's eyes met his gaze, and Kyle forced himself to his feet. His clothes in hand, he turned as Eden quizzed groggily, "Is . . . is something wrong?"

"We have to get going."

"But—"

Crouching beside her, Kyle whispered, "It's too dangerous to delay any longer . . . and if I touch you one more time, we won't get away from here before noon."

Her abrupt flush was apparent even in the cabin's limited light. Eden threw back the coverlet and reached for her clothes. Intensely aware of his physical arousal, Kyle dressed, then turned woodenly toward the locker in the corner of the cabin. He rummaged inside, delaying as long as possible before turning back toward Eden with the supplies he sought.

Relieved to see Eden fully clothed, he mumbled, "I left these things the last time I was here."

Eden did not respond. She was standing as still as stone.

"What's wrong, Eden?"

She was staring at the doorway behind him.

Kyle turned at the same moment the hammer of a gun clicked in the silence.

"Don't shoot!"

Freed from her shocked immobility, Eden rasped, "Please, Witt, put the gun down!"

"I knew I'd find you!" Witt stood squarely in the doorway, his gun steady. His fair skin was an unnatural color and his eyes were cold as he continued in a low growl bearing no resemblance to his normal tone, "I saw you leave the ranch, but I couldn't believe it at first. I went to your room. I couldn't believe you'd really go with him."

"You followed us?"

"I tried damned hard, but I lost the trail in the dark. Funny thing was, I closed my eyes to rest. When I woke up it was dawn—and this cabin was no more than a stone's throw away."

Funny . . . but no one was laughing.

"Why did you follow me?"

"Do you really need to ask that question, Eden? Did you really think I'd let this Injun talk you into runnin' off with him?"

"Kyle didn't talk me into anything'!"

"Didn't he?"

Eden's voice dropped a note softer. "I'm not goin' back with you, Witt."

His gaze filled with incredulity, Witt rasped, "What're you thinkin', Eden? Or ain't you thinkin' at all? Don't you know what your pa's goin' to do when he wakes up this mornin' and finds you gone?"

"It'll be too late for him to do anythin'. Kyle and I will be far enough away that—"

"You can't run far enough, damn it! He'll come after you! He won't stop until he finds you, and there'll be hell to pay for anybody who gets in his way!"

"You're wrong, Witt! Pa will realize he's just wastin' time chasin' us."

"Do you really believe that?"

"Yes . . . no . . . I mean—"

"There's goin' to be blood flowin' over this unless you come back with me now."

"I won't go back with you."

"Eden, listen to me!" Witt attempted reason. "You're not doin' this right! You need to talk to your pa first . . . let him think about your side of things for a while."

"So he can lock me in my room and bar the windows again?"

At the other side of the cabin, Kyle stiffened.

Ignoring him, Witt pleaded, "You need to give your pa time."

"So he can try to kill Kyle again?" Eden shuddered. She glanced at Kyle, who stood immobile, the supplies on the floor at his feet where he had dropped them. He was too quiet. She saw the twitch of his jaw, the tense set of his shoulders. Fear choked her throat.

"Witt, please, go back to the ranch. Tell my pa that I'll let him know where I am when I can."

"You're comin' back with me now, Eden, one way or another."

"Witt—"

"I mean it, Eden."

Eden shook her head. "I know you. You won't use that gun."

"Won't I?" Witt's gaze intensified. "Maybe neither one of us knows what I'm capable of, but I found out somethin' about myself when I saw you ridin' away last night. Seems like your pa and me ain't too different, because I won't let you go off to live your life in a dirty Injun tepee surrounded with savages who might turn on you the first chance they get. I won't take that chance, Eden, even if you will."

"Witt—"

"One way or another, Eden."

Kyle inched toward a nearby chair where his gunbelt hung out of Bradley's view. Eden was wasting her time trying to reason with Bradley. The cowpoke meant every word he said.

Eden pleaded, "Witt, please, you of all people know how I feel!"

No reply.

Her jaw tight, Eden backed away from Bradley. "I'm not going back with you, Witt. And there's no way you can make me. I—"

Tumbling suddenly backwards over an unseen stool, Eden cried out when she struck her head against the stone hearth. Bradley started spontaneously toward her and Kyle dove for his gun. He pulled it out of the holster just as Bradley turned back toward him, his finger on the trigger.

Leaping sideways when a shot sounded, Kyle fired.

Bradley fell to the floor with a thud at the same moment that Kyle turned to see Tom Richard's men charging into the cabin.

Knocked back against the floor, Kyle looked up as a gun barrel was jammed against his jaw with the words, "Move and you're a dead man!"

Gunshots. A rush of movement. The sound of racing steps. A cry of alarm. The cabin, which had been silent and filled only with love minutes earlier, had exploded into sudden violence.

Disoriented, Eden touched the throbbing lump on the back of her head to find it wet with blood. She winced, standing shakily amidst the furor around her.

Her thoughts still unclear, Eden gasped when she saw Kyle lying pinned to the floor by her father's cowhand, a gun pressed to his jaw.

"Kyle!"

She started unsteadily toward him, halting when her father blocked her path.

"Stay away from him!"

"Let him up, Pa!"

"No!"

"Let him up!"

"That Injun bastard's all right. He ain't the

one you should be worryin' about. The fella lyin'
on the floor behind you is the one you should
be thinkin' about."

Eden turned toward the doorway and gasped
aloud. Witt was lying prone, a pool of blood
welling underneath him.

Beside Witt in a moment, Eden watched as
McGill turned Witt to his side to look at the
wound. The grim-faced wrangler paled, then
laid Witt back with a shake of his head.

Witt's eyes were closed, his breathing shallow. Eden brushed a strand of sandy hair back
from his forehead with trembling fingers, and
his eyelids flickered. His eyes opened.

"Witt, I'm so sorry." Eden clasped his hand in
hers. It was cold . . . like death.

Witt's brown-eyed gaze touched hers. "Still
. . . mad at me?"

"Why did you have to come after me, Witt?"
Eden struggled against tears. "Why didn't you
just let me go?"

". . . couldn't."

"Why?"

Why?

Eden's question reverberated in Witt's mind
as he struggled to breathe.

Didn't she know why?

Eden was holding his hand, her gaze intent
on his face. He felt no pain, only an aching
weight in his chest as he tried to respond.

His breath gurgled in his throat, and Eden
clutched his hand tighter. Fear touched the bril-

liant blue of her eyes as she rasped, "No, don't try to answer me. You'll be all right, Witt. Pa and the boys will take you back to the ranch and get Doc Bitters."

"Your pa . . . hates Doc Bitters."

"Yeah." Eden's small smile trembled.

A sudden bubbling within stole his breath, and Witt gasped. The light was fading.

"Don't close your eyes, Witt!" Eden's voice pierced the growing darkness. The sound drew him back as she pleaded, "Don't give up!"

"Eden—"

"Don't try to talk."

"—have to tell you—"

"Witt, please."

"—just wanted you to be safe."

"Save your strength, Witt."

"—wouldn't have shot him."

"I know."

"I . . . love you, Eden."

He had said it, at last.

Witt gasped for breath. His chest was heavy. He could taste blood in his mouth. He was going to die.

But Eden was holding his hand. Her face glowed in the darkness rapidly enclosing him— her face, the last he would ever see.

Yes . . . just as he had always dreamed.

"He's gone."

"No!" Eden shook Witt's arm.

"Let go of him, Eden."

Eden looked up at her father. "He isn't dead, Pa!"

"Yes, he is."

Eden looked back down at Witt. Yes, he was.

The shuffle of footsteps turned Eden toward the corner where two wranglers held Kyle between them, their guns tight against his sides.

Her head pounding, Eden swayed to her feet and started toward Kyle. She halted when her father stepped into her path. His voice harsh with disgust, he rasped, "Can't nothin' make you see that Injun bastard for what he really is? Witt's lyin' dead on the floor with that bastard's bullet in him!"

"Kyle didn't want to kill Witt!"

"Didn't he?"

"He thought Witt was goin' to shoot him!"

"Witt wasn't even lookin' at him! That bastard shot him in the back!"

"No, he didn't!"

"No?"

"Kyle wouldn't do that!"

"Are you goin' to deny what you can see with your own eyes?"

Eden looked back at Witt, at the pool of blood under his body.

. . . *under* his body.

"I . . . it was a mistake."

"It was deliberate!"

"No!"

"Yes!"

Eden's head throbbed harder. Her thoughts

were whirling. She looked at Kyle, but he made no denial. His dark eyes were cold.

Cold and dark—like death.

Yes, death.

Darkness abruptly consumed her.

Chapter Four

Kyle covered the length of his cell in three tense strides. Turning, he retraced his steps in the opposite direction as he had countless times since being confined.

Kyle halted abruptly, then looked up at his cell window to see a sky lit by the golden glow of late afternoon. A day that had begun with soft words of love had turned hot and violent so swiftly that the morning was still a blur in his mind. Within moments, Witt Bradley was dead and Eden was being carried out of the cabin unconscious, the back of her head bloody from a jagged cut. His hands bound, he was then forced up onto his horse and delivered directly to jail while two of Richards's wranglers took Eden off in the opposite direction. He hadn't seen Eden since—nor would anyone tell him if she was all right.

Shouted epithets and angry voices filtered into Kyle's cell from the street. He had been charged with Witt Bradley's murder, and it was obvious what the mood of the town was like. He was an Indian—a Kiowa—and one of their own was dead. It didn't make any difference to those enraged men that Kyle had been shot by "one of their own" a few days previously and had barely escaped with his life. Nor did it make a difference to them that Bradley had been holding a gun on him, or that if he hadn't leaped out of the path of Bradley's bullet, it might have been him instead of Bradley who was lying dead. In fact, he knew they would have preferred it that way.

Protesting voices on the street grew louder. Kyle turned to face the inner doorway to the cells when he heard the street entrance open. The mumbled tones of a bitter exchange preceded the sound of approaching footsteps. He watched silently as the inner door opened and Tom Richards took a few strides toward his cell. He went still when Richards halted, then stepped aside to allow the smaller figure concealed by the rancher's large frame to pass.

Eden.

Relieved at the sight of her, Kyle struggled to maintain an impassive facade. Eden was pale. Her step was unsteady. Dark circles shadowed her red-rimmed eyes as she looked at him for a long moment, then turned to address her father hoarsely.

"I want to talk to Kyle alone."

"No."

"I want to talk to him alone!"

"No! I ain't goin' to leave you alone in here with this murderin' Injun!"

"Now or later, Pa. If you make me come back, I will, but I'm goin' to talk to Kyle alone."

"How can you stand to look at him, Eden? He killed Witt! He shot him dead without battin' an eye! Don't you feel nothin' about that, or were all them tears you shed when we put Witt in the ground a while ago nothin' but show?"

"Pa . . ."

"All right!" Pure hatred twisting his face into a snarl, Richards turned back toward Kyle and spat, "I'll give you a few minutes alone with this bastard, but don't try my patience, Eden . . . because there'll be hell to pay if you do."

Waiting only until Richards stomped out, Kyle strode toward the cell bars. But Eden did not move. Standing as if frozen to the spot where her father had left her, she stared at him. When she spoke at last, her voice quavered with pain.

"Why did you shoot Witt in the back, Kyle?"

There . . . she had said it.

Eden's question hung on the silence. Looking at Kyle now, she could hardly believe that the words had left her lips. Only the previous night she had acknowledged the full scope of Kyle's

69

Kiowa heritage and denied its significance to their love. She had lain in his arms as he had made her a part of him with exquisite tenderness. In the glowing aftermath of consummation, she had indulged the wonder of the intimacy they had shared, believing with all her heart that nothing could ever come between them.

Eden awaited Kyle's reply. The violence in the cabin that morning had somehow numbed her. She had awakened in her own bed hours afterward, as the noon sun reached its zenith. Doc Bitters was leaning over her, his thin face sober while he explained that he had closed the gash on her head with six stitches, that she might be dizzy for a few days, and that she would do herself a favor if she rested as much as she could.

She had discarded Doc Bitters's advice, however, when she discovered that the hammering she heard in the yard was the construction of Witt's coffin, that Sheriff Duncan and Reverend Mills had already arrived, and that Witt would be buried in Diamond R ground near her mother's final resting place as soon as the coffin was finished.

Eden took a shuddering breath. She would never forget her last glimpse of Witt before the lid was nailed into place. He had looked so young.

Kyle stood at the barred door of his cell. His gaze had not left her face and he had not spoken. Sober, his demeanor unrevealing, he stood stiffly, hands curled around the metal bars.

Oddly, the sight of him so confined somehow magnified the innate power that was so much a part of him, while giving him the same feral quality that had struck her so strongly the previous night.

He's a Kiowa. He'll always be a Kiowa.

Witt's words haunted her. She needed an answer to her question. She needed the truth.

"Kyle . . ."

Kyle turned his back on her unexpectedly, bringing Eden forward in a rush. Unconsciously gripping the bars in the same manner he had moments earlier, she rasped, "Witt didn't even fire his gun! He could've shot you anytime he wanted to, but he didn't!"

Standing at the bars, Eden was unprepared when Kyle turned back toward her abruptly, covering her hands with his own. "He shot first . . . but I shot straighter."

"No." Eden closed her eyes. She couldn't bear the lie. "He never fired a shot. You shot him in the back. I saw the wound."

"He shot first."

"He didn't."

"Eden, look at me!"

Eden opened her eyes. Kyle was so close. His gaze burned into hers. "Bradley fired the first shot, Eden. I didn't have any choice."

She couldn't bear the lie!

Slipping his arms through the bars when Eden jerked her hands free, Kyle crushed her close, rasping, "Listen to me, Eden. I—"

The inner door burst open. Startled at the

sight of the gun in her father's hand, Eden remained speechless when Kyle released her. She fell back a step back, leaning heavily against the supportive arm her father slipped around her as he growled, "Touch her again and you're dead."

Her head was pounding. Her thoughts were confused. Only one thought remained. *She couldn't stand the lie.*

Physically sickened, Eden turned toward the door.

All was quiet in the street outside the jail as Kyle continued his anxious pacing. The angry crowd had finally been dispersed a few hours earlier. To his credit, Sheriff Duncan and his three deputies had maintained a firm hand in dealing with the mob, but Kyle knew he had not seen the last of it. News of Bradley's death had not yet reached the outer ranches where Bradley was well known and liked, and where feelings ran high because of past bloody encounters with tribes in the area. When it did, he had no doubt the reaction to Bradley's death would be more violent. In the dark hours while silence prevailed, he had accepted a simple fact: If he was still in this cell when that happened, he would not survive.

Unable to sleep, Kyle looked up at the window high on his cell wall. He saw a sky free of clouds and a brilliant crescent moon which skewered the darkness with shafts of silver light. Activity in the sheriff's office beyond the inner door had also halted and snoring had begun. The sheriff had stationed a deputy on guard outside his window, and the occasional click of bootheels against the wooden floor indicated that another man remained awake inside.

Frustration at his impotence swelled Kyle's anger anew. He had returned to the land of his birth and found welcome and a sense of belonging only with his father's people . . . and fulfillment only in the arms of a woman who was now beyond his reach.

Why did you shoot Witt in the back?

Kyle's jaw hardened.

Witt didn't even fire his gun!

Lies, which Eden obviously believed! The accusation in her voice had cut as sharply as a knife. His first reaction had been incredulity, then a fury so intense that he had turned away from her. But the plea in her voice had turned him back to her to say that he had not lied . . . and that he loved her.

He didn't have a chance. He knew the moment Richards burst through the door with his gun in hand that the man was looking for any excuse to kill him.

Only a fool risks his life for a white woman.

No.

Her arms cling to you and your heart answers, but the woman will never be yours.

No!

Touch her again and you're a dead man.

Kyle's denials ceased. Richards had meant every word.

The hoot of an owl sounded outside the cell window, and Kyle went suddenly still. He remembered that sound.

Jumping to stand atop the bunk, Kyle peered out the window. He saw the guard lying motionless on the ground. His heart pounding, he also saw a gun being raised to the bars atop a tall pole. At the other end of the pole stood a figure that was unmistakable even in the semidarkness.

Grabbing the gun when it came within reach, Kyle looked at Lone Bear, realizing when he saw movement in the shadows that his uncle was not alone. Lone Bear signed to him in a silent language he had almost forgotten. When the message was clear at last, Kyle climbed down from the cot and his uncle disappeared from sight.

Kyle waited the necessary minutes, then lay face down on the cell floor, the gun concealed beneath him. He moaned aloud. When there was no reaction from the outer office, he moaned more loudly, then thumped the floor to simulate the thud of falling.

"What's goin' on in there?"

Sheriff Duncan's hoarse tone was unmistakable. Kyle responded with another groan.

The inner door opened. "What the hell—?"

Two sets of footsteps approached his cell as a third voice called out from behind them, "What's wrong with him, Sheriff?"

Springing to his feet at the sound of sudden scuffling in the outer office, Kyle leveled his gun at the startled sheriff and deputy. He barely reacted when Lone Bear appeared in the doorway and felled both men with swift blows to the head.

Lone Bear unlocked his cell and grated in their native tongue, "We must leave quickly."

Kyle started toward the door. He turned back as Lone Bear bent toward the unconscious men with his scalp knife. Staying him with a touch of the hand, Kyle saw his uncle's brief, bitter smile as he deferred to the unspoken request.

"Your Kiowa heart does not yet sing a song of war—but the time will come."

The words rang in Kyle's mind as he followed Lone Bear out into the darkness.

Unlike the previous night, the sky was free of clouds. A brilliant crescent moon rent the darkness with silver shafts of light, illuminating Eden's room. Her head ached, but Eden was aware that physical distress was not the true cause of her torment.

Bradley fired first . . . but I fired straighter.

That wasn't true! Her father had showed her Witt's gun before she went to see Kyle. She had recognized its carved handle immediately, and it didn't take an expert to see that it hadn't been fired.

I wouldn't have hurt him, Eden.

I just wanted you to be safe.

Eden closed her eyes against the tormenting

words. Everything had happened so fast! She would have accepted any explanation Kyle gave her—a mistake in the darkness, uncertainty, miscalculation. She would have pleaded his case to everyone, even if she wasn't able to accept it in her heart. But she couldn't accept the outright lie Kyle had told her—not with Witt's dying image so clear in her mind—not while knowing that if not for her, he would still be alive.

I love you, Eden.

Witt had struggled for breath as he said those words, but there had been no recrimination in his eyes.

The haunting image suddenly more than she could bear, Eden threw back the coverlet and began an anxious pacing. What was wrong with her? Witt was dead because of her! His warm brown eyes were closed forever, and his easy laugh was silenced. She would never see him again—yet despite it all, she wanted with all her heart to believe that Witt had fired the first shot.

Moving to the window, Eden looked out at the bright crescent moon. She had stood in the same spot only a few nights previous, before Kyle had come to take her away with him, earnestly believing that she had reached the lowest point of her life. She had been so wrong.

Her eyes blurred with tears, Eden did not immediately see the mounted figure approaching on the moonlit trail. She heard the pounding hooves before the shadow took form, heading directly for the ranch house.

Her heart pounding as well, Eden jerked open her bedroom door and started down the hallway at the same moment that her father emerged fully clothed from his room. She gasped at the look in his eye and the gun in his hand. Refusing to be shrugged aside when they reached the front door, Eden stood beside her father, hardly aware of the cowhands filtering out of the bunkhouse as the horseman slid to a shuddering halt in front of them.

His bearded face shining with perspiration, the rider didn't bother to dismount as he gasped, "That Injun escaped! A bunch of them heathen Kiowas broke him out! Sheriff Duncan's started formin' a posse and he sent me out here to tell you."

Rigid, Tom Richards questioned, "When did this all happen?"

"About an hour ago."

"What direction did they head in?"

"The sheriff said as far as he could tell, they was headin' south."

"Get yourself a fresh mount. Me and the boys'll be goin' back with you." Not waiting for the rider's response, Richards turned to his men and ordered, "Booth, Whitney, McGill—get yourselves armed and find yourselves a spot where you won't be seen. I want you to stay at the ranch just in case that Injun bastard changes direction and comes here. The rest of you boys, make sure you have enough ammunition before you mount up."

Aware that her father deliberately ignored her, Eden snapped, "If you're leavin' McGill and the others behind because of me, you can forget it. I'm goin' with you."

"No, you ain't!"

Her cotton nightgown billowed in the night breeze, reminding her of her state of undress, and Eden turned back to the house, responding, "I'll be ready in a minute."

"Listen to me!" Jerking her back toward him, Richards spat, "I'm not givin' you no leeway this time. You're stayin' here, where you belong! I already done too much listenin' to you, and Witt's lyin' six feet under because of it."

His words as powerful as a blow, Eden gasped, "Don't say that!"

"Why not?" His fury visible even in the limited light, Richards continued, "Your precious *Kyle* is joined up with the rest of them murderin' bastards now. He ain't even pretendin' to be a white man, and you can't deny what he is anymore. He's a Kiowa! He's out for blood like all the rest of them, and that's what we're goin' to give him!"

"You're wrong!"

"Hell . . ." Richards's lips twisted with disgust. "There are times when I can't believe you're my own flesh and blood. How many of us do you have to see lyin' dead in front of you before you'll admit what that Injun really is?"

Her throat tight, Eden was not able to respond when her father directed, "Whitney . . . Booth—make sure she goes back to her room and stays there. McGill, you take the first watch out here."

"Pa—"

"Get her back in the house!"

His sharp command still ringing on the night air, Richards strode toward the barn. A burning irony seethed within him. Eden's physical resemblance to her mother had been so strong when she had faced him a few minutes earlier that he had almost been overwhelmed—her mother, murdered by the same kind her daughter was defending.

Familiar agonies returned. Her hair had been a shade darker than Eden's, and her eyes a lighter blue, but Eden's fine features and clear skin duplicated the beauty that had fascinated him from the first moment he saw Bonnie Carson. A rough-and-tumble wrangler without a cent to his name those many years ago, he was distinguishable from a hundred other wranglers working local Texas ranches only by the bright color of his hair. He wasn't good enough for the educated daughter of the town banker, who miraculously loved him as much as he loved her. He swore the day they took their vows that he'd cherish and protect her until the day she died.

There was never any doubt that he fulfilled the first part of that vow. Nor was there any question that he failed on the second.

His throat tight, Richards recalled that day of horror twenty years ago. A severe, unseasonal storm struck the Diamond R that year, stranding his herd. As soon as it was possible to travel on the trails, he left two men behind at the ranch and went out with the other hands to round up the surviving calves. When he returned at sundown, he found his two wranglers dead in the front yard, his house ransacked, his beautiful Bonnie lifeless in a pool of her own blood, and Eden's cradle empty. He was past consolation when he heard whimpering from the root cellar underneath the house. He knew he would never forget the moment when he pulled up the trapdoor and saw Eden lying safe and sound where her mother had hidden her. He pledged that day to avenge Bonnie's death, and to protect Eden as he had failed to protect her mother. He had learned the hard way that no amount of heathen blood shed since that time could erase the bitter memories from his mind.

Malice shuddered through him. He remembered just as clearly the first day he saw *Kyle Webster*. Wearing the clothing of a white man, the Kiowa bastard had walked boldly down the main street of town—where he was neither wanted nor had any right to be. But nothing had prepared him for the rage he felt when he saw Eden in the fellow's arms. He had sworn to himself in that moment that he would not allow Eden to be defiled as her mother had been. He hadn't realized how great a price would have to be paid to keep that vow.

His rage deepening with each step he took, Richards snatched up his saddle inside the barn entrance. Ignoring his startled mount's snort, he slapped the saddle onto his back and turned toward his approaching foreman, snarling, "Damn it, Mullen, that Injun bastard got away. I knew I should've stayed in town."

A similar zeal burned in Mullen's eyes as he grated, "He ain't goin' to stay free very long, boss."

"One minute's too long! If it wasn't for him, Witt wouldn't be dead."

Mullen's expression hardened. "It wasn't your fault."

"I know it wasn't!" Richards slipped the cinch strap through the loop and pulled it tight. "Witt never would've took that bullet if that Injun didn't jump aside when he did. My shot would've hit that Kiowa bastard square, and everythin' would've been settled, once and for all."

"The boys all know it wasn't your fault that you shot Witt instead."

"He ain't goin' to get away with it, Mullen. I'll make him and every lyin', thievin', murderin' Injun in his tribe pay."

"The boys wanted me to tell you, just so it's clear, that as far as we're concerned, that Injun's bullet killed Witt, just like everybody thinks. There ain't a one of us who ain't got a debt to settle with them Kiowa butchers. We ain't goin' to say nothin' different, and that's the way Witt would want it."

Richards nodded, then slapped down the stirrups. "Tell the men I'm leavin' in five minutes, and I ain't waitin' for nobody."

Digging his heels into his mount's sides minutes later, Richards spurred the horse onto the trail, a full contingent behind him.

Eden did not look back as the two grim-faced cowhands pulled her bedroom door closed behind her. Joey Booth and Bart Whitney. She had ridden alongside the two wranglers for years. She had considered them friends. Now they were her jailers.

Uncertain how long she had stood motionless in the spot where she entered, Eden walked slowly to the window. Jolted suddenly back to reality by the sight of her father's party as it disappeared into the shadows of the trail, Eden ran to the door. She pulled it open to find Whitney's barrel-chested figure blocking her way. She turned back to the window to see Booth take up a position there.

Whitney pulled the door closed behind her. The sound cracked the silence with harsh finality, sweeping Eden with a wave of sudden incapacitating sadness. Irrefutable truths returned that tears could not erase.

Witt was dead. Kyle was running for his life. *All because of her.*

Eden sank to her knees.

* * *

They had been traveling silently and steadily for more than an hour on the moonlit trail. Kyle glanced at the stalwart braves behind him— Gray Fox, Standing Man, Yellow Dog, Black Snake—all men renowned within the tribe for their hunting and riding skills, and for their bravery. Their faces were grave.

Lone Bear signaled their party to a halt and dismounted. Kyle followed Lone bear as he climbed to a vantage point that allowed him a clearer view of the moonlit terrain. The older man turned toward him, his expression solemn as he broke the silence between them.

"No one yet follows. We may rest briefly before continuing on."

"The sheriff can't be far behind." Kyle spoke uneasily. "Nobody's going to let him forget that Witt Bradley is dead. They want me for murder."

"White man's justice."

"I'm not guilty—not of murder! The other man shot first. I'd be dead now if his aim was better. If I were any other man, they'd call it self-defense."

"Because of the woman."

Refusing to respond to Lone Bear's comment, Kyle continued, "I would've been dead by noon if you hadn't come."

"Such would be the fate of any Kiowa so confined."

"Where're we going, Lone Bear?"

"We travel south until I am sure no one is behind us. In two days or three, when it is safe, we will return to camp and move north with our people, to a place where these men will not follow."

Nodding, Kyle then questioned, "How did you find out so quickly that I had been arrested?"

"Tom Two Fingers lives in the white man's town with his white woman. Many there call him half-breed and revile him. We call him Kiowa. When so many gathered outside the jail after you were confined, he knew what would soon happen, and his heart rebelled. He rode toward our camp and met our hunting party on the trail. Because of him, you were saved."

"No, because of you. For that, I thank you."

"I do not ask gratitude for sparing Kiowa blood!" Suddenly angry, Lone Bear spat, "I ask only for similar concern! It is time to cast thoughts of the white woman aside so you may find your true path. Noble blood flows in you, Young Hawk. You have the spirit within you to lead. Your people need you! Our numbers dwindle, and my time grows short. My hair will soon whiten. My vision will fade and my limbs will weaken. I will not then be fit to lead my people."

"No!"

"I am yet strong, but I do not deny that which awaits us all. You have returned to your people from the land of the white man where you were raised and where you felt no truth within. White Horn has looked into the flames and read the course which has been set for you. He has seen glory, and he has seen pain . . . but in all, he has seen honor and courage. With you to lead, the Kiowa will not be driven into homelessness from the land that the Great Spirit gave us."

"I'm a hunted man, Lone Bear. I can't lead anyone without attracting trouble."

"All Kiowa are hunted men!"

"There are things I must settle before I can consider what you say."

Lone Bear's expression tightened. "The woman."

His respect for Lone Bear never greater, Kyle replied earnestly, "White Horn looks to the future, but I can't while I'm still unable to see past the present."

"The woman will never be yours!"

"She will!"

Pausing, his flash of anger subsiding, Kyle studied his uncle silently. Lone Bear spoke of noble blood. Never clearer to him than at that moment was the realization that any nobility he might possibly earn in his lifetime could not compare with the nobility Lone Bear innately possessed. Kyle knew it was in the heart of the man standing before him, who lived the values of his people with a selflessness that enabled him to place the welfare of the tribe before his own; a man who so honored the memory of his dead brother that he accepted his brother's son unconditionally, with true faith, despite his failings.

Kyle recalled his childhood dream, of matching this man's stature. He knew he could not aspire higher.

Hesitating briefly, Kyle then spoke from the heart. "You say you don't want gratitude, Uncle, but it's yours anyway."

Silent for long moments, Lone Bear replied, "You speak your gratitude in words, Young Hawk. I ask for more. The time will yet come when there is no further need for entreaty."

Terminating their conversation with those words, Lone Bear walked back to his mount and their escape resumed.

Chapter Five

Eden awakened at first light of the new day. Groggy, she groaned and touched the throbbing wound on her skull. The previous day had begun before dawn with the rider from town and the news that Kyle had escaped. In the endless hours following, she had dressed and waited in her room, enduring an agony of uncertainty. There had been no bars on her window and her bedroom door had not been locked, but she had been a prisoner nonetheless. Her stomach unsettled and her head aching, she had dozed fitfully during that time, awakening anxiously to find that nothing had changed.

Afternoon had slipped into evening before her father and the wranglers returned. Unwilling to face him, she had listened at the door as

McGill's anxious question opened the conversation.

"Did you find him, boss?"

"No."

A weary shuffling sounded before Mullen interjected angrily, "We picked up his trail, all right. That Kiowa and the rest of his band headed south, just like the sheriff said. The trail was pretty fresh, too. Then they split up and started circlin'. We split up to follow them and ended up runnin' into each other left and right and gettin' nowhere."

"Them damned savages sure know this country!" Hawkins added. "They led us around by the nose all day!"

"Them bastards . . ." She had never heard Curry speak with such venom. "When we catch them, I'm goin' to drag each and every one of them on their backs over the ground we covered today."

"We'll get them. Don't worry." Her father's voice had been deep with conviction, the most frightening of all with the antipathy that rang in each word as he grated, "And we'll make them all pay for every drop of Witt's blood."

Grunts of agreement sounded all around before her father ordered gruffly, "You boys get somethin' to eat. McGill pulled some things out of the smokehouse and left them on the table."

Her father's distinctive step sounded.

"Where you goin', boss?"

"I ain't hungry. I'm goin' to bed." His footsteps halted; then he spoke again. "Make sure you get yourselves some sleep tonight, too, because we'll be startin' out tomorrow at dawn. I'm goin' to make sure that Injun gets what's comin' to him if it's the last thing I ever do."

Her father had walked down the hallway and turned without hesitation into his bedroom. He had made no attempt to come to her room, and she was glad.

It was now morning, and despite her fervent hope that she would awaken to discover the entire nightmare had dissipated with the light of day, still nothing had changed.

The familiar squeak of her father's bedroom door pulled Eden erect in her bed. She jumped to her feet, grateful that she had slept fully clothed when she opened her bedroom door and her father turned toward her, dressed for the trail. Her emotions fluctuating between anger and despair, she was certain of only one thing. Another day of waiting would be intolerable.

Boldly breaking the silence between them, Eden asked, "Where're you goin', Pa?"

His gaze chilling, Richards responded, "Where do you think I'm goin'?"

"You're goin' out after Kyle again." Eden held his gaze. "I'm goin' with you."

"No, you ain't."

"This is crazy, Pa!" Eden tried a softer appeal. "I . . . I know how you feel, but—"

"How *I* feel? How about the way *you* feel—or don't you feel nothin' at all, except for that heathen redskin?"

"Pa, please—"

"Please what? Please forget that we buried Witt yesterday because he wanted to save you from somethin' that would make you suffer for the rest of your life?"

"That was *my* decision to make, not his!"

"Was it? Witt thought it was his—because he cared about you."

"Pa . . ."

Richards was silent for long moments. "You're the picture of your ma, you know that, Eden?" His lip twitched revealingly as he then spat, "But you're a damned fool like she could never be!"

"My mother was a good woman. You *told* me she was!"

"Damned right."

"A good woman wouldn't look down on a man just because he was an Injun!"

"Oh, yes, she would." Richards took an aggressive step toward her. "You're alive today because she knew what them Kiowa were and what they were after, and she had the good sense to hide you where they couldn't find you. She'd be alive today, too, if she'd stayed in that root cellar with you instead of comin' back up to help fight them bastards off."

"You don't really know how it all happened that day, Pa! Maybe your wranglers . . . maybe they shot first!"

The words were out of her mouth before she could stop them. Appalled, Eden waited for the thunderous response that was not long in coming.

"What did that redskin do to you? Did he steal every bit of common decency you got?" Richards's chest heaved with fury that was barely restrained. "Your ma died fightin' to save you from the same kind as the Injun you tried to run off with! Witt knew what would happen to you if you did. Like your ma, he died tryin' to save you, and you're *still* defendin' that bastard! Listen to me, Eden." Advancing toward her, he grasped a lock of her hair and spat, "It's been twenty years since then, and a day never goes by that I don't think about your ma's beautiful yellow hair—hair just like yours—hangin' on a scalp pole in a Kiowa village somewhere until it turned to rot!" Releasing her hair with utter disdain, he added, "Lucky, ain't it, that we was there when Witt was killed, or we might be thinkin' the same thing about him right now."

Her stomach churning, Eden fought for stability. "You . . . you're wrong, Pa. Kyle wouldn't do anythin' like that."

"No?" His eyes suddenly wild, Richards rasped, "Well, I'm tellin' you now, your *Kyle* thinks he's goin' to get away with what he did, but he ain't. We lost his trail yesterday, but we're goin' to be takin' up where we left off, today. We ain't goin' to give him a chance to get to that Kiowa camp so he can rile up the rest of them savages and turn them on us!"

"You're wrong, Pa! Kyle isn't even headin' toward the camp."

"He's ridin' toward that Kiowa camp, all right, and I'm goin' to make sure he don't make it!"

"No . . . no, that isn't true! If he was headin' for the camp like you said, he'd be ridin' west!"

"What're you talkin' about?"

"The camp's west of here, near Sweet Water—not south! I know because Kyle told me. You're wrong about him. Whatever happened, Kyle doesn't want to go back there and start a *war*. He's runnin' away now to give everyone time to cool off. He'll come back again to straighten everythin' out. I know he will."

"Yeah."

Richards turned away abruptly, and Eden caught his arm. "Where're you goin'?"

Richards shook off her hand. "I told you where I'm goin'."

Suddenly more frightened than before, Eden controlled her quaking with sheer force of will. "I'm goin' with you."

"McGill!" Turning toward the burly wrangler who stepped into the hallway in response to his summons, Richards spat, "Me and the boys are leavin'. Make sure she stays here."

"No, Pa! Pa—"

He was gone.

Kyle observed Gray Fox and Standing Man as they talked quietly. They had all awakened at dawn and eaten sparingly from provisions originally packed for the hunt. There had been little conversation between the other braves and him, yet there somehow existed between them an instinctive accord of mutual support that went beyond spoken words.

Kyle studied the men as they prepared to mount. He had spent many hours in friendly conversation with Yellow Dog during his stay at the camp after first returning to Texas. He had hunted with Gray Fox and Black Snake, and it was Standing Man's sister, Running Deer, who had brought him food while he recuperated from his wound in White Horn's tepee. In all contacts, these men had treated him as they treated him now, as if he were one of them, not a man who had come back to Texas almost a stranger.

They were his brothers.

Contrasting sharply was the townsfolk's reaction to his return. Clearer to him than ever before was the reality that while his brothers were called "savage," it was the supposedly civilized society that was truly worthy of the term.

Except for Eden.

A familiar torment returned. Eden hadn't meant what she'd said when she came to the jail, he was sure of it. She was confused by the lies others had told her. As soon as he was able, when the shock of Bradley's death had faded, he would find Eden and explain again what happened. He had already accepted the fact that he might never be cleared of Bradley's death in this country where the Kiowa were hated so intensely, but Eden wasn't like the others. However much she mourned Bradley's death, she still loved him. He was sure of it. In her heart, she must know he would come back for her when he could. He wouldn't disappoint her.

Kyle turned toward Lone Bear as the older man prepared to mount. Kyle remained silent for long moments—standing eye to eye with this man who looked on him as a son.

Under Lone Bear's intense scrutiny, Kyle offered, "I rode out earlier to scout the trail. I didn't see any sign of a posse."

Lone Bear nodded. "The trail is difficult for the white man to follow."

"You think we've lost them, then?"

"Perhaps. We will see."

Kyle frowned.

"You do not like delay."

Kyle did not respond.

Lone Bear frowned as well. "Your mind drifts from the danger at hand. The woman still occupies thoughts that should be turned to your people's survival."

Kyle accepted the reprimand. Honesty forced him to respond, "I respect what you say, Lone Bear, but I want you to know that I intend to go back for Eden when everything calms down."

"If she will accept you."

"She will."

"She calls you murderer."

"She was confused. She loves me."

"She loves you as a Kiowa?"

"She loves me—for the man I am."

"Such a woman would be welcome in our camp."

Terminating their conversation abruptly, Lone Bear mounted. Allowing Lone Bear's reply to stand despite its apparent conflict with his previous statements, Kyle mounted as well.

The sun had penetrated the shadows of dawn with golden shafts of light when Kyle realized there had been no conflict in his uncle's statements. Lone Bear had said "such a woman" as Kyle had described would be welcome in their camp. Lone Bear had made that statement with ease for the simple reason that he did not believe that woman truly existed.

There it was, just where Eden had said it would be.

Concealed in a dense grove of trees that had muted the sound of their posse's approach, Tom Richards stared at the Kiowa camp. His heart pounded. The taste in his mouth was as bitter as bile.

Scrutinizing the scene, he saw even rows of tepees basking in the midday sun, with little sign of movement between them. The barking of a dog and a shouted reprimand briefly shattered the silence as smoke from unattended cooking fires rose in lazy, curling spirals toward the clear blue of the sky. A woman emerged from a hide shelter to stir a pot and jab the fire before again slipping out of sight. A man stepped into view between the tepees when the dog's barking continued. He scanned the terrain casually, then silenced the animal with another sharp command before disappearing from sight.

Richard heard a woman laugh, then a baby's cry. He heard the crack of newly cured hides flapping in the brisk spring breeze. How quiet and peaceful it all appeared. No one looking at the indolent tableau where daily life appeared to be progressing so harmlessly would believe that within those simple shelters lived a people whose sudden rabid violence and vicious raids had destroyed so many lives.

But he knew better.

His venomous wrath building, Richards glanced at Sheriff Duncan, who sat his horse nearby, then at the mounted men behind them. He had met up with Duncan's posse shortly after leaving the Diamond R. It had been difficult to convince him to abandon the trail they had followed the previous day and accompany him in the opposite direction. He supposed he owed his eventual success in that regard to the frustration of the men in the posse, a group that had grown larger after word of Witt's death reached the outlying ranches.

Richards surveyed the newly arrived recruits. He saw Sam Hart and his wranglers. Sam's son had been killed by a Kiowa scouting party months earlier. He saw Jesse Walters and his men, who still remembered the raid on Jesse's ranch when he lost his family years earlier. He saw Martin Lane, Michael Drew, Larry Neece, Justin Worth, and a dozen others who had suffered similar losses over the years, men who swelled the posse's number to a formidable force. He knew these men as well as he knew himself. He knew what they wanted.

His chest heaving with an enmity so deep that it almost stole his breath, Richards turned back to Duncan when the mustached law officer quietly addressed him.

"All right, the Kiowa camp is exactly where you said it would be, but there's no way we can tell from this distance if Kyle Webster is hiding there."

"He's there."

"We can't be sure of that. And there ain't much chance that anybody there'll turn Webster and the Injuns who broke him out of jail over to us, even if they are."

"So what are you sayin', Sheriff?"

"I'm sayin', now that we know where the camp is, we can get the Army to take over for us. There's no way a camp of this size can move and hide again before a contingent gets here. It'll be better if soldiers go in and get him out. They're better equipped to handle it."

"*Why* are they better equipped?" Richards was beginning to shake. "Because they're wearin' uniforms? We've got guns just like they have!"

"Because they represent the Federal Government, that's why! With all the talk in Washington about treaties bein' broken left and right, this is their job! They have the power to negotiate!"

"None of them Kiowa bastards negotiated when they raided Jesse Walters's ranch and killed his whole family! Them murderin' redskins didn't try talkin' peace when they shot young Billy Hart, stole his horse, and left him for the buzzards a couple of months ago! What about the way them savages slaughtered Larry Neece's stock when they was all liquored up and fit to kill, and how they burned Marty Lane's house to the ground? Three of his men died in that fire!"

Richards took a tight breath, continuing more softly, "They killed my Bonnie without battin' an eye . . . and Witt's lyin' dead now because another of them redskin murderers wanted my daughter."

"So"—the sheriff's small eyes bored into his—"what are you sayin', Tom?"

"I'm sayin' it's time to show them heathens that they ain't goin' to get away with it no more! I'm not waitin' for nobody! I'm goin' in there now!"

"I ain't goin' to allow it!"

"You ain't goin' to be able to stop me!" Not waiting for Sheriff Duncan's reply, Richards turned toward the mounted men behind them. He spoke in a grating rasp that traveled with a deadly chill on the clear midday stillness.

"You heard what I said to the sheriff! I'm goin' in down there! Are you with me?"

Harsh grunts of accord sounded spontaneously, and exhilaration flushed Richards's face hot with color. Looking back at the sheriff, he was surprised to see the lawman's gun pointed at his stomach.

"I'm not goin' to let you do it."

"Yes, you are." Never more sincere, Richards spat, " 'Cause you'll have to pull that trigger in order to stop me!"

Duncan's lined face twitched. "I'm warnin' you—"

Startled when his gun was knocked from his hand by the man beside him, Duncan hissed into the unyielding faces of his posse, "You're askin' for more trouble, don't you know that? If you do what you're thinkin', it won't end here!"

His rage exploding as Bonnie's bloody image flashed before his mind, Richards snapped, "It'll end here—for this camp, at least!"

Turning to the mounted men behind him, Richards shouted, "All right, men! Light those torches!"

Eden awakened with a jolt from an uneasy sleep. She glanced around her room, a sudden panic besetting her at the realization that the chill crawling up her spine had no relation to the room's temperature. She raced to the window to see it was not past midday. Pa and the boys hadn't returned yet, but something was wrong! She could feel it.

Silent, Eden stared at the sunlit terrain. She hadn't wanted any of this! She had only wanted Kyle, but the cost of loving him was becoming too great.

Where would it all end?

Outside the window where he stood his turn at guard, McGill turned to look up at her. His bearded face was unsmiling, his lips tight. She saw the accusation in his eyes, and she saw the growing apprehension there.

Another chill set Eden shuddering. Yes, something was terribly wrong. Her gazed locked with McGill's.

The sun was descending toward the horizon in a sky that had been free of clouds throughout the daylight hours. Lone Bear had continued to lead their party in a cautious southward direction calculated to confuse any posse that might be following. Satisfied a few hours before noon that further subterfuge was unnecessary, they had then turned back toward the Kiowa camp. Kyle was relieved. The camp was over the next rise—home and safety to his brothers, who had already risked too much for him.

Kyle slowly stiffened as his mount continued its steady forward pace. Something was wrong. The sky ahead was too dark. He smelled . . . smoke!

Glancing at the men beside him, Kyle saw a fear that mirrored his own as he kicked his mount into a gallop. His horse was wheezing from the breakneck pace when they reached the wooded glade that blocked the camp from view.

Hardly aware of the pounding hooves beside him, Kyle emerged out into the clearing with a gasp of horror at the devastation that met his view. The camp was in smoldering ashes. Motionless bodies lay scattered between piles of debris where neat rows of tepees had formerly stood.

Dying cries . . . sorrowful wails . . .

Turning, he saw Lone Bear galloping forward into the smoke with Yellow Dog close behind—while beside him Gray Fox, Standing Man, and Black Snake remained as motionless with incredulity as he.

Freed from his momentary immobility, Kyle spurred his mount forward. He leaped to the ground where a young squaw knelt beside her fallen husband, almost hidden within the black smoke from a stack of newly cured hides. He pushed the woman aside to check the young brave's wound. One touch and he knew the man was dead.

Looking up, Kyle saw Lone Bear rein his horse to a halt beside the remains of his tepee. He heard Lone Bear call Rain Woman's name. Pain unlike any he could recall shuddered through him when there was no reply. He saw Yellow Dog swatting at lingering flames, his voice growing increasingly shrill as he called his young daughter's name. He watched as Gray Fox, Standing Man, and Black Snake each disappeared within the smoke.

"Many white men came . . ."

Kyle turned back toward the squaw. He responded hoarsely, "Soldiers?"

The woman's smoke-stained face twitched. "No. The men came upon the camp with torches while we slept through the heat of the day. Some were able to escape, but others could not elude the fire." Her eyes growing suddenly wild, she rasped, "The white men chased those who tried to hide. They cut them down, shouting *your* name."

Kyle stared at her, stunned, as the squaw repeated, "They called for Young Hawk, and when there was no response, they called for Kyle Webster! They demanded to know where you were. The leader had hair the color of flames. He shot those who would not reply!"

Kyle's spinning mind jarred to a halt. The woman's description fit only one man.

"What happened then?"

The woman's eyes blazed with hatred. "When fires burned all around . . . when all was quiet within the camp, they called your name again so all who escaped might hear and remember."

The barbarity of the woman's tale resounded in Kyle's mind. He rose slowly to his feet under the young squaw's accusing gaze, shaking with outrage as he surveyed the burning remains of the camp. To have slaughtered so many, just to find him!

His Kiowa blood crying for retribution, Kyle stepped out into the open where he might view the carnage more clearly. He had dismissed White Horn's visions. He had ignored Lone Bear's warnings. He had held himself above their advice with the conviction that he could meet the white man in peace—*but he was wrong!* There was no justice for his people! The wanton shedding of Kiowa blood was the price others had paid for his refusal to accept the truth, but he would not allow so high a price to stand! He would answer with a charge of his own! He would repay with blood to be shed for every drop of Kiowa blood that now stained the ground! That was his solemn vow! And when the day came that he—

A sudden gunshot knocked Kyle to his knees.

A second shot had him sprawling on the ground.

Consciousness fading, Kyle tasted dirt between his teeth. He smelled anew the scent of blood. He heard heavy footsteps approaching. They halted beside him as a gruff voice commented, "You're a good shot, but you were a little off the mark. He's still breathin'."

"I'll fix that."

Kyle heard the click of a gun barrel, then the same gruff voice saying, "He's done for. You're just wastin' a bullet."

Kyle's breathing grew more pained.

The voice continued, "He ain't goin' to last much longer."

Consciousness drifted as Kyle strained to open his eyes to see the person who had shot him and was now watching him die. He succeeded at last, managing to peer out through slitted lids before the darkness claimed him. He saw . . . *Eden*.

Kyle's labored breathing grated on the silence of her room as Eden looked down at him, numb with fear.

"Kyle . . . can you hear me?"

Kyle did not reply. He was so pale. Witt had been as pale as he, and now Witt was dead.

Shuddering, Eden held Kyle's limp hand tightly. She remembered looking down into McGill's apprehensive gaze when he stood guard at her window at midday. She recalled sensing that McGill was as worried as she, and that the right words spoken at that moment would unite them in a common cause. It was only when she, McGill, and Booth were mounted, however, that she learned her father's true destination that morning had been the Kiowa camp.

Cursing her stupidity in revealing the camp's location to her father, she had turned her mount west and set off at a frantic pace. The smoke-darkened sky over Sweet Water spurred her on anew when they approached. She was unprepared for the devastation when the camp came into view, but she knew she would never forget the sight of her father and Mullen standing over Kyle's fallen body.

The horror of that moment . . . the agonizing fear that she might be too late! She remembered falling to her knees beside Kyle, and her moment of elation when she realized he was still breathing. She had demanded that Kyle be brought back to the ranch so Doc Bitters could treat him there. She had dismissed her father's protests and his insistence that Kyle would be better off in town. She knew he realized that if he refused her this time, he would lose her forever.

Sheriff Duncan had dispatched a deputy for Doc Bitters, who was waiting for them at the ranch when they arrived. If not for that, she was sure Kyle would not have survived.

Eden scrutinized Kyle more closely. Doc Bitters had removed the bullets from his chest. Kyle still had difficulty breathing, but the bloody circle on his bandage had not widened. He would get well. He had to.

"Kyle . . . can you hear me?"

Silence.

Eden stroked his cheek, recalling the gentleness with which Kyle had caressed her as they had lain side by side. She remembered the warmth of his lips when he clasped her close, the hunger in his eyes, the tenderness in his touch, and their mutual joy when he claimed her at last.

Eden pressed her mouth to Kyle's jaw. She kissed his lips. She whispered into his ear, "I love you, Kyle. I'm so sorry. I wish you could talk to me and tell me how all this happened. I need to know if—"

Kyle's breath rattled in his throat, and Eden panicked.

"Doc!"

Beside her in a moment, Doc Bitters attempted an encouraging smile. "He's all right, Eden. He needs to rest—and you need to get away from here for a while. Go get something to eat. I'll stay with him until you come back."

Get something to eat. Eden's stomach rebelled at the thought—but Doc Bitters was right. She did have something to do . . . something that couldn't wait any longer.

Eden stood up abruptly. She looked down at Kyle, then released his hand and turned toward the door.

His hard features tensely drawn, Tom Richards watched unseen as Eden strode down the hallway, then out into the yard without a break in stride. He continued staring when the door banged shut behind her. She was still protecting that heathen redskin! Damn her, did she have no shame?

The thought revived a burning rage within him. He had been so close to having it over with! If Mullen hadn't made him hesitate when he was about to fire that final shot . . . if Eden hadn't ridden up at that moment . . . if he hadn't known that he would lose Eden forever if she saw him pull the trigger . . .

Instead, the bastard was in his own house!

Damned if he'd stand for it much longer!

His lined face twitching, Richards strode into the hallway. He was at his daughter's bedroom door—the room where the savage was lying in his daughter's bed—when a tall figure stepped into his path.

"Get out of my way, *Sheriff*!"

Sheriff Duncan's wiry mustache twitched. "Where do you think you're goin'?"

"This is my house, not yours! I do what I want here!"

"No, you don't!"

"Get out of my way!"

"No!"

"This is your last chance, *Sheriff*. Get out of my way!"

Richards reached for his gun.

An angry, buzzing sound penetrated the black void that encompassed him. Kyle sought to escape it, but he could not.

Squinting through heavy eyelids, Kyle saw a familiar room. It was Eden's. He was lying in her bed.

His chest was heavy. It hurt to breathe. The angry buzzing grew louder, shattering his disoriented thoughts. It became the sound of irate voices outside the bedroom door.

"Cool down, Tom!"

"I want that Injun out of here!"

"We can't move him yet. If we do, he'll bleed to death."

"Do you think I care!"

"You'd better care."

"Don't threaten me, *Sheriff*."

"Listen to me, Tom! It don't affect me none—your callin' me Sheriff like it's a dirty name. You're actin' crazy and you're not thinkin' clearly! You fellas all went wild out there at that Injun camp! There's no excuse for what happened. I couldn't stop it, and when it was over and done, there was nothin' I could do about it, short of throwin' half the county in jail. But when you and Mullen sneaked back to lie in wait for that fella, when you shot him without givin' him a chance just because he—"

"Just because? Don't it make no difference that Witt's dead *just because* he was tryin' to save my daughter from that bastard?"

"Your daughter didn't want to be saved."

"My daughter didn't know what she was doin' then, but she's changed her mind a bit, now."

"Yeah, that's why she talked that hard-nosed McGill into ridin' out with her to find out what was happenin', and that's why she came ridin' up and stopped you from finishin' the job on that Injun. And that's why she made sure we brought him back here so's he wouldn't bleed to death."

"She cares about him, all right. Hell, it shames me to admit it! But she hates all them other murderin' savages just as much as we do."

"Yeah . . . right."

Kyle heard an angry scuffle.

"Take your hands off me, Tom."

Silence.

"I said, take your hands off me—or, I swear, I'll arrest you right here."

A silent pause, then a wry laugh. "In my own house, *Sheriff*?"

"Yeah."

"All right!" Another pause. "But you'd better watch what you say about my daughter from now on."

"I only spoke the truth."

"You don't know what's the truth! Eden has feelin's for that fella in there because she's still foolin' herself that he's more white man than redskin—but she don't have no use for the rest of them Kiowa."

"Believe what you want to believe."

"It's the truth, I tell you! How do you think I found out where them Kiowa moved their camp to? She told me because she knew *Kyle* wasn't there! She didn't care what happened to all them others! She never figured that he'd come back in time for me to catch him, is all!"

"That ain't my problem, Tom. My problem is how I'm goin' to explain what happened when the Army hears about this."

"They don't care! Hell, they done worse in their time."

"They'll have to make a report—to *Washington*."

"Tell them anythin' you want. They'll believe it."

"What about that fella in there? He knows what happened, and he's not just some ordinary Kiowa. He lived back East. He's got friends back there."

"Any friends he's got are *back East*, just like you said. They ain't goin' to change nothin' here."

"I wouldn't be so sure."

"I *am* sure . . . because I'll *make* sure."

"Tom, I'm tellin' you—"

A shadow moved unexpectedly into Kyle's line of vision and he started. The discussion continued beyond the bedroom door, but he was no longer listening. He strained to sit up as a man crouched slowly over him.

"No, don't move. You'll start bleedin' again."

The image slowly cleared. Doc Bitters.

"Seems like you got an earful of what's bein' said out there."

Kyle could not manage a reply.

"If you did, you'd best put it out of your mind. It won't do you no good to get yourself agitated. You're lucky you're alive."

Alive . . . while others were not.

"Just close your eyes and try to rest. You can't do much else right now, anyway."

Not right now.

"Here, drink this. It'll make you feel better."

Kyle felt a cup against his lips. He drank as directed.

"In case you're wonderin', Eden just stepped out for a minute. She'll be here when you wake up next time."

Eden.

The pain was fading. The voices were drifting away.

Eden . . . who had betrayed him.

"Tell me what really happened out there, Quinn."

Eden faced the sober wrangler squarely. He was the youngest of her father's hired hands. He was quiet. He didn't talk much to the rest of the men, but he had been close to Witt. She had cornered him in the barn when she saw he was alone. She knew she didn't stand a chance of learning the truth, otherwise.

Eden waited for Quinn's reply. She glanced

toward the doorway. Satisfied they were still alone, she pressed, "I need to know the truth, Quinn. Everybody's tellin' the same story. They're sayin' the Kiowa were waitin' when the posse rode up to the camp, that the Injuns attacked when the sheriff told them he was lookin' for Kyle and the Injuns who broke him out of jail, and you all had to defend yourselves. Is that what really happened?"

"That's right."

"If the Kiowa attacked, how come only Kiowas were killed? Not a man in the posse got anythin' much worse than a scratch."

"Lucky, I guess."

"Why did my father and Mullen stay behind at the camp when everybody else in the posse started back?"

"What're you askin' me for?" His beardless face coloring, Quinn snapped, "Ask your pa."

"I did ask him. He said the smoke was so thick from those hides that were burnin' near Kyle that they didn't see him lyin' there when they first checked the bodies. He said he went back to check again. He said he found Kyle just a few minutes before I rode up. He said he doesn't know who shot him."

"So, what do you want from me?"

"I want to know if it's the truth!"

"Yeah, you want to know if it's the truth!" Quinn's flushed face tightened into a sneer. "You don't care about Witt! All he ever did was want the best for you—because he thought you was the greatest thing that ever walked the face of the earth. But he wasn't good enough for you. You wanted that redskin instead, and because of you, Witt's dead!"

Eden steeled herself against the wrangler's verbal assault. She repeated, "I just want the truth."

"Well, you got it! Now what are you goin' to do with it?"

Quinn turned away from her abruptly and strode out of the barn.

Shaken, Eden stood motionless for long moments before starting back toward the house. She saw Quinn pull the bunkhouse door closed behind him as she passed. The men still avoided her. Their former affection for her had become disdain. She supposed that under other circumstances their attitude would hurt her, but she was somehow too numb to react.

Startled to see Sheriff Duncan leaning against the wall outside her bedroom door, Eden felt anxiety rise anew. Halting beside him, she asked, "Is somethin' wrong, Sheriff?"

The sheriff's full face twitched in an attempt at a smile. "I'm thinkin' I should be gettin' that fella in there back to jail as soon as possible. It ain't too safe for him here."

Eden's heart began a slow pounding. "Y . . . you can't move him yet. He won't survive."

"Eden . . ." All sign of a smile fading, the lawman continued, "He might not survive if I don't."

"Nobody'll hurt him here, Sheriff."

The sheriff did not respond.

Unwilling to face the meaning behind his silence, Eden pushed the bedroom door open and slipped inside. She stopped short at the sight of Doc Bitters, bag in hand.

"Where're you goin', Doc?"

"Home, that's where. There's nothin' more I can do for this young fella tonight. I'll come back in the mornin' before the sheriff moves him to town."

"The sheriff isn't movin' Kyle tomorrow!"

"Yes, he is."

"I won't let him!"

"I don't think you have much choice."

"I—"

"Listen to me, Eden." Closing the distance between them, Doc Bitters took her hand. "Let the sheriff move him. It'll be better that way."

"What're you sayin'?"

"I'm sayin' if the bleedin' doesn't start up again durin' the night, this fella here will probably be able to survive bein' transported."

"*Probably?*"

"There are too many hard feelin's here. The sheriff's only one man. He can't fight everybody."

"The sheriff's one person. I increase the number to two."

"Nothin' you say or do is goin' to change the situation here. The fact stands—it's better for all concerned if he's moved as soon as possible."

"I—"

"I'm leavin'. I'll be back in the mornin'. I gave Kyle a sedative. He's goin' to sleep for a few hours. If I were you, I'd get a few hours' sleep myself, so's I'd be in shape to keep a keen eye on things when we move him tomorrow."

Eden stared into Doc Bitters's steady gaze. There was something he wasn't telling her. He was trying to warn her. She could either listen to him, or she could fight the inevitable.

"All right. But I'm not leavin' this room."

Doc Bitters stared at her a moment longer. "The sheriff's taken up watch outside the door. Kyle's safe enough while he's there. Don't be a hard nose. Get somethin' to eat. Take care of yourself and your horse so's you'll both be ready to travel in the mornin'. You know damned well there ain't a man on this ranch who'll go out of his way for you right now, so you'd better take care of things yourself."

The hard truth. Eden nodded reluctantly. "You're right, but I'm stayin' here until I'm sure everybody's asleep for the night."

"I'm goin'. I'll see you tomorrow."

"Thanks."

"Yeah."

Turning back toward Kyle when the door snapped closed, Eden forced back tears. She needed to be strong. Kyle was helpless. He needed her.

"Kyle." Eden sat beside him and slid her arm across his chest. She felt the rise and fall of his breathing, and her throat choked tight. He couldn't hear her, but she had to say the words.

"I love you, Kyle." Her lips trembling, she

continued more softly, "Whatever you did, I love you."

Laying her head on the pillow beside his, Eden closed her eyes.

Eden awakened with a start. She looked up to see that Kyle was still sleeping. Uncertain how long she had been asleep, she glanced at the window to see the sky bright with stars. Hours had passed. The stillness of night had silenced the sounds of the ranch. There would never be a better time for her to ready things for the trip to town without interference from her father or the others.

Kyle moved in his sleep and Eden hesitated. She wanted him to open his eyes. She wanted to tell him she'd be back as soon as she could.

Eden studied his motionless face a few minutes longer. The warm hue of his skin had paled, but his chiseled features remained somehow strong. She had been drawn to his strength the moment she saw Kyle. Despite the bloodshed and the hatred on all sides, she still felt the unspoken union of heart and mind that she had experienced when his dark eyes first met hers. She had no true regrets for loving him. Nothing could change that.

Brushing Kyle's lips lightly with hers, Eden drew herself wearily to her feet. She had no doubt that her horse was still standing where she'd left it, unfed and untended. She had neglected it long enough.

Sheriff Duncan was sprawled asleep in a

chair outside the door. It occurred to her as she pulled the door closed behind her that he had taken Doc Bitters's advice and was getting some well-needed rest while everything was quiet. She'd do the same as soon as she was finished.

Anxious to be done, Eden headed for the barn.

A stabbing pain in his chest awakened Kyle to the darkness of the room. A sudden uneasiness stirred his senses, and he forced his eyes open. The shadows of the room moved, forming a familiar outline. The broad figure moved toward him.

Lone Bear.

He was dreaming.

"Young Hawk." Lone Bear's harsh whisper dispelled the unreality of the moment. Crouching beside him, Lone Bear said, "The scent of death fills my nostrils and sadness fills my heart—but it is rage that brings me to you. Your wounds are of the body. They will heal, but your people endure a greater suffering. Your people cry for vengeance against the great wrong that was done to them. The spirit of Rain Woman calls out to me and to you, who share my blood. It is time for you to stand beside me. It is time to embrace your destiny, Young Hawk."

Still disoriented, Kyle grated, "How did you get in here?"

"The guard at the window was easily overcome. Gray Fox and Standing Man await us with horses. You must come with us now."

Kyle nodded. Yes, he must.

Kyle fought the waves of dizziness sweeping over him as he attempted to stand. Lending his strength, Lone Bear assisted him to his feet. So intent were they that they did not hear the sound at the door before it flew open with a bang.

"Don't move!" Tom Richards's sharp command jerked Lone Bear upright. Kyle sensed Lone Bear's hot flush of hatred as his hands dropped to his sides and he turned fully toward the rancher's drawn gun.

Richards laughed aloud. "This couldn't be better. Eden was right when she said we needed to bring *Kyle* here. Hell, she was smarter than anybody gave her credit for. She knew it would flush more of you heathen redskins out into the open. Now we have two of you to hang!"

Kyle swayed, silently cursing his weakness. He looked at Lone Bear. He knew that stance, and he knew the look on Lone Bear's face. Only a bullet would stop him.

Addressing Lone Bear, Richards continued, "You Injuns ain't as good as you think you are. I saw you climb in here, and I sent one of the boys back to the bunkhouse to rouse the men. They'll be here any minute—too soon for anythin' you're plannin'!" Richards laughed again. "Yeah . . . you're *both* goin' to hang."

Kyle turned toward the window at the sound of angry voices in the yard. The cowhands were coming!

His attention momentarily diverted by running footsteps in the hallway, Richards turned toward the sound. Leaping forward in a flash of movement, Lone Bear drew his knife from his waist and plunged it into Richards's back.

A sudden gunshot shattered the silence.

Watching as if mesmerized, Kyle saw Lone Bear's powerful frame shudder with the impact of the bullet. Unable to move, he saw Lone Bear turn to meet his gaze a last time before falling heavily to the floor. He looked up to see Eden in the doorway, a smoking gun in her hand.

Kyle heard Lone Bear's dying rasp.

He saw Eden's unwavering stare.

He knew it was over.

Chapter Six

Kyle glanced around the cell where he had spent the last two months of his life. He remembered being delivered from the Diamond R in a daze, with only the image of Lone Bear's lifeless form vivid in his mind. He recalled the countless empty days of recuperation. His physical wounds had healed. He was strong again, but silent rage festered within.

Strangely, a part of him had died when Lone Bear breathed his last. With that part of him, his illusions had died as well. The man who survived was not surprised that Lone Bear's death, the slaughter of the Kiowa camp, and the attempt on his own life went ignored and unpunished, while he was brought to trial for Witt Bradley's murder.

His lips twisting with bitterness, Kyle rubbed

his scarred wrists. His ankles bore similar scars from iron shackles that had not been removed since the day he took his first, unsteady step. Delivered to the courtroom in chains as a waiting crowd shouted angry epithets, he had known from the outset what the verdict would be. Found guilty, he heard the crowd roar its wrath when the judge spared him the death penalty in favor of imprisonment at hard labor—*in a place where few survived the first year.*

A late autumn sun shone beyond his cell window, but Kyle felt none of its warmth. He was cold inside, as dead as the brave warrior whose lifeless image was burned indelibly into his mind.

A debt of blood had yet to be repaid.

As for the softer image that haunted him— blue eyes glowing with love, smooth skin flushed with passion—he had reminded himself over and again that those eyes hid betrayal, and that they had been cold as ice when Eden stood in the bedroom doorway, a smoking gun in her hand.

He hadn't seen her since. There was no need to question why. He knew the answer.

Distracted from his thoughts when the inner door to the cells opened, Kyle turned toward Sheriff Duncan. The lawman announced soberly, "They'll be here to pick you up soon."

To deliver him to prison.

"But there's somebody here to see you first."

Eden stepped into view and Kyle's heart leaped with rage. Infuriated by the traitorous, aching hunger the sight of her evoked, he rasped, "Get her out of here!"

Rigid, Eden stared at the manacled man separated from her by iron bars—the man whose dark eyes raked her so venomously. He was thinner than before, almost gaunt. His weight loss and the black hair that now hung unbound past his buckskin-clad shoulders emphasized a savage demeanor she had once dismissed, but which she could no longer ignore.

But it wasn't the physical change in his appearance that affected her most strongly. Rather, it was the hatred in his gaze that chilled her.

Eden's throat tightened with pain. The conflict within her had never been greater. So much had happened. How could she find the words to convey her horror when she saw Lone Bear plunge his knife into her father's back? How could she explain her anguish in knowing that her father lay bleeding and near death because of her? How could she describe her guilt? How could she tell Kyle that she hated him at that moment for making her love him—but that she loathed herself even more? How could she make Kyle understand that her refusal to visit him was a way of punishing herself and him for her father's suffering—but that ultimately she'd realized the only offense they had committed was to love each other?

The answer was suddenly clear. She could

not. It was too late. This man who had once loved her was her enemy.

"Get her out of here, Sheriff."

But she had to try!

Her voice devoid of the emotions rioting within, Eden responded, "I'm not goin' anywhere until I say what I came to say."

The chill in Kyle's gaze turned to ice.

Hardly aware that Sheriff Duncan had left and pulled the door closed behind him, Eden forced herself to begin.

"You're angry. You have a right to be, but I couldn't let them take you away without trying to explain. So much has happened. My pa almost died."

Almost.

"When the shock of it was over, I wanted to come to see you, but the sheriff wouldn't allow it. He said it was too close to the trial date. He said my visit would inflame the townsfolk—that you'd be the one to suffer if I came."

Lies.

"Then Pa had a relapse and I couldn't come to the trial."

Tom Richards, who survived.

"The wranglers had calmed down a bit by the day of the trial. I talked to them. They promised me they'd testify about the confusion in the cabin when you shot Witt. They did what they said. I couldn't believe it when you were convicted."

He could.

"I . . . I want to do *something*. You said you

have friends back east. Tell me who they are. I'll contact them to see if they can help. I'll get you another lawyer. I'll—"

"You waste your breath!"

"Kyle—"

Kyle took an angry step forward. His chains scraped against the stone floor, and Eden shivered.

"Do my chains bother you?" Kyle's smile was bitter. "Strange, because you're the one responsible for them."

"I'm not!"

"You told your father the location of the Kiowa camp so the posse could satisfy its blood lust by massacring my people!"

"No!"

"You thought the posse would lose interest in chasing me, and it would all be over and done then. You didn't think I'd go back there, and you didn't care what happened to the people in the camp. They were only savages, after all."

"I didn't send the posse there!"

"No one else knew where the camp was."

"I didn't realize my father would—"

"So, you *did* tell him!"

"Yes, but—"

Silence.

Eden took a shaky breath. "I didn't intend to tell my father where the camp was. I don't even remember why I mentioned it!"

"The camp was already destroyed when I got there. The posse left, but your father didn't. He waited. Too bad his shot was off the mark."

"He didn't shoot you!"

"I've had plenty of time to think about the voice of the man who shot me. It was your father, all right. He shot me without a second thought—just like you shot Lone Bear."

Suddenly as angry as he, Eden retorted, "It wasn't the same thing! Lone Bear was a savage! He tried to kill my pa!"

"He was a Kiowa . . . like me."

"You're not like him! You're . . . you're—"

"I am Kiowa! When you spilled Lone Bear's blood, you spilled mine!"

Eden gasped, "My pa was right all the time, wasn't he? He said you were a Kiowa first, and that nothin' I could ever say or do would make a difference when the time came."

"Your father and his men killed Kiowa women and children while shouting my name. They burned everything they left behind so survivors would suffer even more because of me. The only reason I'm alive now is because your father's shot didn't hit its mark—and you call Lone Bear a savage!"

"Lone Bear *was* a savage! He stabbed my pa. Pa's crippled! He'll never walk again!"

"Lone Bear is *dead*."

"That's right, he's dead and I killed him." Shaking with sudden overwhelming fury, Eden rasped, *"I killed him, and I'd do the same thing again."*

Silence marked the significance of the moment.

It was over. She had lost him.

Turning when voices sounded at the door behind her, Eden saw Sheriff Duncan walk into view, followed by two strangers wearing badges.

Sheriff Duncan addressed her quietly. "You'd better leave now, Eden. These fellas are here to take the prisoner."

Eden glanced back at Kyle. His eyes were cold . . . dead.

They had already said goodbye.

Eden was leaving.

Despising himself for the aching yearning that soared to sudden blinding heat within him when she turned away, Kyle spoke softly, in a tone that filled the silence with the power of a shout.

"Eden."

Eden stopped short.

"Tell your father . . . tell them all . . . I'll be back."

Chapter Seven

Summer, 1850

The burning sun did not affect him. The shackles no longer irritated his skin. He raised his pickaxe over his head and drove it into the ground, raising a cloud of grainy dust that was swept away by a warm gust of wind. He paused to brush aside dark, heavy strands of hair that adhered to his sweaty bare back—a back muscled and corded by years of physical labor. The expected response to his pause was not long in coming.

"Hey, Injun!" The senior guard approached, rifle in hand. "Keep swingin' that pick if you want to eat tonight."

He met the man's gaze with eyes that spat hatred.

127

"Bastard! Don't look at me like that!"

He raised his pick again over his head, restraining a smile when the sweating guard took a spontaneous backward step. He drove it into the ground with earth-splitting force. His manacles slammed against the bones of his wrist, abrading flesh already callused and scarred from long years of such abuse, but he dismissed the chafing. Iron shackles and heavy chains, long days in the scorching sun, and endless nights of silent rage had molded him into the man he was now—a man taller, harder, more powerful—a man without fear.

He glanced at the guard as he raised his pick again. Satisfaction pulled at the corners of his lips when the fellow muttered a low curse and retreated another step. He celebrated that man's fear, just as he had celebrated the final demise of Kyle Webster and of Young Hawk years earlier. The new man forged in their stead was stronger than the metal constraints he wore.

That man's name was *Iron Hawk*.

And tonight, Iron Hawk would be free.

"You mean you didn't get up to the north pasture yet?" The tone of Tom Richards's voice raised his weary wranglers' heads from their plates. His scowl turned them toward Eden where she sat at the far end of the table, frowning back at him.

"That's right, Pa, we didn't. You know

damned well the kind of problems we've been havin'."

"Yeah, I know, but that ain't no excuse. You know what's goin' to happen if you don't drive them beeves in close where we can watch them better."

Eden knew what was coming. She recognized the signs. Another rampage was beginning, and neither she nor the men were in the mood for it.

"Pa—"

"Don't 'Pa' me! Just do what you have to do!"

Slamming his fork down onto the table, Richards turned his chair and propelled it toward his room at a speed that tightened Eden's frown. His bedroom door slammed shut, and Eden put her fork beside her plate, her appetite gone.

"What're you doin'?" The blunt question turned her toward Jesse Rowe, where the whiskered cook stood in the kitchen doorway, holding a platter with hands that could no longer handle the task of roping, but still turned out the best biscuits in the county. Short, wiry, his legs bowed from long years in the saddle, and his skin like weathered leather, he had been hired the week before her pa was first lifted into his chair. He ran the kitchen with an iron hand and a steely stare that even her pa was seldom able to ignore.

Not waiting for her reply, he continued, "You ain't goin' to let your old man get to you again, are you? Hell, you're runnin' this ranch as good as any man could—your pa included. He knows it, too! He's frustrated, is all, and he's takin' it out on you like he always does."

Eden glanced toward the assenting grunts that sounded around the table. Whitney, Booth, McGill, Quinn, Hawkins, Curry, Masters—even Mullen, who she'd thought would never come around—all looked back at her in silent support that had been hard-won. They had surrendered their resentment with great reluctance, accepting her in her father's place only after she had successfully overcome the past by proving to them a day at a time that she was determined to rise to the task she had undertaken.

Her throat suddenly tight, Eden shrugged. "I'm not hungry."

"You are, too!" Rowe's small eyes pinned her. "Eat. I'll take care of your pa."

"No, leave him alone. He'll get over it."

"He ain't got no right to act the way he does! It ain't your fault if the Army ain't been able to stop them Comanches from makin' life hell around here."

"He'll calm down in a couple of hours." Eden pushed back her chair.

"You ain't finished your dinner."

"Yes, I have."

Ignoring Rowe's grunt of disapproval, Eden left the room with an uncompromising stride which did not alter until she reached her mare's stall. Halting abruptly, she stood as still as stone in the empty barn, her teeth clamped tightly shut.

Damn it all! No matter how hard she tried, nothing ever went right!

Eden struggled to subdue her anger. Rowe was right. Every ranch in the area faced the same problems as the Diamond R. It was bitter irony, indeed, that her pa had ended the "Kiowa menace" in the area with his raid on the Kiowa camp five years earlier—only to have the Comanches take over with a savagery that surpassed the Kiowa in every way. The establishment of Fort Worth on the Trinity River earlier that year had done little to change matters. The Comanches raided at will, disappearing into the wilderness like ghosts in the darkness.

Eden raised a weary hand to massage her aching temple. The escalation of attacks earlier that year had forced her into a decision that she had long avoided. She had hoped by the time summer arrived, the Army would have things under control. It hadn't happened. Instead, Comanche attacks had worsened and the situation was growing dire. She only hoped that when—

"Eden."

Eden jumped. She turned, her anger fading at the sight of the man behind her. Curt Masters's dark eyes were level with hers as he searched her face with the squinting gaze of a man who had spent his life in the saddle. Hired a few years earlier, he had fit easily into the routine of the ranch. The men liked him. She liked him, too, most of the time, but he was frowning. She had seen that frown many times over the past year—when her day stretched too long, when Pa started riding her about something she had no power to change, when they accidentally brushed against each other in passing. She had tried to ignore it.

"Masters . . ." Eden attempted a smile. "I almost jumped out of my skin."

"I didn't mean to scare you. You know you don't have nothin' to worry about on the Diamond R. There ain't an Injun in the state who'd be dumb enough to try sneakin' up on this ranch."

Eden was somehow annoyed. "I wasn't worryin' about Injuns."

"About your pa, then?"

Eden shrugged. "What's the use of talkin' about it?"

"You're right, there ain't no use." Masters took a step closer and Eden felt a flush of uneasiness. Masters was thirty years old, healthy and good-looking, and even if his temper occasionally turned vicious, he had an easy smile that most females couldn't resist. She knew he had his choice of almost any woman he set his eye on—but she wasn't *any* woman.

Eden reached for the pail hanging nearby. "I have to feed my horse."

Masters stayed her hand. His palm was warm and callused. His gaze was direct, but his smile was absent. "Your husband's been dead for more than two years, Eden. It's time for you to move on. You're a beautiful woman, and you're too young to block that part of your life off like you're doin'."

Eden's throat tightened. James Broker—her husband, and one of the gentlest men she had ever known.

Eden tried to smile. "You're a good man, Masters. You've been workin' on the Diamond R for almost five years, but the truth is, you don't really know me as well as you think you do."

"I know as much about you as any other fella on this ranch does."

Eden's lips tightened. "Meanin'?"

"Hell, a man don't live in a bunkhouse with the same fellas for as long as I have without gettin' to know the way of things."

"The way of things . . ."

"I know how you was raised the apple of your pa's eye after your ma was killed by Injuns. I know he went to war with that Kiowa fella when he found out you was meetin' him on the sly."

Eden bristled. "What else did the fellas tell you?"

"They said that Injun wasn't what he made himself out to be, that he talked you into runnin' off with him, and when one of your pa's wranglers followed, tryin' to make you see the light, that Injun bastard shot him in the back."

Eden went cold. "What else did they say?"

"That the Injun got shot when the sheriff's posse finally caught up with him, that the sheriff was afraid of some friends the fella was supposed to have back East, so he dragged him back here for the doc to look at. They said that was how your pa got knifed, when some Injun from his tribe tried to rescue him."

"Did they tell you I shot that Injun dead?"

"Yeah. They was proud of you, and I am, too. They said that Kiowa fella's still behind bars for doin' what he did to Bradley, and that's where he deserves to be."

Eden's stomach twisted tight.

"Eden . . ." His expression softening unexpectedly, Masters clasped her shoulder. "With everythin' happenin' the way it did, it must've hit you hard when you took your pa to that big hospital back East and them doctors said the same thing the doctors here did, that your pa'd never walk again. You was all alone. That Broker fella was in the right place at the right time. It ain't no secret that you was out of money and you probably would've lost the ranch if it wasn't for him. Everybody knows that would've killed your pa."

Eden could not reply.

"Everybody here knew why you married that fella, especially after he took care of things at the hospital. How was you to know he was goin' to up and die on you, and leave you with a son to raise without a pa of his own?"

Masters smiled for the first time. "He's one helluva boy, that little Jimmy. I'm thinkin' the fellas miss havin' him around as much as you do. As for your pa, I'm thinkin' that accounts for a part of his sour disposition of late—him missin' the boy and all." Masters paused. "Any man would be proud to have that boy for a son."

Eden remained purposely silent.

"I ain't got no doubt his grandma back East will be sorry to be sendin' him back here soon." Masters's strong hand cupped her chin. His voice grew husky. "So, is there anythin' I left out?"

Softening her action with an attempt at a smile, Eden stepped away from his touch. "No, just the part about how after James died, I told myself I had enough men in my life and that I wasn't goin' lookin' for more."

"Seems to me you're the kind of woman who'd never have to worry about lookin' for a man. The boys told me why that Witt Bradley followed you and got himself killed. It wasn't hard for me to understand why he felt so strong about you, why he wanted to prove to you how much he cared, or why he wanted to help you shoulder the troubles you was facin'."

"Witt was my *friend*. As important as that was to me, it was *all* he was. The reason Witt's dead now is because he wouldn't listen to me when I told him that whether he thought I was doin' right or wrong, what I did was *my* business."

"He knew what was goin' to happen. He wanted to help you."

"I didn't want Witt's help then, and I don't want anybody's help now."

"Yes, you do."

Eden's patience snapped, "That's how Witt got himself killed!"

"Don't get mad!" Masters shook his head.

"Hell, the last thing I wanted was to make you mad."

"I'm not mad." Eden paused, then continued more evenly, "I was finished a long time ago with lookin' back on things that're over and done and can't be changed. I've got more important matters to take care of now—things that are botherin' my pa as much as they're botherin' me."

Eden tried again to smile. "You're a nice fella, Masters. Do yourself a favor and go into town this weekend and take a good look around. Becky Neil's grown into a fine woman, and she's got an eye for you. For that matter, Sissie Walker—"

Masters's full lips twitched. "Thanks, but I don't need you to tell me somethin' I already know. I ain't interested, and I ain't listenin'." He took a step closer. "All right, I'll back off, if that's what you want, but make no mistake—my feelin's for you ain't somethin' you can talk away."

"You're wastin' your time."

"Well, I guess it's my time to waste then, ain't it?"

Masters was about to turn away when Eden halted him with a hand on his arm. "I'm sorry."

"Don't be. I ain't givin' up, you know."

"Masters . . ."

Suddenly more sober than she had ever seen him, Masters continued more softly, "I know what I want, and what I want's worth waitin' for. I'm a patient man."

Masters's declaration rang in her mind as

Eden worked unconsciously in her mare's stall minutes later. She didn't need this. Thoughts of Witt still tormented her. She missed him, but she had meant what she said to Masters. She had no time for distractions. She was a woman with responsibilities, not the headstrong, immature girl she had once been, who refused to consider the impact of her actions on those she loved. She had made mistakes—plenty of them. She had ruined lives beyond repair. She had learned hard lessons that she would not forget, and she would not make the same mistakes again.

Her mare was feeding leisurely when Eden hung the pail back on the wall. She stood staring blindly at the animal for silent moments, then raised her chin determinedly. The past was over and could not be undone. She had put it behind her.

Eden strode toward the barn doorway. She halted as she emerged into the yard and looked upward. Darkness had fallen. The clear night sky was ablaze with stars. She wondered if—

No. She was finished with wondering, too.

Resolute, Eden walked back to the house.

Darkness had fallen. The clear night sky was ablaze with stars, but Iron Hawk's small cell was dark and airless. The heat was a heavy mantle on his bare shoulders, a weight he had long ago learned to bear.

Moving quietly, Iron Hawk slid his wooden bunk away from the wall, then removed the packing that concealed his route to freedom. He had lived for the few inches he progressed each night toward his goal. When it was within his reach, he had endured long, frustrating nights while he worked diligently at his chains until the selected links were sufficiently weakened. And during the few hours when he allowed himself to sleep, he dreamed of what freedom would bring.

A solitary cloud slid across the moon, and Iron Hawk smiled. Gripping the chains that linked his wrists, he broke the weakened link, then snapped his ankle chain as well. He did not bother to bid farewell to the misery he had endured as he slid into the tunnel and inched his way forward.

The dark corridor grew progressively airless as Iron Hawk made his way toward the exit beyond the prison grounds. Showers of sandy soil accompanied each forward inch, impeding his progress. He was painfully short of breath when a gust of air from the end of the tunnel bathed his face at last. He stilled. The air was sweet and fresh with the scent of freedom.

Iron Hawk's heart began a heavy drumming. Previous attempts by inmates to tunnel free of their confinement had failed. The punishments exacted were heavy, but he was unafraid. The time was right.

The air grew clearer. The tunnel lightened. The end was in sight.

Pausing an inch from freedom, Iron Hawk waited. He listened. Satisfied, he thrust himself forward, using the iron manacles on his wrists for greater traction as he dug into the ground to pull himself free.

His powerful body crouched like a wary animal, Iron Hawk searched the shadows. Four hours, perhaps five, and his escape would be discovered. He must run like the wind while the darkness still concealed him. He must make his way to the river. The current was his ally. It would carry him away.

Slowly drawing himself erect, Iron Hawk surveyed the silent terrain a last time. He had dreamed of this moment, and it was his.

Eden awakened with a start. She glanced around her room. She stared into the shadows, her heart pounding. She recalled a night when those shadows came alive with a familiar form. She remembered the broad stretch of shoulders and the fluid step that stealth could not disguise as it approached her. She recalled her exhilaration when she realized the moment was not a dream, that it was reality, and she remembered—

No! She would *not* remember!

The heat of the room was suddenly oppressive. She needed air.

Striding out into the yard moments later, Eden breathed deeply, but her anxiety persisted. Something was wrong. Was it Jimmy? He was so far away.

Eden closed her eyes. Jimmy, four years old, with sandy brown hair, an inquisitive mind, and a smile that lit her heart. She remembered when he was placed into her arms for the first time. The moment could not be matched. The decision to send him back East to visit his grandmother earlier that year was one of the most difficult decisions she had ever made—but she knew in her heart it was right.

Comanche raids had intensified with the coming of spring. The ranches in the area had been particularly hard hit: cattle slaughtered and scattered; outbuildings burned; fences destroyed; riders killed. With the need to leave a sizable force behind to protect the ranch, she and the wranglers had been forced into especially long hours to repair the damages. She had reluctantly accepted that Jimmy would be asleep when she returned each night, and that she would ride out before he awakened in the morning. But she could not accept his nightmares.

Eden's throat tightened. Her poor little darling. He tried so hard to be a man, but he was only a little boy, after all.

A familiar anger flashed. She knew who was to blame for those nightmares. Pa was relentless in his vivid descriptions of Indian attacks. He did it deliberately, she knew. He was desperate to pass along his hatred of the Indians to the grandson he loved without qualification. The only problem was that Jimmy was too young for real hatred. He was not too young, however, to be *afraid*.

The nightmares rapidly worsened, and when

James's mother wrote that she wanted her grandson to come back East for a visit, Eden knew she must get him away.

Pa had fought her decision furiously, right up until the moment when Emily Broker's servant arrived to escort Jimmy back East. Eden's only consolation as the stagecoach faded from sight was the hope that when her child returned in the fall, the Indian raids might be under control.

But the raids continued. That hadn't gone right, either.

Everybody here knew why you married that fella, especially after he took care of things at the hospital. How was you to know he was goin' to up and die on you, and leave you with a son to raise without a pa of his own?

Yes, everybody knew. Eden closed her eyes as tears threatened. But they couldn't know that she would not have survived those dark, desperate days without James's kindness, his selflessness and unconditional love. He was exhilarated when Jimmy was born. He used the short time he had with his son well, and his love for them never faltered. She was devastated when he breathed his last.

Another chill shook her, and Eden snapped her eyes open. Suddenly sure somehow that her uneasiness was not related to her beloved son, Eden stared into the shadows. It was foolish, she knew—just imagination that made those shadows appear to take on human form ever so briefly. The past was dead. It had died with the thrust of the knife that had put her father in a wheelchair, and with a twitch of her finger—the gunshot that still echoed in her dreams.

The past was dead. It was over and done.

Yet she still ached—

Eden shivered, abruptly cold despite the heat of the night. Angered by her wandering thoughts, Eden turned back to the house.

The river was cold and the current was strong. Iron Hawk fought to keep his head above the churning rapids, silently cursing the power that dragged him relentlessly downward even as it aided his escape. He could not measure the time that had passed since he'd entered the river. He knew only that his limbs were weakening and his breathing was pained. He could not last much longer.

Pulling free of the powerful current with a mighty effort, Iron Hawk struck out strongly for shore.

Moonlight lit the silent terrain with the brightness of day as he drew himself up onto the bank and staggered to his feet. He gasped for breath, standing stiffly as a soft night breeze caressed naked flesh covered only by a breechcloth. He stared at the stars above him. The night was so clear. He breathed deeply of its freshness, filling his lungs with freedom.

Turning sharply toward a sound behind him, Iron Hawk saw a small animal scurry into its burrow, and his moment of exhilaration faded. A sign. The meaning was clear. There was no time for celebration when his freedom was not yet secured. He knew where he must go. He knew what he must do.

Tossing back the long, black strands that hung against his shoulders, Iron Hawk surveyed the moonlit landscape before him, searching out his path. In its stead, a familiar image appeared in his mind with sudden brilliance, tormenting him with flowing gold hair and blue eyes bright with love. A remembered gunshot echoed, and Iron Hawk's jaw hardened.

The night lost its beauty. The wind lost its caress. Iron Hawk pressed on.

Standing in the shadows outside the bunkhouse, Curt Masters watched as Eden turned and strode back into the house. He stared at the door that closed behind her. Sleep had eluded him despite the long day he had spent in the saddle. Forced from his bed in frustration as his conversation with Eden ran over and over again in his mind, he had emerged from the bunkhouse to see Eden standing just beyond the ranch house door, and his frustration had increased.

Masters recalled the first time he had seen Eden. Hell, he had almost been knocked breathless. He had seen yellow hair before, but none the likes of hers. Blue eyes were nothing new to him, but hers stopped him dead. He had known a lot of pretty women, but not a one of them could match her. He remembered the irrational anger he had fought to conceal when he discovered she was married to that James Broker fella. Broker was nice enough, but Masters had known instinctively that Broker wasn't half the man she needed.

Then he heard the rest of the story.

Masters's full lips pulled into an unconscious sneer. Eden and a Kiowa. An Injun! He had been outraged. He knew how her pa must've felt. Knowing the old man now, he wondered how Eden had managed to stand up against him. The thought of her being with that red-skinned devil made his flesh crawl, but she was redeemed in his eyes when he heard how she pulled the trigger on the Injun who knifed her pa.

Masters considered that thought. The truth was, none of that really mattered to him now. He had watched Texas sunlight shine on Eden's yellow hair for almost five years, and he had looked into her blue eyes until he almost drowned in them. He had watched Eden ride and rope better than a man. He had seen her bend her back to work right alongside the men at the heaviest tasks. He had heard her bark orders and he had heard her cajole. He had heard her laugh, but he had seldom heard her complain. She was tough as any man, but when she walked, it was with an unconscious sway that was all woman.

His decision was made before he even realized it. She was the woman for him.

"You're wastin' your time, Masters."

Masters turned toward the unexpected voice.

Somehow he wasn't surprised to see Mullen standing in the bunkhouse doorway. The keen-eyed foreman always seemed to know everything that was going on.

Masters responded without any attempt at denial. "That so? I think you're wrong."

Mullen's gaze did not falter. "Let me tell you somethin'—for your own good. For a while, I wouldn't have wasted the time of day on that girl. I was right beside her pa when she put him through hell because of that Kiowa. If I was him then, I would've let her go with good riddance."

"But he knew better."

"Maybe . . . but my opinion of the woman Eden turned out to be is different. Truth is, I ain't never seen nobody, male or female, who's tougher than she is. It took a while for me to admit it, but she's as much of a *man* as her pa ever was when it comes to this ranch—and she's a damned good mother, too. Only one thing ain't changed. She knows her mind, and there's nobody goin' to change it once it's set. If I were you, I'd save myself a lot of trouble and stop lookin' her way."

"But you're not me."

Mullen sneered. "I've seen that hard-nosed attitude before. Witt Bradley—"

"I ain't interested in Witt Bradley! That's in the past."

"Witt Bradley didn't say much, but everybody knew how he felt about Eden. Everybody knew how Eden felt about him, too."

"It ain't the same."

"Ain't it?"

"That was a long time ago. I'm a lot older than Bradley was."

"What difference does that make?"

"I've been around. I know how to handle myself."

"If you're talkin' about your experience with the ladies, you'd best keep in mind that Eden ain't like them saloon women you're used to botherin' with."

"I know she ain't. But I know the way of things. I know she's killin' herself to keep this ranch above water and her pa won't meet her halfway. She needs somebody on her side."

"We're all on her side! She knows that!"

"Maybe . . . but it ain't enough. She needs her own man to turn to. She needs somebody she knows she can trust, somebody she can lean on when she gets tired of fightin'."

"That's you, huh?"

"Yeah, that's me."

"You're thinkin' she's had a hard time of it."

"That's right."

"You're thinkin' she deserves better."

Masters didn't bother to reply.

"Hell, you ain't no different from Witt . . . not one little bit. He was always makin' excuses for her and lookin' out for her, whether she wanted him to or not. That's what got him killed!"

"Don't worry. I ain't got no intention of dyin' that way."

"Neither did Witt."

Masters stiffened. "I'm done talkin'."

Mullen's small eyes narrowed into assessing slits. "Really care for her, do you?" When Masters did not answer, he shrugged. "Good luck to you, but I wouldn't push her too hard. If you do, you might find out she's more than you bargained for."

"I can handle it."

"Maybe."

Allowing his last word of reply to stand for a silent moment, Mullen strolled back into the bunkhouse.

Masters stared after him, then grated, "I can handle it."

Exhaustion claimed Iron Hawk as dawn made its way across the night sky. He had crawled through an airless tunnel, his lungs bursting. He had ridden the merciless river downstream. He had run the moonlit trails until his bare feet bled, with only a star to guide his direction.

But morning approached. The star was fading and his strength was dwindling.

His breathing short, Iron Hawk leaned back against a fall of rocks and closed his eyes. He dared not lie down. He would allow himself only to rest a few minutes until he regained his breath.

Iron Hawk did not hear the sound of approaching hooves until they were almost upon him. Jumping up, he slid behind a boulder and listened intently as the hoofbeats drew nearer. His heart pounding, he remained motionless as they halted beside the place where he was hidden.

Rage infused him. He would not be put back in chains. He would not return to the place that drained a man's spirit before it took his life. He would breathe his last breath in freedom, cursing those who sought to destroy him and his people.

Springing from concealment, Iron Hawk took a racing step forward. He halted abruptly, staring with disbelief at the man looking back at him.

"You return at last." White Horn's voice quaked in the silence. The gray light of dawn exposed the new lines that ravaged the shaman's face, but the old man's gaze was keen and unwavering as he continued, "You have journeyed long to this place and time. Your body has suffered torment and your spirit has raged. You have faced many perils, but you have persevered. The man within has been purged by these hardships. His thoughts are pure and clear. His destiny awaits him, Young Hawk."

"Young Hawk is dead."

Unfazed by his response, White Horn replied, "How do you call yourself now?"

Raising powerful arms toward the aged shaman, he clenched his fists as he displayed the iron cuffs on his wrists from which chains still dangled. He rasped, "My jailers thought they would enslave me with these manacles. They thought they would kill my spirit, but these bands didn't weaken me. They made me

stronger. They're a part of the man who survived, and from them I take my name—Iron
Hawk."

White Horn's enigmatic gaze grew intense.
He nodded, then motioned to the horse he led
behind him. "Iron Hawk's ordeal is over."

Iron Hawk was mounted when the aged shaman added in solemn declaration, "And now
Iron Hawk's time has come."

Chapter Eight

Eden was in his arms at last. Her womanly flesh was hot against him. Her scent was sweet in his nostrils. Her lips were inches from his.

Shuddering with emotion barely held in check, Iron Hawk looked down into Eden's eyes. They were so blue. He had tried to forget the glow that suffused them when their naked flesh met. He had struggled to strike from his mind her muted sounds of yearning when he crushed her close. He had fought to cast forever from his thoughts the words of love she uttered.

Iron Hawk slid his fingers into her hair. The silky strands were liquid gold against his palms. He smoothed her cheek, skin that was fine and clear beneath his callused fingertips. He pressed his mouth to hers, and the glory swelled. The taste of her shook him with hunger.

Joy became bliss when her lips separated under his. Rapture encompassed him as she turned to him fully, giving as he gave, wanting as he wanted . . . as he wanted . . . as he—

Iron Hawk awakened with a start.

His heart pounding, Iron Hawk glanced around the tepee. Dawn lifted the shadows of night from its interior and reality rapidly returned. Curling his hands into tight fists, he fought to curtail the shuddering his dream had evoked. He had returned to the tribe two months earlier and had cleansed his spirit with fasting and prayer. With White Horn's guidance, he had confirmed his direction in a vision quest that had cast forever aside a youth spent estranged from his people. He had discovered a heart that was true Kiowa, and he had then ridden the land for endless hours until communion with his Kiowa blood was complete. His people recognized the man he now was, and accepted him instinctively. Yet in all he did, he was still powerless against the golden vision that haunted his dreams.

A sudden fury rose, drawing Iron Hawk to his feet. But he was no longer dreaming!

The bite of fall nipped Iron Hawk's naked flesh as he reached for his clothes. He donned the soft buckskin garments given to him in celebration of his return. Still clear in his mind was the bittersweet moment of his arrival in the Comanche camp when he recognized fully, for

the first time, the lasting change that the deci-
mation of the Kiowa camp had wrought on his
father's people. The survivors had been forced
to make desperate choices. Some had traveled
north to join larger Kiowa bands, while others,
hardened to vengeance, had remained to join
the Comanche.

Familiar warriors within the camp had renewed his acquaintance—Yellow Dog, whose
easy smile was now seldom seen; Gray Fox and
Black Snake, who hunted men as they once
hunted game; Spotted Elk, Black Cloud, Red
Crow, Sitting Bear, Standing Man—all men
with one purpose in mind. Theirs was a solemn
reunion, with a mission that united them as
one.

His acceptance in the Comanche camp had
been gradual. The Comanche chief studied him
with caution, while other warriors kept their
distance, but he had not awaited their recognition to embark on the path that was set for
him.

He had ridden to the new fort and observed
it covertly, studying its fortifications with silent
determination. Impatient to strike at the heart
of his people's enemies, he had returned to the
camp to participate in sporadic raids against
the steady encroachment on his people's lands.
He had proved himself fully at last when leading Kiowa warriors in a victorious attack on a
supply train that brought new prosperity to the
Comanche camp. Once regarded with scorn,

the iron cuffs he still wore on his wrists were now celebrated as bands of honor.

Iron Hawk emerged from his tepee. He stretched his powerful frame to its full height as he scanned a camp stirring slowly to life. He remembered another peaceful camp, one that had been destroyed in his name. He had vowed retribution, and he served that cause in all he did. He had honored Lone Bear's memory at every step of redress . . . but he had yet to serve his personal vengeance.

Iron Hawk turned toward the place where his mount leisurely grazed. He approached the animal with a determined stride, knowing that with each dawn, the time drew nearer when he would address that goal as well.

Patience was difficult, but it would not be much longer.

"Do you want me to help you with that?"

Tom Richards's jaw hardened at the sound of the voice behind him. Ignoring the question, he stretched up to the wall rack beside the ranch house door. He retrieved the hat hanging there with pure strength of will, then jammed it onto his head before turning back toward Jesse Rowe. "I may be a cripple, but I ain't totally helpless!"

"I know what you ain't." The balding cook eyed him coldly. "What you are is an ornery cuss who ain't got no sense at all!"

"I'd watch what I said if I was you. You ain't the only cook in these parts, you know."

"Maybe not, but I'm the best, and I'm the only fella in these parts who's not afraid to tell you that you're goin' too far by pushin' your daughter like you do, and that you might end up regrettin' it."

"Did it ever occur to you that Eden can take care of herself?"

"She usually does."

"Then you might try mindin' your own business."

"She takes care of herself and everybody else on this ranch, includin' *you*—"

"Eden don't take care of me!"

". . . includin' *you*! And just because she's your daughter, that don't give you the right to abuse her!"

"What're you talkin' about?" Richards was rapidly losing his patience. He had emerged from his room that morning to find the breakfast table had been cleared before dawn and there was no one in sight. He didn't like it. "What's goin' on here, anyways? Where is everybody?"

"Where do you think they are? You've been harpin' about roundin' up the last of the herd so's they could sort out them steers to drive to that buyer before he lowers his prices. Hell, Eden's been workin' the men from sunup to sundown to make sure the job gets done, and you ain't had a decent word to say to any one of them."

"They're doin' their jobs. They won't get no medals from me for that!"

Approaching in a few quick steps, Rowe deliberately blocked his path as he asked abruptly, "You got pain in them dead legs of yours, is that it?"

Richards glared. Yes, he had pain. He'd had pain every day of his life since the time that heathen Kiowa stuck that knife in his back. He sneered. "No, I ain't got no pain."

"And you're a damned liar, too."

"What's that to you, anyway?"

"Let me tell you somethin'. Pain or no pain, I'm gettin' damned sick and tired of seein' you drive that young woman the way you do."

"It's goin' to be her ranch when I die. She's not workin' for me. She's workin' for herself!"

"Don't tell me you're doin' it for her own good!"

Richards didn't even attempt it.

"I seen it change, you know. I seen the way the fellas looked at Eden when I first came here, when you was first put in that chair. They was with you, then, blamin' her for the bad things that happened. Then I started seein' things change, and I started hearin' things."

Richards stiffened. "You started hearin' what things?"

"I started hearin' things like, maybe you was as much to blame for what happened as Eden was, what with you barely missin' killin' that young Kiowa fella she had her heart set on."

"Who are you talkin' about?" Richards responded sharply. "That nice young Kiowa fella who shot Witt Bradley in the back, you mean?

That same fella who got shipped off to prison where he belonged, but not before he told Eden to tell everybody on this ranch that he'd be back to get them?"

Rowe didn't respond.

"You're talkin' about that same young Kiowa fella who broke out of the jail two months ago, and then showed everybody what he was made of by joinin' up with them Comanches who've been makin' life hell around here—the same bastard who's been wreakin' havoc ever since?"

"You ain't about to let her forget she made a mistake, are you?"

"No, I ain't."

"Hell, how does she stand you?"

Watching as Rowe turned away from him in disgust, Richards wheeled himself determinedly toward the porch. Fixed in his customary spot moments later, he squinted into the distance to survey the surrounding landscape. His hand slipped unconsciously toward the gun on his lap as he fought to overcome a seething anger.

They all thought they knew what he was feeling, but they didn't! Nobody knew that he was as proud of Eden as any pa could be, what with the way she took over when he was stuck in a wheelchair. He was proud of her because she did the job as well as any man, and because she never backed down, even against him. He rode her hard the same way he would ride himself, knowing the ranch was just hanging on, and that a bad year or the loss of a single herd might make them lose it all. Nobody knew his fear that his grandson—that beautiful boy he loved more than he'd thought he ever could—might never have this land for his own.

Richards struggled to rein his shuddering under control. And everybody thought he blamed Eden for his being in a wheelchair—but he didn't. It was that Kiowa he blamed. He had gone over it a thousand times in his mind. That Injun had done something to Eden somehow. She wasn't the same after that first day she saw him.

But Eden had come through for him. She had chosen him over that redskin . . . and though there had been no love lost between him and that Broker fella she married, in the end, she had given her pa something that he valued more than his legs. She had given him his grandson.

Richards paused at that thought, his jaw hardening. He hadn't taken any chances with Jimmy. He had made sure his grandson would never be soft on Injuns like his mother was. The boy hated them all—just like he had taught him. Eden had punished him for makin' his grandson see them redskins for the butchers they were by sending the boy away. He had been at war with her ever since.

Now that bastard Kiowa had escaped! He was free again—at a time when things at the Diamond R were looking like they just might work out after all—when Jimmy was coming home soon, and it seemed they might be able to round up enough beeves to satisfy the loans that were pressing hard.

Sheriff Duncan had stopped by a few days earlier to report the latest news. That bastard Kiowa was calling himself Iron Hawk now—but that didn't make no difference. That Injun would still drop just as fast when a bullet hit him.

Richards's hands twitched on his gun. He didn't know what that Injun was waiting for, but there was one thing he was sure of. The bastard would come to the Diamond R sooner or later, just like he had once before—and that would be the end of him.

Richards's face creased into an unaccustomed smile.

A brisk wind buffeted Eden as she looked up at the sky. It was mid-afternoon, but it was almost as dark as night. The black, swirling clouds left no doubt what was to come.

Eden surveyed the surrounding terrain. Grainy dust rose ever higher as wranglers chased and cut the straggling beeves. They needed to have their cattle ready for the buyer when he came through. It would be a close call, and when the storm hit, the dust would become mud and slow them down even more.

"Come on, boys! Put your mind to it! Get those beeves movin'!"

Eden winced at the sound of her own voice. She didn't need to push the men like that. She was getting like her pa.

Eden glanced around her again. She was edgy. A funny feeling had been crawling up her spine for the past half hour. She supposed she was letting all the rumors get to her.

Tightening the reins when her mare took a nervous sideward step, Eden continued to scan the surrounding terrain. She remembered Sheriff Duncan's face when he rode up with the news. She had known something was wrong immediately, and when he bluntly announced that Kyle had escaped from prison, she had gone numb. Without a hint of apology, he continued that he hadn't come out to warn them until he was sure it was true. He said Kyle had joined up with the Comanches and was responsible for the increasing raids in the area, and the word was that Kyle had vowed vengeance on every rancher who had taken part in the burning of that Kiowa camp.

Tell them . . . tell them all . . . I'll be back.

The nightmare returned with vivid clarity—her paralyzing guilt at Witt's death and her fathers disablement. She had been unable to think about Kyle without remembering the hatred in his eyes when they parted. Then the horror of those months back East, when the doctors told her that her pa's operation had failed, and that he'd be in a wheelchair for the rest of his life—*if he survived*.

Her money had run out. She'd fallen sick. Her world was collapsing around her.

Then James had entered her life. He took care of her pa and her until she was well, and he took care of everything else. He loved her, and if he heard her call Kyle's name in her sleep, he never said a word.

She had married James, then forced Kyle from her every conscious thought.

Eden took a shuddering breath as the sky continued to darken. Kyle . . . now riding with the Comanches.

There she was.

Concealed on a rise of land, Iron Hawk watched Eden drew her mount up alongside the trailing Diamond R cattle to scan the surrounding terrain. His heart began an erratic beating. He had watched her at work many times since his return. He had occasionally been so close that he could see the pulse in her throat beating. He remembered resting his lips against that pulse, and he recalled thinking that nothing could ever come between them.

A familiar hatred seethed. Eden's love had been short-sighted and short-lived. She'd revealed its limited scope when she sacrificed his people to simple expediency. She had betrayed the words she'd spoken so passionately when she married another man only months after he was gone.

Since his return, he had learned everything he could about her. She had a son. His name was James Broker and he was four years old. He was said to be cherished by his mother, and by his grandfather, on whom Lone Bear had wreaked a lasting vengeance. The boy was due to return from a visit with his grandmother soon.

Iron Hawk considered that thought. There were many paths to retribution. He had yet to make his choice.

Ignoring the rapidly darkening sky overhead, Iron Hawk brushed back the dark hair that whipped his face as the wind grew bolder. He was intent on the tableau below him when a clap of thunder snapped the anxious cattle into a sudden explosion of forward motion. Wild-eyed, the beeves were building to a wild run when the point riders cut them off and turned them expertly, averting a stampede by swinging the surging wave back on itself.

The resulting melee of bawling steers, snorting horses, flailing ropes, and shouting cowhands began. Riding boldly, Eden entered the crush as the dust clouds rose higher, thicker.

Another deafening clap of thunder intensified the clash. Eden's mare stumbled within the fray of flashing hooves, and Iron Hawk tensed. He grunted as the mare stumbled again and Eden lurched forward in the saddle. He jumped to his feet when she disappeared momentarily from view within the dust. He halted his forward rush when she became visible again, this time with a rider at her side who protected her horse from the colliding beeves with his mount's superior size.

It was over in a moment. Again secure in the saddle, Eden shouted brief orders to the fellow who had come to her aid, then spurred her

horse forward. The wrangler followed her, and
Eden shouted at him angrily. Iron Hawk saw
Eden stiffen when the fellow remained beside
her despite her obvious order to the contrary.

Iron Hawk's scrutiny intensified.

Eden shouted again, "Curry's in trouble, Masters! Get over there and help him—now! I'll
keep these beeves in line here!"

Ignoring her, Masters remained beside her,
and Eden felt a rush of fury. Masters had saved
her hide and she was grateful, but she was all
right now, and *she was the boss!*

The dust was thick in her throat as another
thunderclap stirred the frightened bovines to
new frenzy. Eden shouted over the pervading
din, "I don't need you to watch over me, Masters! Get over there and help Curry!"

Masters glared back at her. "I'm not goin'—
not unless you pull that mare over to the side
and rest her up! She's ready to fall again!"

"She's all right!"

"No, she ain't!"

"Masters, I—"

Grabbing her reins unexpectedly, Masters
wrested them from her hand. Eden shouted a
curse as he dragged her protesting mount
through the pummeling beeves. She swore
again when Masters pulled her onto the side-
lines, then turned aggressively toward her.

"Stay here!"

"I'm the boss of this outfit! Not you!"

"Look at your horse, damn it! Use your head!

You're both goin' to get trampled if you don't!"

"Give me those reins!"

"No."

"I said—" When her attempt to wrest them from Masters failed, Eden spat, "Give me those damned reins or you're fired!"

"Don't be so damned stubborn. Look at your horse!" Furious, Masters demanded, "Look at her!"

Her mount gave a sudden wheezing cough that drew her attention, and Eden went still. The mare was breathing hard, her eyes were bulging, and her stance was slightly off balance. The animal took an unsteady step forward, and Eden raised her chin. She looked back at Masters.

"Hand me those reins . . . now!"

His jaw locking suddenly tight, Masters slapped them back in her hand. "Do what you want, damn it!"

Eden held his gaze and nodded. "I will!" She paused, then added with obvious difficulty, "You're right. My mare's done in. Thanks."

Masters blinked. He reached toward her.

Iron Hawk stiffened. He had seen the angry encounter between Eden and the wrangler. He saw the man defy Eden's commands and he felt the intensity between them.

Heated emotions flooded his senses as the wrangler reached toward Eden. Iron Hawk drew himself upright, then strode deliberately to the edge of the rise to stand in clear view of those below him.

Another thunderclap was followed by an ear-splitting crack of lightning. One drop, then two, and the rain came down in earnest. The deluge pelted the melee below as Iron Hawk stood unmoving.

His eyes dark with hatred, Iron Hawk stood boldly within view as thunder again boomed and lightning splintered the sky with the brightness of day.

The downpour was sudden and drenching. Soaked to the skin in a minute, Eden shivered, but her chill was somehow unrelated to the icy rain.

Masters grasped her arm. He rasped urgently, "Eden—"

Eden unconsciously shook off his hand. She wasn't listening. Instead, she scrutinized the surrounding terrain. Her gaze halted abruptly at the familiar outline silhouetted against the stormy sky. She gasped.

Masters followed the line of her gaze. His even features tightened.

"That's him, ain't it?"

When she was unable to look away from the motionless figure, he demanded, "Answer me! That's him, ain't it? That Injun . . . that Kiowa?"

Eden swallowed, but no words emerged from her throat.

"The bastard's been watchin' you. I'll get him!"

Masters drew his gun but Eden slapped it from his hand.

Infuriated, Masters grabbed her arm again. "Are you crazy? What do you think you're doin'?"

Eden shuddered.

The wrangler was holding Eden's arm. Iron Hawk felt the heat that flared between them. With two backward steps he took up the rifle he had looted a day earlier. He raised it to his eye and fired in rapid succession.

Eden heard the cracking shots. She jumped when Masters slumped forward, blood spurting from his shoulder. Gasping, she nudged her mount closer to him, instinctively shielding him with her body. The reports sounded again and again, and steers milling only yards away fell lifeless to the ground.

Masters drew himself erect as the animals continued to fall, one with each succeeding shot. He shouted to the startled wranglers, "He's up there on the hill! Get him!"

Two more steers fell to the muddy ground before a barrage of fire was returned from within the milling herd.

The figure outlined against the stormy sky slipped abruptly from sight. "They hit him!" Masters was jubilant despite his wound. "They got him!"

"No, they didn't." Eden untied the bandanna from around her neck. She stuffed it under his shirt where a bloody circle widened. "He's gone, but they didn't hit him."

"He's down, I'm tellin' you!"

"You're so damned stubborn . . . go up and see for yourself!" Eden ignored the shuddering that shook her as the chill rain streamed in rivulets from the brim of her hat. She grated, "Go up and try to find him! Bleed to death, just like he wants!"

Drawing herself under control, Eden rasped, "He's gone . . . and that's the end of it!"

Masters was swaying in the saddle when Mullen reached their side. She saw Mullen's eyes go cold before he spurred his mount abruptly toward the rise with Curry close behind.

Ignoring them, Eden shouted, "Booth, Whitney, Quinn—get these beeves movin' again. McGill, give me a hand! I have to get Masters back to the house."

"I don't need no help gettin' back to the house!"

McGill ignored Masters's protest. Taking the reins from his hand, he knotted them around his saddle horn, then clucked Masters's mount into motion.

The storm continued its relentless assault as they rode with Masters slumped between them, but Eden was hardly conscious of its pounding. Masters's head was drooping. Despite what he had said, she knew he would never have made it back to the ranch alone.

Eden swallowed convulsively. She knew something else as well. Despite what she had said, this clash with Kyle wasn't the end of it. It was just the beginning.

The rain hammered Iron Hawk's shoulders. Biting gusts battered his face. Thunder rolled and lightning struck through the sky above him, but he closed his mind to nature's abuse as he held his mount to a steady forward pace. He reviewed the hour past as he neared the Comanche camp.

He had missed. The wrangler lived. Infuriated when Eden shielded the man with her body, he had chosen instead to leave his mark on the herd that the Diamond R depended on so heavily.

Bullets had whistled past him in return, but none had drawn his blood. Riders had attempted to follow him, but he had easily eluded them. It was a bitter irony indeed, that he was impervious to everything—except his own weakness.

That thought remained as Iron Hawk neared his tepee. He saw the fire burning within and dismounted. He did not hesitate to enter.

Running Deer looked up from the fire when he closed the flap behind him. Running Deer, sister of Standing Man, the same woman who had brought him food when he lay in White Horn's tepee, wounded from Tom Richards's bullet those many years ago. Her dark eyes were searching. Her youthful cheek was scarred by the fire that had destroyed their camp. The devastation that day had changed her life forever, yet she had welcomed him. She had raised his tepee and cooked his food, and he had brought to her a portion of the proceeds from his raids in payment for her kindnesses.

Running Deer approached. Her body heat filled the space between them when she halted a hairsbreadth away. She brushed the wet strands of hair back from his face. She stroked the raindrops from his cheek. She had offered him food and comfort. She now offered him more.

Hair as gold as the sun, eyes as blue as the sky, lips that spoke of love and then betrayed him—he would be a slave to that vision no longer!

Iron Hawk grasped Running Deer close as she raised her mouth to his.

"You had him in your sights and he got away?"

Tom Richards glared at the rain-soaked wranglers around him. They had returned a short time earlier. Steaming platters lay ignored on the dining room table behind him while the hungry men stood silent and motionless, water pooling on the worn carpeting under their feet. He grated incredulously, "All of you were shootin' and none of you hit him?"

"It isn't their fault, Pa!" Eden struggled to control her agitation. She had arrived at the ranch with Masters before the men, after dispatching McGill for Doc Bitters when they were near enough to be sure she could get Masters back alone. Doc Bitters had come and gone after tending to Masters, who was presently sleeping in the back room. She had listened to her pa's ranting as her clothes gradually dried on her chilled skin, and she had had enough of it. She spat, "It was dark, it was raining, and he was gone before the boys had a chance to set their sights."

"It was dark, but that Injun bastard didn't miss Masters! And he brought down a steer with every shot!"

"That's right, Pa, he got Masters and a steer with every shot, but Masters is all right. Doc Bitters says he won't be off his feet long."

"That Injun's playin' with us, Eden! He thinks he's goin' to make us suffer awhile before he does whatever he has in mind."

Eden stared at her father, her jaw tight. "The boys are hungry. Let them eat."

"Sure, let them go ahead and eat! Hell, we'll be eatin' good for a long time with all them steers that was slaughtered today!"

"Pa!"

"What's the matter with you?" Rowe interjected impatiently. "Didn't you hear what these fellas told you? Your daughter almost got trampled in that herd today. Then she just missed takin' the bullet that hit Masters. She didn't budge an inch even though them shots kept comin'. You can thank your lucky stars she's still alive—and you still ain't got nothin' good to say to her!"

"I don't need nobody to put words in my mouth!"

"You don't, huh?"

"That's enough!" Eden interrupted the heated exchange. Her face was white and her eyes were cold as she continued, "I'm goin' in to change my clothes, Pa. The boys did the best they could, and nobody got killed. I don't want to hear anythin' else."

"Nobody got killed *yet*."

"Nobody's *goin'* to get killed."

"You sure of that?"

"I'll *make* sure of it!"

"All right!" Rowe's bellow turned all heads toward the whiskered cook as he grated, "Supper's on the table. It's hot, but it ain't goin' to stay hot long. This conversation's gone as far as it can, and no amount of hollerin's goin' to change things."

"Rowe's right, there's nothin' else to say, except to make this clear." Eden drew herself erect. "If *any* man, Injun or white, goes after somebody on this ranch again, he's a dead man!"

Rowe turned a beady eye toward the man in the chair. "Does that satisfy you, *Mr.* Richards?"

"I don't give a damn what any of you do!"

Wheeling his chair around, Richards propelled it toward his room. The slam of his door echoed in the silence.

The wranglers were seating themselves silently at the table when Eden walked past her father's room. She closed her bedroom door behind her and stood motionless as she forced herself to make a solemn acknowledgment. Pa had been right, from the beginning. Kyle Webster never truly existed. Kyle had been a veneer disguising the true man underneath, the man who stood boldly on the rise that afternoon. That man's name was Iron Hawk, and he was a Kiowa who shot to kill.

Eden took a shuddering breath. She'd never be sure if that bullet was meant for Masters or her, but it didn't matter. Iron Hawk had made the first move, and there was only one way to stop him.

Running Deer spoke softly to him in their native tongue. She clung to him, pressing her naked flesh against his. She drew him closer. Her musky scent teased his nostrils, and Iron Hawk covered her mouth with his.

There was gentleness and consolation in the meeting of their lips. Drawing back, he looked down into her face. Her features were small and fine and her eyes were bright with emotion. The scar that twisted one cheek was a badge of honor which he revered. She was his sister as the Kiowa braves were his brothers. She was earth. She was warmth. She was the heart of his people.

Iron Hawk tightened his arms around her. She moved instinctively against him as she again offered him her lips. He returned her kiss. He crushed her closer, straining to share her fervor—but he could not.

His body failed him.

Moving her gently from him at last, Iron

Hawk saw the distress in Running Deer's gaze. He stroked dark strands of hair from her cheek and whispered hoarsely, "My mind desires you, but my body yields to a vengeance I can't push aside. I can't think past it. I won't be free until I've avenged Lone Bear's death and the blood that was shed. I ask your pardon, Running Deer."

Silent for long moments as tears welled, Running Deer responded, "My heart dwelled in vengeance for many years. I was unable to see past my pain. I looked forward only to the day when the blood shed in our camp was returned measure for measure. But with your return I was able to see beyond the past. In your arms I am again able to see the future."

"Running Deer—"

"No." Placing her callused fingers against his lips, Running Deer whispered, "Do not speak. I ask no further words. You have spoken to me from a Kiowa heart which leads your way. I will not stand in the path it dictates."

Running Deer dressed quickly and slipped out into the night, and Iron Hawk's regret flashed into sudden anger. Consoling himself that the last of the Diamond R cattle were being gathered, and the drive would soon begin, he centered his thoughts on the vengeance that would soon be his.

Chapter Nine

The pale light of dawn fell on the mounted men surrounding her. The air was heavy in prelude to a hot day to come. There had been no rain since the storm two days earlier, and the ground was dry.

Eden scanned the herd milling quietly nearby, then scrutinized the silent wranglers with a frown. She felt their tension and she knew what they were thinking. Months of grueling work had culminated in this moment. Everything depended on this drive, but it was quiet . . . too quiet.

Eden counted heads. Mullen, Hawkins, Booth, Whitney, McGill, Quinn, Curry . . . and Masters, who refused to remain behind. They had left the ranch protected only by Pa and

Rowe—a necessary risk. This drive was too important.

Eden glanced again at the herd, then scrutinized the shadowed terrain surrounding them. She took a breath, then ordered, "All right, boys, let's get them moving!"

Iron Hawk sprang to a seated position on his sleeping blanket at the sound of hoofbeats approaching their camp. He was on his feet in a minute, his fellow braves beside him. Unconscious of the sun's brilliant display as it dissipated the last fragments of dawn, he watched as the scout neared.

His heart pounding, he heard the words of confirmation he awaited when Yellow Dog shouted, "They begin!"

The tension remained as midday approached. The terrain showed no trace of the violent storm of two days before. The temperature was steadily climbing, but the cattle were moving well.

Riding alongside the herd, Eden frowned at the dust clouds that rose ever higher. Their trail could be seen for miles.

Eden's assessing gaze narrowed. The terrain was growing rougher. As aware of the increasing danger as she, the men pushed steadily forward despite the long hours already spent in the saddle. She had not needed to tell them that they would travel as far and as fast as possible, and that they wouldn't stop until they found a

NAME:_____

ADDRESS:_____

_____

_____

TELEPHONE:_____

E-MAIL:_____

_____ I want to pay by credit card.

__ Visa   __ MasterCard   __ Discover

Account Number:_____

Expiration date:_____

SIGNATURE:_____

Send this form, along with $2.00 shipping and handling for your FREE books, to:

Historical Romance Book Club
20 Academy Street
Norwalk, CT 06850-4032

Or fax (must include credit card information!) to: 610.995.9274.
You can also sign up on the Web at www.dorchesterpub.com.

Offer open to residents of the U.S. and Canada only. Canadian residents, please call 1.800.481.9191 for pricing information.

If under 18, a parent or guardian must sign. Terms, prices and conditions subject to change. Subscription subject to acceptance. Dorchester Publishing reserves the right to reject any order or cancel any subscription.

spot where the herd could be adequately defended.

Eden scanned the rocks around her, noting the pass ahead. A chill moved down her spine. She had had this feeling before. She didn't like it.

Turning toward the herd, Eden shouted, "Get them movin' faster, boys!"

Yips and calls sounded within the herd, accompanied by shrill whistles and the slap of coiled ropes. The herd's pace increased, and Eden dug her heels into her mount's sides.

The afternoon sun burned into Iron Hawk's bare back where he lay motionless against the dry overcropping of rock. Perspiration beaded his skin as he squinted down at the herd moving swiftly through the narrow pass below him. He shifted cautiously for a clearer view, his gaze intent.

He spotted her. The dust raised by the longhorns could not obscure the bright color of Eden's hair. Nor did it conceal the tense set of her shoulders as she rode alongside the herd, or her wary scrutiny of the steep rock walls.

Her searching gaze halted abruptly. Turning, she shouted a command to her drovers and whipped the cattle into a run, but it was too late.

Raising his hand in a prearranged signal, Iron Hawk struck the ground with his palm. He leaped onto his horse as gunfire erupted below, and raced across the crest of the bluff. Riding recklessly down the opposite side, he arrived on the canyon floor where silent braves massed, awaiting his command. He glanced at the barricaded passage, then at the resolute faces of his warriors as the stampeding cattle pounded into sight.

Locating Eden where she rode alongside the herd, Iron Hawk noted the moment she saw the barricade and turned back to her men with a shouted warning. He raced toward her, pulling up beside her as the first of the herd slammed into the barrier.

He saw her shock when she recognized him.

And when she raised her gun toward him, he swung his fist with all his might.

The darkness was heavy with pain.

Eden opened her eyes slowly. She saw a hide shelter above her head and heard a rustling sound nearby. She started, realizing her wrists and ankles were tied, as a shadow figure loomed over her. Wincing at the pain in her jaw, she sneered in recognition.

"It's you."

"That's right, Eden. It's me."

The unspoken threat in his voice sent warning tremors down Eden's spine. There had been a time when that deep voice had caressed her with warmth, and when the eyes looking coldly into hers had shone with loving heat. She knew now that time was past.

A sudden hatred swelled in her. "I don't know how I was ever fooled by you. You really are a bastard, Kyle."

"My name is Iron Hawk."

"That's right. How could I have forgotten? You're a Kiowa. The Websters educated you and changed your name, but it didn't take long for you to revert to your true self when you came back here. My father was right. A savage is always a savage!"

"Your father taught me more about savagery than any Indian ever could."

"Liar!"

"And he's going to pay for the lessons he taught."

"Blood and revenge, that's all you're after."

"I live in the *real* world now, Eden." Iron Hawk's voice dropped to a sudden whisper. "Look around you, Eden. This is the real world where I live."

"What happened to my men . . . to my herd?"

Eden struggled to maintain her composure as Iron Hawk replied, "I wouldn't worry about them. They didn't worry about you. They made a run for it the first chance they got, and they didn't look back."

"Liar!"

"That's the second time you've called me a liar, Eden." His face was so close that Eden could feel his warm breath against her lips, so close that his dark eyes singed her with their intensity. "You believed whatever I said to you once," he whispered.

"I was young . . . and I was a fool."

"I was young, too." Iron Hawk's tight smile sent a tremor down Eden's spine. "I believed all the things I was taught in those white man's schools. I believed that the heart of the man meant more than the people he came from, but I was wrong. The blood of my people washed away those beliefs, the blood *you* caused to be shed."

"That's not true!"

"Don't waste your breath with denials. I believed you once, but I learned a hard lesson. Now it's my turn to do the teaching."

Iron Hawk strode abruptly from the tepee and Eden closed her eyes.

Facing Elk Dancer boldly within the circle of grim-faced braves, Iron Hawk grated flatly, "The woman is mine."

Elk Dancer's heavy Comanche features darkened. Of medium height and barrel-chested, he stood a head shorter than Iron Hawk, but his power within the camp shone in eyes that grew increasingly menacing. Iron Hawk had been uncomfortable with Elk Dancer's participation in the attack on the herd, but he had also known that Elk Dancer and his braves were necessary to his plan's success. All had gone well. The ambush had been successful and the captured cattle had been distributed equally among the braves. He had not expected the bone of contention that had arisen. Nor had he been prepared to be accosted by the Comanche warrior and his braves, but his reaction was spontaneous. He repeated, "The woman is mine."

The Comanche took an aggressive step. "The

soldiers will appeal for the woman's return and she will bring much in exchange."

"The woman will remain with me as long as I want her."

"So stands the honor of Iron Hawk!" Elk Dancer taunted him openly. "He who comes to the camp and is received in welcome, now shows his true self when he cheats his Comanche brothers."

"I cheat no one!"

"You claim more than your equal share from this raid!"

"I do not!"

"The Comanche will not be cheated by his Kiowa brothers!"

"I took the woman. She is mine."

Elk Dancer slipped his hand to the knife at his waist. "She will be yours only if my blade allows."

Drawing his blade as well, Iron Hawk watched as Elk Dancer began a slow circling. His knife flashing, Elk Dancer sprang unexpectedly forward, and Iron Hawk gasped as first blood was drawn.

Blood dripped warm and hot from the slash in Iron Hawk's side as he retaliated with an unanticipated thrust. Elk Dancer took a backward step as Iron Hawk's blade found its mark and blood surged from his forearm.

His eye on a more vital target, Iron Hawk prepared to thrust again when a frail figure stepped between the two men. Iron Hawk drew back abruptly, his lips tight when White Horn spat,

"Only a fool sheds his brother's blood while a greater enemy waits."

"I am no fool!" Enraged by the aged shaman's words, Elk Dancer turned again to Iron Hawk. "I would have what was promised—an equal share of the spoils that were won this day!"

"You have an equal share!"

"The woman—"

"The woman is mine!"

"Enough!" White Horn's feeble frame quaked as he raked each man with his gaze. "When anger speaks, wisdom is silent."

The truth of those same words spoken by White Horn at an earlier time returned vividly to Iron Hawk's mind as the old man addressed him directly. "Elk Dancer's claim is just. The matter of the woman must be settled to the satisfaction of all."

A warm spill of blood continued from the slash in Iron Hawk's side, but he felt none of its sting. Instead, his rage soared as he repeated with greater intensity, "The woman is mine!"

White Horn replied sharply, "The woman or the cattle . . . the choice is yours."

Iron Hawk sneered, almost amused. "The cattle . . ." He felt Elk Dancer's surprise before he continued, "Take them! They won't be the last herd that I'll bring to this village."

White Horn faced Elk Dancer coldly. "Does this satisfy our Comanche host?"

Drawing himself slowly erect, Elk Dancer eyed Iron Hawk in silence. He touched a finger to the slash on his arm, then addressed Iron

Hawk flatly. "My blade has tasted your blood, and yours has tasted mine—and so it stands. Your cattle for the woman—a fair exchange."

Holding Elk Dancer's gaze a moment longer, Iron Hawk turned abruptly and strode back to his tepee, the irony of the moment strong.

Your cattle for the woman—a fair exchange.

Tom Richards's heart pounded as a trio of riders appeared in the distance. Never despising his dead legs more, he called out to the cook, who had disappeared into the house minutes earlier.

"Get out here, Rowe! Hurry up!"

Refusing to end his scrutiny of the approaching horsemen, he did not turn as Rowe's footsteps sounded on the porch behind him. He rasped, "Are they who I think they are?"

"It's Mullen . . . and Booth and Masters. Somethin's wrong! It looks like they're hurt!"

"Get on your horse, damn it! Get out there and help them!"

Watching impatiently as Rowe accompanied the swaying riders into the yard minutes later, Richards shouted, "What happened? Where's Eden? Is the herd all right?"

Sliding to the ground, Mullen stood unsteadily, his shirt stained with blood. Masters dismounted to lend him support as Rowe dragged Booth's semiconscious form off his saddle and threw the man over his shoulder. He was carrying the wrangler toward the house when Richards pressed, "I asked what happened and I want an answer!"

"What do you think happened?" Swaying visibly, Mullen rasped, "Them Injuns was waitin' for us when we reached the pass. An ambush . . . hell, we didn't stand a chance. Eden realized what was comin', but it was too late. We got the beeves runnin', but them bastards had a barricade set up."

"A barricade . . ."

Following as the men entered the house, Richards waited only until Rowe had settled the semiconscious Booth on the couch to press, "Tell me the rest of it! Where's the herd?" He took a tight breath. "Where's Eden . . . and the others?"

Rowe checked Booth's wound and shook his head. "I'd better try to stop some of that bleedin' before I go for Doc Bitters."

Rowe disappeared into the kitchen, and Richards exploded, "I want some answers now!"

Bent over Mullen's chest wound, Masters looked up. His tone contemptuous, he snapped, "What do you want to know first, about the herd or your daughter?"

"Damn you, Masters—"

"Them Injuns got almost half the herd before we managed to run the rest through the barricade. The savages wasn't interested in chasin' the steers or the fellas that got away, so Mullen told the rest of the men to keep the steers runnin' right up until they got to that buyer, like we set out to do. He said gettin' half a herd there was better than gettin' none of it through. But him and Booth was too bad hit to make it, so Mullen told me to start back with them because he knew Booth wouldn't make it by himself and he wouldn't be able to help him."

"What about Eden?"

"I don't know what happened to her."

"What do you mean, you don't know?"

"I said, I don't know!" Glancing at Mullen, then at Booth, Masters grated, "I think that bastard Kiowa got her."

"That bas—" Abruptly short of breath, Richards was temporarily unable to continue. Forcing himself to speak past the sudden weight in his chest, he rasped, "Tell me the rest!"

Masters's voice shook with barely controlled fury. "We was racin' them beeves through the pass when gunfire started comin' from both sides. I looked for Eden where she was ridin' alongside the herd—and I saw *him*. That Injun came out of nowhere, and there he was, right next to her. The next thing I knew, they was gone."

"What makes you think it was him?"

"It was that Kiowa, all right. I couldn't miss him! He's so damned much bigger than the rest of them heathens."

"Eden . . ."

"She ain't dead." Masters's jaw was tight. "I know that. I looked back when all the beeves had cleared the pass, and she wasn't there. If she was dead, the Injuns would've left her where she fell."

Shuddering, Richards ordered, "Rowe can take care of these two. You ride out and tell that doc to get himself here, and then go straight to town and tell the sheriff to get himself a posse and chase them savages down!" Richards struggled for breath. "I ain't goin' to leave my daughter in that bastard's hands."

Masters stood up, his eyes hot with hatred. "He was waitin' for her, you know that, don't you? Just like the last time—he was waitin' for her."

"Go get the sheriff!"

Breathing heavily, Iron Hawk paused outside his tepee. Blood dripped from the gash in his side, staining his buckskin leggings, and he grimaced. He had no time for such a wound. Nor had he time for the complications Eden's capture had brought.

Iron Hawk struggled for control. He hadn't consciously intended to bring Eden back to the camp. His intention had been to reveal himself to her so she would know he was responsible for the raid. But then Eden had drawn her gun and everything changed.

Iron Hawk's jaw tightened. Had she been anyone else . . . had the moment when her gaze met his not briefly stilled his heart, he would have drawn his blade and put an end to her meager challenge. But Eden wasn't anyone else.

Snatching her from her horse when she was unconscious from his blow, he had held her on his saddle as he joined the other braves in rounding up the portion of the herd that the wranglers had abandoned to them. As for those who escaped, neither he nor his people felt any regrets, for the sport could then continue.

Sweeping aside the entrance flap, Iron Hawk caught and held the gaze of blue eyes that burned him. He muttered, "The cattle for the woman . . . a fair exchange."

Eden fought to subdue the wild pounding of her heart as Iron Hawk entered the tepee and dropped the flap closed behind him. She scrutinized him in silence, noting clearly for the first time the changes that the years had wrought on his person. He was taller, his frame more heavily muscled. Abandoning any semblance of civilized attire, he was bare-chested, wearing only buckskin leggings and moccasins. His hair hung long and straight to his mid back, and his chiseled features were sharper, more tightly drawn than before. But it was his eyes that reflected the greatest change . . . eyes that regarded her with unrelenting enmity as he inquired, "Are you comfortable, Eden?"

"Do you really care?"

Silence met her response, and Eden silently cursed her throbbing jaw and the numbness besetting hands that were bound behind her as she attempted to pull herself upright on the sleeping bench. It did not miss her notice that Iron Hawk made no motion to aid her as she drew herself erect at last and demanded, "What are you goin' to do with me?"

When Iron Hawk made no reply and then turned toward supplies piled near the entrance, Eden saw for the first time the blood that streamed from a gash in his side. She glanced up to see Iron Hawk observing her reaction with a narrowed gaze. She smiled. "So, you didn't get away with my cattle as easily as you said."

Iron Hawk's eyes turned to ice. "You think one of *your* men marked me?" He shook his head. "Your wranglers didn't waste any effort trying to fight. They just *ran*."

"I don't believe you!" Incensed, Eden spat, "You don't want to admit that one of my men came so close to bringin' you down!"

Crouched beside her in a moment, Iron Hawk grasped her chin, forcing her gaze to meet his as he rasped, "Believe what you want, Eden. The truth never did mean much to you, so that won't be difficult. But the truth is, your men never touched me." A hard smile grazed his lips. "They never even tried."

"Lies! That's all you're capable of!" Struggling to shake off his touch, Eden spat, "whatever your intentions are, you're wastin' your time. My pa doesn't have any money to pay for my return."

"I don't want his money."

"What *do* you want? Revenge on the ranchers who raided that Kiowa camp? It wasn't their fault! They entered that camp peacefully and the Injuns attacked." Eden's eyes widened. "But what you really want is my father's blood, isn't

188

it?" Shuddering with sudden rage, she rasped, "Isn't it enough that he's crippled?"

Iron Hawk's eyes were cold.

"Whatever you want, you can't win. You know that! You lived away from here long enough to realize that your people are outnumbered. Sooner or later they'll lose!"

"Perhaps . . . but if it's later, just think what we can do until that time comes."

"Bastard!"

"Sticks and stones, Eden . . ."

She sneered, "A *white man's* rhyme."

Drawing her closer, Eden felt the warmth of Iron Hawk's breath against her lips as he whispered, "No, a *youth's* rhyme that means the same in any language."

Iron Hawk's touch was gradually gentling. Fingers that had gripped her chin with fierce anger now caressed her cheek. His mouth brushed hers and she attempted to draw back, but he held her fast.

"What are you afraid of, Eden?"

"N . . . nothing."

Iron Hawk's lips brushed hers again, and Eden fought to still her quaking as he whispered, "You taste the same . . . warm and sweet, like honey."

Eden's heart pounded as Iron Hawk slid both hands into her hair, holding her fast as his lips met hers fully. Somehow powerless to resist him, she closed her eyes as his mouth separated her lips, as his kiss pressed deeper and he—

"Iron Hawk."

A feminine voice outside the tepee yanked Iron Hawk away from her. The unexpectedly savage quality in his gaze stunned Eden.

"Iron Hawk . . . I may enter?"

Iron Hawk released Eden abruptly and drew himself to his feet. He stood looking down at her for another silent moment before he turned to the door.

"You may enter."

The squaw was young. Her features were pleasant except for the scarring on one cheek. The woman glanced at Eden with pure malice, but when the woman looked at Iron Hawk, Eden's stomach twisted in abrupt realization.

Hatred seethed within Running Deer. She knew who the woman sitting on Iron Hawk's sleeping bench was. She was the daughter of the man who had burned their camp. She was the woman who had betrayed Iron Hawk. She was the person whose treachery had left her face and her heart forever scarred.

And she was the woman who kept Iron Hawk from her.

Running Deer's hands tightened on the articles she carried. If she'd had her blade now, she would have put an end to this life that threatened hers. But she was accustomed to waiting. She would bide her time.

Deliberately addressing Iron Hawk in their native tongue, Running Deer spoke simply.

"I have come with medicine to dress your wound."

The frigidity of Iron Hawk's gaze pierced her heart as he responded, "I don't need medicine. It's only a scratch."

"Such a scratch will heal more quickly with White Horn's salve."

Iron Hawk's gaze flickered. He sat abruptly to avail himself of her ministrations, and Running Deer breathed a silent sigh of relief that the woman would not see her repulsed.

Kneeling before him, Running Deer moistened the cloths she had salvaged from a white man's coffer and wiped away the blood that was already congealing on Iron Hawk's wound. His flesh was firm and smooth under her hand, and she yearned for him with a loving hunger she felt for no other man.

Speaking to him softly in their native tongue as she worked, Running Deer whispered, "The wound is slight, as you said. It will heal quickly." She picked up the pouch of salve and dipped her finger inside. She smoothed the medicine against his skin.

Her heart beating rapidly, Running Deer looked up at Iron Hawk when her task was completed. She spoke to him gently.

"This woman brings disruption to our camp. The blood of our people is on her hands. There are many who would take vengeance on her."

His voice devoid of emotion, Iron Hawk replied, "This woman is my captive. I satisfied Elk Dancer's protest with my portion of the spoils from the raid. She is my property. Anyone who touches her will feel my wrath."

Running Deer held his gaze. "Your people have waited for your return. I would not have this woman come between you and those who look to you now for leadership."

His eyes wavered, but Running Deer was not prepared for the abrupt softening of his gaze when Iron Hawk reached up unexpectedly to stroke her scarred cheek and whisper, "I made the mistake of believing this woman once before. I let thoughts of her take precedence over my duty to my people, and many died. The images of that day are too clear in my mind for me ever to forget them. I won't let that happen again, Running Deer." Iron Hawk paused, then continued, "Don't be concerned for me. I know what I must do."

Running Deer stood and gathered her cloths. Iron Hawk stood as well. He accompanied her outside the tepee and dropped the flap closed behind them. "You are the heart of our people, Running Deer," he whispered. "You are my sister, and you will always be in my heart."

Running Deer's throat tightened with pain as she turned away. The significance of the moment burned keenly within her as she walked back to her tepee. Iron Hawk had attempted a gentle goodbye.

Running Deer raised her chin where the memory of Iron Hawk's touch still lingered. Her heart wept—but hers was a Kiowa heart! It was proud and strong! She would claim Iron Hawk for her own in the end. She would find a way.

* * *

"What are you sayin'?"

Astounded, Tom Richards stared at Sheriff Duncan. He had been momentarily elated when he saw the mustached law officer approaching the ranch with Masters riding beside him. His helplessness had forced him out onto the porch in frustration while Doc Bitters and Rowe worked over Booth's and Mullen's wounds in the living room. He wanted the blood of that Kiowa with a burning intensity, but the bitter reality was that he was totally dependent on others to do that work for him. His brief elation at Sheriff Duncan's approach had drained, however, when he realized belatedly that the sheriff and Masters were *alone*.

His gaze intent on Sheriff Duncan's jowled face, Richards continued incredulously, "You're sayin' you can't do nothin' about them Injuns raidin' my herd and takin' Eden off with them?"

"Things have changed, Tom!" Sheriff Duncan stood his ground. "It ain't like it used to be before the Federal Government built Fort Worth. We've got a Federal presence here now. It's the Army's job to handle the Injuns."

"You don't mean what you're sayin'!" Richards flushed a hot red. "You know as well as I do that them soldiers are ridin' around in circles. They ain't done nothin' since they got here but blow their damned bugles and go out on patrol!"

"That's right, they ain't." Sheriff Duncan's wiry mustache twitched. "I know how you feel,

Tom. Hell, Eden's like my own daughter."

"No, she ain't! And you ain't got no idea how I feel."

Sheriff Duncan's small eyes narrowed. "Say what you like. I know you want me to go out with a posse that'll shoot up the first Injun camp it comes onto. Well, it ain't goin' to happen. I did that once, remember?" When Richards did not reply, the sheriff continued, "I sent word to the commander at Fort Worth like I'm supposed to, but I ain't goin' to lie to you. You know as well as I do that they won't get Eden back until that Kiowa's ready to let her go."

Richards shook his head. Struggling to conceal his increasing difficulty in breathing, he rasped, "You're wrong, *Sheriff*. What I know as well as you do is that it ain't really Eden that Kiowa's after. It's *me!* He's wantin' to see me suffer, and he knows takin' Eden is the best way to do it." Richards took a shaky breath. "Well, I'm goin' to make it easy for him."

Turning toward Masters, who had been listening with a darkening frown, Richards ordered, "I want you to ride out to that new Fort Worth, but I don't want you to talk to the fort commander. I want you to talk to them Injun scouts they hired. Them Injuns will find a way to get my message to Iron Hawk. I want them to tell Iron Hawk that if he lets Eden go, I'll turn myself over to him so he can settle up with me personally, once and for all, like a *real* man!"

Sheriff Duncan took an angry step forward. "If you're plannin' on trickin' that Injun, you're makin' a mistake. He ain't no fool. He'll see through it in a minute."

"I mean every word I said."

"Then you're a crazy man!"

Speaking for the first time, Masters grated, "I ain't takin' that message nowhere."

His gaze darting back to Masters, Richards spat, "Oh, yes, you are! The thought of that Kiowa puttin' his hands on Eden is eatin' at you just like it's eatin' at me!"

"That's right, it is." Masters's face flamed. "I'll get the bastard, too, and I won't need the Army to do it."

"But you won't get him soon enough! Listen to me, Masters." Leaning forward in his chair, Richards rasped, "If you really care about Eden, you'll get that message to Iron Hawk—now—before it's too late!"

Masters hesitated, and Richards grated, "It's gettin' dark, damn it! Eden's first day at that camp is endin'. What do you think is happenin' to her? Do you think that Kiowa's got her, maybe? Do you think he might be—"

"That's enough!" Masters's gaze was deadly. "I'll get that message to the fort for you."

Richards turned back to the silent sheriff. "And you, Sheriff, just go back to that little town of yours and leave the rest to us."

"You're makin' a mistake, Tom."

"Am I?"

Watching as the sheriff strode back to his horse without responding, Richards turned abruptly toward Masters.

"You're wastin' time."

*   *   *

Eden looked upward at the patch of sky visible through the smoke hole in the tepee. Stars were beginning to appear in the darkening expanse. She had spent the greater portion of the afternoon alone, with her hands and ankles bound. Night had fallen with no end to her ordeal in sight.

Her frustration soaring, Eden worked desperately at the leather strips that bound her wrists. Her flesh was raw from attempts to loosen the thongs that only seemed to grow tighter with her continued efforts, and her ankles ached. She winced as another abused piece of skin peeled back painfully from her wrist, then raised her head when conversation sounded outside the hide walls.

Eden stilled as the conversation hours earlier between Iron Hawk and the woman who dressed his wound returned to mind. She hadn't understood a word they said, but words weren't necessary. The message between them had been conveyed in the warmth of the woman's gaze when she looked at Iron Hawk, and in Iron Hawk's tenderness when he stroked her cheek. The conversation had continued briefly when they walked outside, and she did not care to speculate about what they discussed.

The woman was Iron Hawk's lover. It made no difference to Eden that Iron Hawk had looked at that woman with a tenderness once reserved for her. The man who had held her in his arms and pledged his love with ardent passion bore no resemblance to the man he now was.

Eden paused at that thought. She was a different person, too. She was no longer the girl who lived for the moment when she would be with Kyle—a man who never truly existed. That person had died a painful death, drowning in the blood that was shed because of her. She had finally accepted the lesson those terrible times taught her and put the past behind her.

Eden took a shuddering breath. The past had risen to haunt her, but she wouldn't let it do her in. Jimmy needed her. She had already determined that she would be there to greet her son when he returned home—at any cost.

A rustling at the tepee entrance raised Eden's head as the young Indian woman entered with a steaming bowl. The woman glanced at her with true venom until Iron Hawk entered behind her. The conversation between the two was short as the woman placed the bowl near the fire and left.

Iron Hawk leaned down to dip a wooden utensil into the bowl, and Eden's stomach gurgled spontaneously. Iron Hawk's head turned toward her.

"You haven't had anything to eat or drink all day. Are you hungry?"

Eden refused to respond.

Picking up the bowl, Iron Hawk approached, and Eden gritted her teeth tightly shut. She would not allow herself to be intimidated by the power he exuded.

Crouching beside her, Iron Hawk looked coldly into her eyes. He dipped the wooden spoon into a stew heavy with gravy and swallowed the contents.

"It's good." He held her gaze. "You didn't answer me. Are you hungry?"

Damn him . . .

"Are you?"

"No."

Her stomach loudly contradicted her, and Eden silently cursed.

He had tried to deny it to himself, but she was more beautiful than ever.

Iron Hawk regarded Eden silently a few moments longer. Even smudged from the trail, her skin had a translucent quality unlike any other . . . and even pressed tight in anger, her mouth tantalized him.

It had taken several hours to finally acknowledge to himself that it was fortunate Running Deer had appeared at his tepee earlier. He had been unprepared for the physical desire that shook him when he yielded to impulse and kissed Eden, and he had been equally unprepared for her reaction. Her lips had parted under his, and had Running Deer not interrupted, he was uncertain where the moment would have ended.

In the time since, he had had time to realize that he had almost fallen into a trap of his own making. He was in control. He would not make the same mistake again. The hours past, spent with Kiowa braves who had suffered as gravely as he from this woman's treachery, had confirmed that resolution.

A fair exchange—the cattle for the woman. Eden was his, to do with as he pleased.

Iron Hawk raised the spoon deliberately to Eden's lips. When her lips remained closed, he urged, "You need your strength, Eden. How else will you be able to escape this camp and bring the Army down on us?"

The slight flaring of Eden's nostrils was the only indication of the anger she withheld. Drawing the spoon back from her tight lips, he consumed the contents again.

Refilling the spoon, Iron Hawk held it again to her lips, warning, "When this bowl is empty, you'll go hungry."

When Eden continued to refuse the food, Iron Hawk tried another approach.

"Your son will return soon."

Eden stiffened.

"You'd like to be strong enough to get a *glimpse* of him, wouldn't you?"

"Bastard . . ."

"Tell me, Eden." Iron Hawk's voice softened to a husky whisper. "What would you do to be free to welcome your son home?"

Eden was shuddering.

"Or does your pride take precedence over all?"

Eden accepted the food abruptly. Iron Hawk took another spoonful for himself as she chewed. When she was ready for more, he held back.

"You didn't answer me, Eden. What would you do in order to be free when your son comes home?"

Eden responded sharply, "You want to intimidate me. You want to make me beg. That won't happen."

"I don't want to make you beg, Eden."

Eden would not reply.

"I just want you to acknowledge that the tables are turned. The hunted has become the hunter, and he now calls the terms."

"Enjoy your gloating!" Eden shook with anger. "It'll be short-lived when the Army finds this place."

"The Army chases its tail."

"You can't win!"

"Neither can you."

His eyes as cold as ice, Iron Hawk dropped the spoon back into the bowl. He sensed Eden's fury the moment before he reached behind her to free her hands and ordered, "Feed yourself."

Eden drew her hands in front of her, and Iron Hawk frowned at the raw abrasions on her wrists. He grated, "You were a fool to think you could work yourself free."

"Was I?"

Iron Hawk stood abruptly and left Eden to the silence of tepee.

Stars brightened the night sky as Masters urged his weary mount through the gates of Fort

Worth. He had been riding for hours. His partially healed wound ached, he was hungry, and he was weary to the bone.

Ignoring his personal discomfort, Masters looked around the fort yard. It appeared the fort had begun to settle in for the night, but he would find the Army scouts and give them Richards's message to deliver as he'd promised. The way Richards had been treating Eden, he had begun to think the old man didn't care about anything but his ranch, but he was wrong. He had to hand it to the old man. He had gumption, even if he wasn't too smart.

Masters's jaw hardened. Richards was setting himself up for a fall. Even if that Kiowa did agree to Richards's terms, he'd never surrender Eden voluntarily. He'd use the opportunity to get Richards, and then he'd take Eden off with him again.

Masters flexed his wounded shoulder. He mumbled a curse at the stabbing pain that resulted. He knew why that Kiowa had shot him. He'd had plenty of time to think about it. The bastard had been watching Eden and him while they talked, and he could see there was something warming up between them. An inch or so lower, and that shot would have killed him dead on the spot, just like that Injun intended.

Iron Hawk had missed his chance—but he wouldn't.

Nudging his mount over to a hitching rail, Masters dismounted stiffly. There was only one reason he had agreed to deliver Richards's message. If that Kiowa pretended to agree to the terms of Richards's offer, he's be there, where they set up the exchange, and he'd get that Injun before the bastard knew what hit him. That was the only way Eden would ever be safe from him.

Masters glanced around him, his gaze halting on a half-breed standing at the far side of the yard. He was wearing an Army cap.

Masters started toward him.

The night sky was a black canopy studded with stars when Iron Hawk reentered the tepee. He looked at Eden where she stood opposite him, then glanced at the empty bowl resting beside the fire. He had instructed Woman Who Walks Lightly to escort Eden to the stream a few minutes earlier. He had had no concern that Eden would attempt an escape. Woman Who Walks Lightly stood taller than most men, and there were times when he had even wondered who might emerge victorious in a match of physical strength between the squaw and himself.

A glance at Eden revealed that she had made good use of her brief excursion. Her face had been washed free of the grime of the trail, and her skin glistened.

Iron Hawk stated abruptly, "It's time to go to sleep." He frowned at the leather ties lying on the ground near his feet, then picked them up. He saw Eden's instinctive backward step.

"You don't want to be tied up again, do you?"

"I don't care what you do."

"Don't you, Eden?" Closing the distance between them in a few swift steps, Iron Hawk grasped her forearms and held her raw wrists up in front of her. "You forget, I know how these marks sting. They're like bands of fire that grow hotter with every minute that you're bound." He paused. "It wasn't my intention to cause you pain, Eden."

Eden raised her bruised jaw. "That's why you hit me, I suppose, so you wouldn't cause me pain."

Iron Hawk's lips tightened. "You know why I hit you."

Eden's face flamed.

"Lie down, Eden."

"So you can tie me up again."

"No. Because it's time to sleep. This camp rises early."

Eden backed up, then sat down on the sleeping bench. She lay down and turned her back to him. Iron Hawk felt the shock that rippled through her when he slid himself down beside her and drew her back into the curve of his body.

He whispered against the golden mass resting just below his chin, "I won't tie you up tonight, but there's a price to pay."

Eden did not reply.

"Don't you want to know what the price is?"

A shudder shook her.

"What are you afraid of, Eden?"

"Nothing."

Iron Hawk drew her closer. "My arms are more gentle than leather ties."

He could feel her heart racing.

"And they're less cruel than the manacles that kept me chained day and night while I was a prisoner."

When Eden maintained her silence, Iron Hawk spoke again in a whisper that cut the silence like a knife, despite its softness.

"The chains are gone, but I still wear the iron bands, Eden . . . because I choose to. They're proof of the mistake that was made the day they were fastened on me. You see, Eden, they made me stronger." Iron Hawk drew her closer. With his lips against her ear, he rasped, "They made me invincible, Eden. I'll remain invincible until my vengeance has been achieved. You're a part of that retribution, Eden."

Eden's buttocks were tight against his male warmth. Her heat scorched him.

"You belong to me, Eden. You're my property."

Eden did not reply.

"I could take you now."

Silence.

Iron Hawk added with slow deliberation, "But . . . *I don't want to*."

After allowing long moments for her to consider his statement, Iron Hawk directed, "Close your eyes. Go to sleep."

Iron Hawk lay awake in the darkness, keenly aware of the irony that prevailed as Eden's breathing gradually slowed. He had protested when Eden falsely accused him twice; but, minutes earlier, he had truly earned the name *liar*.

Chapter Ten

"Up! Get up!"

The harsh commands that penetrated her sleep were accompanied by sharp jabs in the ribs that woke Eden abruptly. She opened her eyes to see the tall squaw who had escorted her to the stream the previous night standing over her.

"Up! Work!"

Eden sat up on the sleeping bench. Iron Hawk was nowhere to be seen.

"Come!"

Eden stumbled to her feet. Prodded into moving outside the tepee, she squinted in the brilliant glow of morning sunlight and fell into step beside the women who walked in the direction of the steam she had visited the previous evening. She turned as a little girl toddled toward them, her arms held up to the squaw. Eden's throat momentarily tightened. Jimmy had done the same thing at that age when she returned to the ranch after a hard day's work. She remembered that the long, tiring days were momentarily erased at the sight of his smile, and when she picked him up and held him tight, she had known that any sacrifice she made for him was worthwhile.

Eden looked at the child a moment longer. Jimmy would soon be coming home.

Snapped back to reality when the woman snatched up the child and the bundle beside her without a break in stride, Eden continued briskly ahead. She would escape. It was just a matter of time. She had already decided that nothing would stop her from being there to welcome Jimmy home.

Eden came into sight of the stream, and the reason she had been awakened so brusquely was immediately evident. Women of all ages and sizes knelt on the sandy bank, some rubbing a foaming substance into the wet clothing in front of them while others pounded garments with smooth rocks. Pulling a buckskin garment from her bundle after putting her child back on her feet, the big woman threw it down on the sand in front of Eden and pointed to the water.

Yes, it was washday.

Eden grimaced. She had refused to be relegated to women's chores at the ranch. She didn't like—

Knocked forward onto her knees with one

208

swipe of the woman's hand, Eden turned with a spontaneous protest that caught in her throat when the woman's small eyes narrowed. No, to make an enemy of this squaw would be a mistake. She already had too many enemies in this camp.

Eden snatched up the buckskin garment, her thoughts halting at the sight of a familiar bloodstain. It was Iron Hawk's.

You're mine now. You belong to me.

Eden unconsciously shuddered. She remembered a time when she would have welcomed those words and responded lovingly in kind. But their meaning had changed—just as the man who said those words had changed.

You're part of my retribution, Eden.

Yes, she was—but not for long.

Instilled with new determination, Eden plunged the garment into a pool at the stream's edge and began scrubbing. She looked up when the squaw dropped a piece of the foaming root onto the sandy bank beside her. Eden picked it up resentfully and rubbed it against the bloody stain. The spot lifted, turning the water at the stream's edge red.

Eden's hand stilled as she stared at the rapidly darkening water. Iron Hawk had obviously bled more profusely than she'd realized, yet he had seemed totally unaffected by the wound, as if it were of no consequence. The pain was insignificant to him, and it occurred to her that it probably paled in comparison to the hardships and torment he'd suffered as a prisoner in the burning heat of a place where so few survived. She had not allowed herself to dwell on his circumstances after he was taken away. She had reminded herself that he had shot Witt in the back without any regret at all. Witt, who had not fired a shot, and she—

Knocked abruptly forward by another whack on the head, Eden turned toward the squaw who knelt beside her. The woman spoke a single word.

"Work."

Angry, Eden was about to respond when she saw the scarred woman—Running Deer—watching them from her position upstream. The look in the woman's eyes left no doubt as to her thoughts. Reluctant to oblige her by drawing the squaw's wrath, Eden turned back to the buckskin garment and started scrubbing.

Engrossed in her anger, Eden did not immediately hear the soft tittering that began among the younger women downstream. Raising her head at last, she saw several of the maidens whispering behind their hands as they looked in her direction. She jumped at the sound of the deep voice behind her.

"I see Woman Who Walks Lightly is supervising your work well."

Eden turned, her response freezing on her lips at the sight of Iron Hawk. Except for a brief breechcloth covering his male portion, he was unashamedly naked. The muscular size and breadth of him was momentarily stunning, and it occurred to her that there wasn't a woman in camp, Comanche or Kiowa, who was immune to the raw power of his masculinity. She also realized belatedly that his masculinity would remain all too obvious until the garment she was washing was again ready to be worn.

When Eden did not respond, Iron Hawk crouched suddenly beside her. He whispered, "You don't like women's work, do you, Eden?" He paused, his dark eyes intent on hers, then added deliberately, "There are worse things."

Standing abruptly, Iron Hawk strode away. She was still staring after him when another heavy swat turned her back toward the squaw.

Eden stared at her coldly. Iron Hawk had called the squaw Woman Who Walks Lightly. Eden was almost amused.

"You ain't goin' to let him do it, are you?"

Major John Henry Peters, commandant of the recently constructed Fort Worth, stared at Sheriff Duncan as the frowning lawman awaited his response. The morning sun slanted through his office window as the sheriff faced him squarely, obviously determined to waste no words in making his thoughts known. He didn't like this sheriff's attitude, and he didn't like being told what to do.

Responding in the straightforward manner that had earned him his reputation in the military as a man of conviction, Major Peters snapped, "How do you expect me to stop him, Sheriff Duncan?"

"How?" The sheriff's wiry mustache twitched.

"Is that what the Army taught you—to answer a question with a question? Damn it, man, you got to do somethin'!"

"Really? Do you have any idea how many miles of wilderness my men are responsible for *protecting*? Do you have any comprehension of how greatly our force is outnumbered by those damned Comanches?"

"Tom Richards ain't intendin' to trade himself off to the Comanches. He's goin' to deal with the Kiowas."

"Same thing. They live together, they raid together, and they *kill* together! Tom Richards knows what Iron Hawk is like. If he's fool enough to go behind my back to offer some kind of deal with that savage, I say he's going to get what he has coming."

"Now look here, Major—"

"Don't you 'look here' me, Sheriff!" Major Peters paused in an effort to bring his temper under control. He had been told, when sent to this wilderness fort after distinguishing himself in the Mexican War, that gaining control of the savage element in the area would be difficult but not impossible, and that success would add additional luster to an already brilliant career.

Poppycock!

It hadn't taken him long to realize the truth. The entire endeavor was an exercise in futility initiated by a Federal committee that had no idea of the size and scope of the country or the operation that was needed. The Comanche and the Kiowa had joined forces in an area where their expertise was second to none. His troops could adequately protect no more than a fraction of the area assigned to them. The Indians were laughing at them, and he resented being made the brunt of anyone's joke—most especially the joke of men who were supposed to be ignorant savages!

Major Peters attempted a rational response. "You did the right thing, Sheriff. You reported the capture of Eden Broker by Iron Hawk, and I've followed through by reporting it to Washington. I was already informed of Iron Hawk's escape and was advised to be on the lookout for him, but you and I both know that there's not a chance in the world that either Eden Broker's or Iron Hawk's location can be pinpointed closely enough for me to be able to send a troop out there to attempt a rescue."

"No? Then what in hell are you here for?"

"I'm here to bring some semblance of sanity to this region! That means dealing with the Indians on a formal level, so I'll be able to demand Mrs. Broker's return in the name of the Federal Government—but that will take time."

"Time? We ain't got time! Tom Richards is goin' to trade himself off for his daughter so's he can get her home, and that means sendin' himself off to be killed!"

"If Richards wants to act prematurely, there's nothing I can do about it." Major Peters held the sheriff's gaze unflinchingly. He added, "I understand your frustration, however, and I'll tell my scouts not to oblige if they're asked to find a way to convey the message to Iron Hawk."

"Don't bother. They've done it already."

"I gave no such order!"

"You didn't need to. Masters took care of it."

"He has no right to command my scouts!"

"Major, you may think them Injuns is *your* scouts, but they're half-breeds, and that makes them lean whatever way they like."

"All right, Sheriff." Aware of the hot color that flushed his face, Major Peters returned with forced civility, "What would *you* have me do?"

"I want you to get a troop out to the Diamond R and make that old man understand that you ain't goin' to put up with him stirrin' up a full-scale war by tradin' himself off to get killed. Then I want you to get that same troop out ridin' so they can impress on the first Injun camp it comes to that you want Eden Broker back."

"And how do you propose I do that?"

"Damn it, man! Use your imagination!"

Major Peters stiffened. "Goodbye, Sheriff."

"Goodbye?"

"You've done your duty. You've reported the situation to me. I'll take it from here."

"What are you goin' to do?"

"Corporal!" Summoning the guard outside the door, Major Peters ordered, "The sheriff is leaving. Show him to the fort yard."

"So that's it?" Sheriff Duncan's jowled face tightened in anger. "That's the end of it?"

"Goodbye, Sheriff. I'll take over the matter from here."

Waiting until the door closed behind the furious sheriff, Major Peters sat abruptly. Damn it all, he'd had enough!

Snatching his pen from its holder, he started to write.

Eden looked up at the brilliant blue of a sky devoid of clouds. She wiped the perspiration from her brow. The afternoon sun was merciless, but it would be setting soon. She had spent the day with the squaws, under the watchful eye of Woman Who Walks Lightly. She was treated roughly but fairly, and when her work was done, her wrists were again bound and she was secured to a tree at the edge of the camp. Through it all, she had made no protest when following the squaw's orders. It occurred to her that the squaws probably considered her faint-hearted, but she didn't really care what they thought. Other priorities had occupied her mind. Her silence had allowed her the opportunity to study the routine of the camp, and she had already begun planning her escape.

Eden glanced at Running Deer where the young woman worked beside her tepee, making no attempt to disguise her feelings. The morning had only begun when Eden realized Running Deer was growing increasingly jealous of Iron Hawk's attentions to her. By the end of the day, Eden also realized that the young woman's attitude could be deadly.

Eden briefly closed her eyes. She had given up trying to anticipate when she would see Iron Hawk again, or what he would do next. She needed to get back home! Pa was probably wild with worry. Despite appearances, she knew he blamed himself for much of the hardships they had suffered. Whatever his faults, he loved her and Jimmy and wanted the best for them. If she could only—

Welcoming cries erupted within the camp, halting Eden's thoughts. She turned to see horsemen approaching in the distance.

Eden stiffened at the sight of Iron Hawk's unmistakable figure within the approaching party. The previous evening flashed back to mind, when he had joined her unexpectedly on the sleeping bench and enveloped her in a passionless embrace that held her captive through the night. The unreality of it all was with her still. She remembered the tremors that shook her when Iron Hawk lay down beside her. His voice was cold, his body strong and hard as it curved around hers, but his powerful arms were so gentle, she almost believed she was safe from any harm that might threaten her. She had slept well, and so deeply that she was startled when she was awakened by Woman Who Walks Lightly.

The fallacy of her thoughts had become obvious, however, when Iron Hawk had appeared unexpectedly by the stream. It had occurred to her as he crouched beside her, enjoying her discomfort, that his was a clever revenge indeed.

In the time since, she had deliberately avoided assessing the conflicting feelings Iron Hawk raised within her. She consoled herself with the determination to prove that *she was as clever as he.*

Eden watched as the riders neared. The women of the camp crowded forward, speaking excitedly at the sight of several horses heavily laden with plunder trailing on leads behind the party. Standing stiffly where she was bound, Eden watched the fawning welcome Iron Hawk received, her stomach tightening at the thought of those who had suffered his retribution that day.

Unaware of the exact moment when Iron Hawk turned to seek her out, Eden felt only the shock when their gazes met. Her heart raced when he dismounted and started toward her.

A flush of anger suffused Iron Hawk as he strode toward the tree at the edge of the camp where Eden was bound. Scanning the camp as he walked, he saw Woman Who Walks Lightly look up, her eyes narrowed in scrutiny. He cared little that she noted his displeasure. He had turned Eden over to that woman's care because he knew that despite her great size, Woman Who Walks Lightly was fair and so keen of mind that she would not be deceived by any ploy that Eden might use to effect an escape. He also knew that Red Horse considered Woman Who Walks Lightly a superior wife, that he was proud of the confidence others placed in her, and that the additional bounty from his raids that he would give the woman for supervising Eden during his absence would be well received by both of them.

But he was not pleased.

Tight-lipped when he reached Eden's side at last, Iron Hawk scrutinized her silently. Her face was flushed and beaded with perspiration, her clothing stained with sweat, and her eyes were weary. He did not doubt that she had stood in that spot, only slightly shielded from the brilliant afternoon sun, since the women had completed their chores several hours earlier.

Turning at a step behind him, he saw Woman Who Walks Lightly approach. He addressed her sharply in their native tongue.

"Why is this woman bound?"

Standing up to his challenge, Woman Who Walks Lightly replied, "She is a captive put in my charge. I would have her here when you return, as I promised."

"Did she work well?"

"Yes."

"Did she attempt to escape?"

"No."

"Then why is she tied?"

"To keep her safe."

When Iron Hawk did not reply, Woman Who Walks Lightly shrugged her broad shoulders in a casual gesture that did not match the intensity in her eyes. She continued, "This woman works well. She is strong and her mind is keen . . . but although I did not fear her strength, I feared the thoughts that kept her silent through the day."

"You feared her thoughts?"

"This woman's mind does not know fear. It knows only anger, and the need to escape. Her eyes revealed the truth when she saw my child in my arms. She has a child of her own. She will risk all to return to it." The mention of the child tightened Iron Hawk's jaw as Woman Who Walks Lightly continued. "There are those in this camp who await an opportunity to act against her. I would not give them the opportunity they seek."

Woman Who Walks Lightly turned back in the direction from which she had come without awaiting Iron Hawk's response. His emotions further heated by the exchange, Iron Hawk stared at Eden for a silent moment, then drew his knife. He saw Eden's eyes widen when the knife neared her flesh, and he felt her relief when he slit the leather thongs that bound her wrists. He saw the grimace of pain she restrained when the strips fell away.

Unmindful of those who watched intently, Iron Hawk grasped Eden's arm and started down the trail toward the stream, dragging her behind him. Her resistance grew stronger with every step they took. They were out of view of the camp when Eden grated, "Where are you takin' me?"

Iron Hawk did not deign to answer.

"I demand to know—"

Halting abruptly, Iron Hawk turned toward Eden, his agitation so complete that his deep voice shook as he responded, "You belong to me! You may demand nothing!"

"You'd like to believe that, wouldn't you?" Returning the heat of his anger, she spat, "You'd like to believe you have me totally in your power, that you have me cowed, but you haven't! I'm not afraid of you!"

"Aren't you?" Slipping his knife from his waist in a blur of movement, Iron Hawk held her fast as he pressed the sharp edge to her throat. He felt her shuddering as he hissed, "Tell me what you think would happen if I chose to use this knife now, Eden. Would anyone come running to save you? Or would the camp sing my praises and then come to admire the bright golden scalp I could then add to my scalp pole?"

"Savage!"

Iron Hawk drew Eden closer. Withdrawing his blade, he gripped her jaw and whispered, "Savage . . . maybe, but I'm not a fool. I have no intention of shedding your blood, Eden. We've just begun."

Releasing her abruptly, Iron Hawk grasped Eden's arm again and pulled her behind him as he continued down the trail. The late afternoon sunlight glittered on the surface of the stream when they reached the sandy bank. He ordered, "Sit down."

"Why?"

His patience thin, Iron Hawk snapped, "Do it!"

* * *

Iron Hawk's sharp command echoed on the sunlit air. Anger displacing the fear Eden had so vehemently denied, she retorted, "I don't like takin' orders!"

"Sit down, Eden."

Iron Hawk's dark eyes burned into hers, and Eden felt a sudden wave of sorrow. Almost disabled by its surge, Eden sat abruptly at the edge of the stream. Her chin high, she refused to look Iron Hawk's way as he crouched beside her. She turned back toward him when he grasped her forearm and lowered it toward the stream.

"What're you doin'?"

Iron Hawk replied with distaste, "You spent the morning washing clothes in this stream, but you didn't have the sense to keep the open flesh at your wrists clean."

"I spent the morning washing clothes, and the afternoon carrying firewood, digging for roots, and—" Halting abruptly, she snapped, "What difference does it make?"

"Even a child knows wounds can fester."

Eden mocked, "You're so concerned for my welfare."

"You belong to me, Eden. I won't have my property damaged."

Forcing her arm underneath the water, Iron Hawk washed the raw flesh with his hand. Eden made no protest, refusing to react to the pain even when he repeated his actions with her other wrist.

Satisfied at last, Iron Hawk withdrew a pouch from his waist. She recognized it, and her gaze slid to the slash at his side. It was dry and mending cleanly.

Iron Hawk replied to her unspoken question. "The medicine of a savage heals well."

Iron Hawk applied the salve to her wrists. His angry touch gentled gradually to soothing strokes as his long fingers worked the salve into the abused flesh. His attention was meticulous, his touch increasingly sensuous. Eden's breathing was ragged when Iron Hawk's gaze snapped up to meet hers at last.

The moment lingered. All pretense stripped away by the sudden intimacy, Eden whispered earnestly, "This is all wrong, Kyle. Let me go. I don't know how everything started turning bad all those years ago. I never wanted it to be that way. It just happened, and there was no stopping it once it began. But we don't have to keep up the hatred! We can put it behind us . . . now. Just let me go. I'll tell my pa that we need to forget the past and start over. He'll listen to me this time. I'll make sure of it."

Without conscious intent, Eden raised her hand to Iron Hawk's cheek. His expression was sober, his skin taut and smooth against his cheekbones, and his lips were parted. She stroked his jaw, searching the dark eyes that returned her gaze. She rasped, "I wish—"

Kyle cut her statement short with his kiss. Swallowing her words, he took them inside him, and Eden felt a familiar elation rise as he crushed her against him. *Kyle* was with her again—and she didn't have to speak the words.

222

He knew what she wished! He held her close. He separated her lips with his, his kiss deepening. He pressed her back against the sandy bank, his weight warm against her as she accommodated it and slipped her arms round his neck. He was holding her as he once did, with love in his touch as he worshiped the contours of her cheek, her jaw, and then found her lips again. He was speaking softly, his words unintelligible as his kisses deepened, as the passion between them soared, but Eden understood their meaning as he slipped away her shirtwaist and his mouth met her breast. Clutching him close as he savored the sweet flesh, Eden felt the joy within rise to wild abandon.

Her flesh freed to meet his at last, Eden gasped aloud as his male length lay flush against her.

"Kyle . . ."

He took her mouth again with his, and Eden indulged him greedily. He was hard and full against her and she gasped at the hunger he awakened. He slid himself inside her in a single thrust, and Eden gave a choked cry of joy.

Kyle's fullness filled her, and Eden closed her eyes at the wonder he evoked with his first surging thrusts. She gasped as his impetus grew, knowing a mindless joy that obstructed all thought as the glory of the moment swelled. She felt the moment approaching. She caught her breath as Kyle's passion exploded inside her, their mutual rapture complete as he throbbed to fulfillment deep within her.

Kyle lay limp against her, and Eden clutched him close. The sun warmed their naked flesh and she closed her eyes, indulging the loving aftermath that lingered. She opened her eyes again as Kyle raised himself above her and looked at her silently. He did not speak when he stood up, then pulled her up as well and drew her into the stream.

Suddenly conscious of the well-traveled trail behind them, Eden whispered, "Someone might come."

Kyle shook his head. "No one will come. They know we're here."

The water was cold. Eden shivered as it reached mid-thigh. Gasping, she splashed the water against her skin as Kyle bathed as well. Troubled when Kyle's face grew increasingly sober, Eden moved closer to him. She did not resist when he drew her against the wet, naked length of him and crushed her close.

Drawing back so he could look down into her face, Kyle whispered, "Your body is so sweet, Eden. Did James Broker enjoy it as much as I do?"

Eden froze. She attempted to pull back as Kyle continued with growing intensity, "Tell me, Eden, did he make you feel as good as I make you feel? Did he make you want him as much as you want me?"

Eden struggled to free herself, but Kyle's arms were too strong as he rasped, "You bore him a son. *Jimmy* will be coming back from his grandmother's home back East soon."

Overcome by a sudden, almost debilitating sadness, Eden whispered, "James is dead, Kyle."

Ignoring her as if she had not spoken, Kyle pressed, "Is that why you gave yourself to me, Eden . . . so I'd let you go and you could return to your son?"

"No, I—"

"—because you thought I wouldn't be able to refuse you anything once I held you in my arms again?"

"Let me go, Kyle."

"Tell me some of your beautiful lies, Eden." Kyle clutched her tighter. "I want to hear them. Tell me that you loved me once, and you could love me again. Tell me you want to forget the past as if it never happened. Tell me your sighs were sincere when I sank myself inside you, and that you want me now, more than you ever did before. Tell me, Eden. . . . tell me what you think I want to hear."

"Kyle, please . . . let me go."

"It might've worked, you know, but you made one mistake." His eyes holding hers, he whispered, "You see, you were depending on *Kyle* to believe you . . . but Kyle's dead. He died in chains, a long time ago. The man who holds you now is Iron Hawk. *Iron Hawk*, Eden! Say it!"

"Iron Hawk."

Releasing her abruptly, Iron Hawk walked back to the bank.

Numb, Eden stood motionless for long moments, then followed.

Dressing with her back to him, Eden raised her chin when she was again fully clothed. She turned toward Iron Hawk. Refusing to flinch under his scrutiny, she did not protest when he grasped her forearms and raised her wrists to scrutinize the abrasions. The unexpected softness in his voice stunned her as he whispered, "Do your wrists feel better?"

Eden nodded stiffly.

"I don't want anything to happen to you, Eden." Drawing her into his arms unexpectedly, Iron Hawk pressed his mouth to hers. His lips were soft . . . gentle as they separated hers. His tongue caressed the hollows of her mouth, coaxing hers into play. His fingers splayed wide as he caressed her back with sweeping strokes, drawing her closer and tighter, until their bodies melded so closely that they were almost one.

When Iron Hawk released her at last, Eden was shuddering.

Passion deepened Iron Hawk's voice as he whispered, "I'll listen to the lies, Eden. I'll enjoy them. Who knows? I might even try to believe them."

Iron Hawk kissed her again, and Eden closed her eyes. She wished . . .

"They are gone a long time. It is getting dark." Bow Woman raised a stubby hand to hide her smile as she nodded in the direction of the stream. "I wonder what they are doing."

Running Deer glanced sharply at her tormentor as the women standing nearby laughed softly. She had emerged from her tepee on a pretext, so she might see if Iron Hawk and the woman had indeed returned, but the squaws were waiting.

When Running Deer made no comment, Bow Woman continued, "He was so angry. Do you suppose he is beating her?"

"I don't think so." Laughing Woman shrugged. "I don't hear her crying."

Running Deer refused to allow the women the satisfaction of her anger. They didn't like her. They were Comanche, and she was Kiowa. She would never be a part of their tribe, and they all knew how she felt. They resented it and hoped to punish her.

Running Deer maintained a stoic facade. She would be the one who laughed when Iron Hawk's vengeance was satisfied and he made her his wife! Iron Hawk and she would then leave this place together and join the Kiowas who had traveled north. Then she would never see the Comanche faces of these women again.

"Here they come!"

Laughing Woman's whispered exclamation turned Running Deer toward the path to the stream. Her heart stilled.

"Look at them! Their hair is wet and their bodies are clean. They bathed together!" Bow Woman snickered. "What else do you think they did?"

"Perhaps they . . . washed their clothes."

The foolish tittering continued, but Running Deer heard none of it as her gaze followed Iron

Hawk and the woman across the camp. She had left a bowl of food sitting beside Iron Hawk's fire. He would eat it and he would remember her when he enjoyed it. Whatever he did during the night that followed was temporary. He would come to her in the end.

Running Deer turned back toward her tepee and walked inside. The white woman would not be here much longer. She had heard the braves whispering upon their return that afternoon. She knew what would soon happen.

Eden closed her eyes, pretending sleep. Iron Hawk lay warm and still beside her on the sleeping bench. They had returned from the stream to the knowing glances of all. She had felt Running Deer's hatred drilling through her, and she had turned in time to see Woman Who Walks Lightly glance briefly their way before she scooped up her child and disappeared inside her tepee. Her heart had ached at that moment with a mind-numbing intensity, and Jimmy had never seemed farther away.

She had eaten woodenly, sharing the food that was waiting when Iron Hawk and she entered his tepee. She had not cared that Iron Hawk's gaze seldom left her. She had refused to think . . . refused to allow thoughts of her own stupidity to surface in her mind . . . but night had come, and she could not keep them away any longer.

How had she convinced herself that Kyle, whom she had loved with all her young heart, had somehow returned? How had she allowed herself to believe, even for a moment, that the savage who had dragged her down to the stream and threatened her with his knife only minutes earlier could ever again become the man he once was?

Why had she allowed herself to believe it?

"What's the matter, Eden?"

Eden did not respond.

"I know you aren't sleeping."

Eden did not move.

"Eden . . ." Iron Hawk cupped her cheek with his hand and turned her to face him. Silver shafts of moonlight glittered on the dark hair that hung against his shoulders, but his features were shadowed as he lowered his mouth to hers. His kiss stirred her with its gentle searching. His caresses tormented her flesh as he turned her toward him fully and fitted his body to hers. He drew her arms up around his neck as he trailed his lips along her cheek. He whispered against her ear, "Your father sent a scout to contact me today."

Eden stiffened. She tried to pull back from him, but Iron Hawk would allow her to move only far enough so that she could look up into his shadowed features as he continued. "The scout came from the fort with a message directly from him."

Eden's heart pounded. She whispered, "Are you tellin' me the truth?"

"Yes."

"What did he say?"

"Your father wants you back. He offered me a bargain that he thinks I won't be able to resist."

"A bargain?" Eden struggled to control her shuddering. She wished she could see Iron Hawk's face . . . his eyes. Were they cold, or did they match the compassion in his voice? She took a stabilizing breath. "What kind of bargain?"

"He said he knew that the person I wanted most was him. He offered an exchange—you for him. He said once you were safe, we could settle everything between us, once and for all, like *men*."

"That's crazy! He's an old man, and he's crippled! There'd be no satisfaction in—"

"Don't worry, I'm not going to do it."

Eden released a relieved breath.

"You're glad."

"Of course, I'm glad! Do you think I'd want my pa here, where everyone hates him? Do you think I'd be able to live with the thought of what would happen?"

Eden felt Iron Hawk tense. "You can't bear the thought of it, can you, Eden—the thought of him suffering? I wonder, did you ever think of me that way—even once during the years I was a prisoner?"

"You killed Witt. You shot him in the back."

"He shot first."

"That's a lie! I saw his gun."

"No, it isn't, but you can believe what you

want to believe. It doesn't make any difference now."

Eden fought to retain control. "What are you goin' to do?"

"Nothing."

"What did you tell the scout?"

"Nothing."

"Did you tell him to tell my pa I'm all right? Did you tell him that I—"

"I told him *nothing*."

"Why?"

"It's better this way—more fitting."

"What are you sayin'?"

"Your pa's wondering what's happening to you. He's waiting for my answer, for a chance to settle things between us. *I* waited five years."

Eden gasped. "My pa's an old man. He's sick. He isn't goin' to live long."

"That's too bad, isn't it?"

Eden rasped, "He needs me, Kyle."

"My name is Iron Hawk."

"I won't let you do this!"

"You don't have a choice."

I do.

"You belong to me. I can do anything I want with you."

No.

"Eden . . ." Iron Hawk's lips brushed hers. "Whatever you're thinking . . . remember, your son will be returning soon."

"What do you mean by that?"

Iron Hawk's lips brushed hers again. They clung, and he drew her closer. She felt the hard rise of his passion as he whispered, "What would you give to be able to welcome him home?"

A tear slipped from the corner of her eye and Iron Hawk wiped it away with the flat of his hand. He whispered against her lips, "Don't cry."

"I'm not cryin'."

"Answer me. What would you give?"

What would she give?

Eden parted her lips under his.

"You talked to the scout. You told him to find Iron Hawk, and he did—that's what you said, ain't it?"

Tom Richards studied the hard set of Curt Masters's face. The wrangler had returned to the ranch, traveling the last hour in darkness. His expression was somber. A new side of the wrangler had emerged after Iron Hawk fired the shot that almost brought him down—a ruthlessness that reminded Tom too much of himself five years earlier.

Disliking the challenge in Masters's eyes, Richards demanded, "That's what you said, ain't it?"

"That's what I said."

Richards waited. He didn't like waiting either—or wondering—or the way Masters looked, as if he were boiling inside and about to explode.

"Tell me what happened, and tell me now, damn it!"

"Nothin' happened!" Erupting into pure fury, Masters shouted, "I talked to them half-breed scouts, like you said. I paid them, and I told them there'd be more waitin' for them when they came back with Iron Hawk's answer. They went right out after him—and then I waited. Hell, I ain't never known time to go so slow! They came back and told me it was easier than they thought to get the message to Iron Hawk—but Iron Hawk wasn't talkin'."

"What do you mean, he wasn't talkin'?"

"Them scouts said he didn't say nothin' at all after he heard what you offered, that he just turned around and rode off with the rest of them Kiowas followin' behind him."

"He—" Richards paused for a breath. He wasn't feeling good. He couldn't sleep with visions of Eden in that Injun's arms haunting him, and he couldn't eat for the knot that twisted his stomach tight. The tremors in his hands had gotten worse, and there were times when he doubted he'd be able to breathe his next breath. But he knew he would—if only to see Eden safe again, and out of that Injun's hands.

Richards demanded, "He didn't say nothin' else, like if Eden was all right, or where she was, or—"

"The bastard didn't say nothin'!"

Speaking up from behind them, Rowe interjected, "How do you know them scouts was tellin' the truth? Maybe they never talked to that Kiowa at all."

233

"They did, all right! I saw the look in their eyes when they talked about him. They don't want to mix with him. The Injuns are sayin' there's somethin' special about him—that the white man's bullets can't hurt Iron Hawk no more."

"My bullet could take him!"

"That won't get your daughter back. That's what's important to you, ain't it?" Masters continued hotly, "Or are you still worryin' about them steers the Injuns got away with?"

Richards grated, "You're steppin' over the line, Masters."

"Am I? If it wasn't for you pushin' Eden like you did, she wouldn't be in this mess now."

"How do you figure that?"

"She wouldn't have been out doin' a man's work with that herd, and that Injun wouldn't have got the chance to get her!"

"You heard the boss, you're out of line, Masters!" With a few aggressive steps, Rowe butted his face up near Masters's, matching his anger. "You're hurtin' inside because you got deep feelin's for Eden—we all know that—but there ain't a one of us on this ranch who ain't feelin' the same. We all know what she's worth, and we don't need none of your rantin' and ravin' to get that through our heads. It ain't skipped our notice that her little boy's comin' home soon, neither, and that he's goin' to be wantin' his mama to meet him when he does—so do somethin' helpful if you're so upset. Get yourself out there and find some Injuns who can tell you where that Iron Hawk's holdin' her!"

Masters took a backward step, then turned to look directly at Richards and said flatly, "I'll be leavin' in the mornin', and I ain't comin' back here again, not unless I got Eden with me when I do."

Richards hissed, "Watch what you do, Masters, because I'm warnin' you . . . if you do anythin' that'll make that Kiowa turn on Eden, I'll come for you myself!"

Not bothering to respond, Masters strode out the doorway. Trembling in his wake, Richards turned toward Rowe.

"I got a bad feelin' about him."

"He won't do nothin' that might end up hurtin' Eden, boss."

"He ain't thinkin' clear. He might do somethin' desperate."

"He ain't crazy. He won't do that."

"I want her back, Rowe. I want her back here, where she belongs."

"We'll get her, boss. We'll get her back."

His hands trembling, Richards propelled himself in an unsteady path toward the porch. He halted his chair, painfully aware as he looked up at a terrain basking in the light of the full moon, that another day had ended.

The hoot of an owl broke the silence of night. Eden's breathing was steady where she lay beside him on the sleeping bench. Warm memories of his childhood flooded back to Iron Hawk's mind when the owl hooted again. He recalled the many times Lone Bear had summoned him with that call. They were happy times, before the hatred, and he smiled. Other memories replaced them, of a time when Lone Bear used that call in rescuing him—a time when Lone Bear did not survive. Iron Hawk's smile faded.

Eden moved in her sleep, jarring Iron Hawk back to the present. The shaft of moonlight streaming into the tepee allowed him to study her face in repose, and he marveled at the realization that her beauty grew greater on closer scrutiny. She was tranquil, but he recalled the shuddering that had shaken her when he told her about her father. He had felt the anger she suppressed. He had flaunted his possession of her, reminding her of her child, but when she turned to him at last, all anger ceased. He accepted her passion then, without allowing himself to question the reason behind it.

Drawing her closer still, Iron Hawk touched his mouth to hers. He had dreamed of the night when he would hold her as he did now. He had vowed that his vengeance would be sweet . . . and it was. He had told himself that he would never again believe the warmth in Eden's voice and the heat in her eyes . . . and he would not. He had promised himself he would enjoy his possession of her fully . . . and he did.

Eden had spoken of returning to the Diamond R. He had allowed her to indulge those thoughts.

Iron Hawk curved his palm over her cheek.

He dipped his mouth again to hers. Eden made a soft sound of protest when he turned her toward him, but when he fit himself flush against her and slipped himself inside her, the protest ceased and the loving began.

She was his . . . as long as he chose to keep her.

Chapter Eleven

Eden straightened up and brushed a damp wisp of hair back from her cheek. The mid-morning sun baked her skin as she covertly scanned the surrounding terrain covered with berry-laden bushes. She had worked with the squaws gathering the sweet berries for hours that seemed interminable, intensely aware that she did not work unobserved.

Running Deer raised her head, and Eden felt a chill run up her spine. The woman hated her.

Woman Who Walks Lightly's gaze burned into her back, and Eden turned briefly toward the squaw. Her jailer. Six days had passed since her capture, during which the daily routine of the camp, and her jailer, seldom varied. She reviewed the routine in her mind.

Dawn—when she awakened in Iron Hawk's

arms. Eden turned to the bush beside her and snatched the ripe berries from their stems with a frown. She did not choose to dwell on those moments when the day was newly born and Iron Hawk lingered beside her, touching and caressing until her body responded to his with compelling heat. Neither did she care to recall the times she had despised the hunger he raised in her, or the promises she had made to herself to reject his touch—promises always broken.

Except for intimate moments, Iron Hawk remained unchanged—coldly detached one moment, warm and speaking straight to her heart the next—an enigma until the moment when he took her into his arms. But when the intimate moments were done, the day began and Woman Who Walks Lightly took charge. Washing, cooking, gathering wood, long walks with heavy loads, and endless work that halted in the glaring sun of afternoon.

The men returned shortly afterwards from whatever endeavors they had chosen. Though few of the other braves joined every party that left the camp, Iron Hawk rode out every day.

Eden considered that fact carefully, as she had countless times before. Her conclusion was the same as always. The hot afternoon hours before the men returned would afford her the best chance of escape. Unfortunately, Woman Who Walks Lightly seemed to realize that as well. When the women's work paused for the day's heat, Woman Who Walks Lightly remained diligent, tying Eden—in the shade—

where she would remain in full view until Iron Hawk returned.

Eden turned to see Woman Who Walks Lightly watching her closely, and annoyance flared. It was as if the oversized squaw could read her mind.

Crouching beside a low-lying bush, Eden was knocked suddenly backwards as a small body propelled itself into hers. She hit the ground in a seated position with a short whuff. She gasped when Bright Bird fell giggling into her lap. She had a true affection for Woman Who Walks Lightly's child, and she hugged the girl with a smile. The girl babbled in the Kiowa language, grasping a handful of Eden's bright hair and putting it up to her own head.

Eden's smile dimmed. Jimmy might be on his way home at that moment. She needed . . . she wanted . . . she *had* to be home when he arrived.

Eden was unprepared when Woman Who Walks Lightly snatched Bright Bird from her lap with a sharp reprimand and walked away. She was sitting still and silent when the women around her picked up their full berry pouches and turned back toward camp.

Woman Who Walks Lightly spoke to her sharply, and Eden stood up to follow them. The berry picking was done, and her decision was made.

Iron Hawk's small party rode slowly back to camp. The day had gone poorly. Their group had been smaller then usual, comprised only of Kiowa braves from the original camp who were as set on vengeance as he. They had ridden out with caution, aware that patrols in the area had increased.

It amused the Comanche that the well-dressed and well-armed soldiers rode so proudly and so blindly across the land. Some of them amused themselves by allowing the soldiers to see them, so they could hear the bugle's repeated report as they led the troop in circles until the day was done.

But Iron Hawk was not amused. His guards had worn those same uniforms. He had not laughed when they drove the prisoners into the yard at gunpoint each day, reserving special torments for the Indians among them as they supervised the merciless labor. He had watched as his brothers dropped, one by one, and he had vowed that he would live to see them avenged.

Many Kiowa and Comanche alike dismissed the importance of the new fort, but Iron Hawk knew what Fort Worth meant. It was the first fort of many, and the time would come when his brothers would no longer be able to outrun the soldiers.

Eden's words rebounded in his mind.

You've lived away from this place long enough to realize you're outnumbered. Sooner or later, you'll lose!

The day was dark with foreboding, and that truth weighed heavily on his heart. Behind him, Gray Fox led a horse carrying Black Snake's lifeless body. Beside him, Yellow Dog hung limply over his mount's neck, blood trailing from the wound in his back. Their small raiding party had easily outrun the patrol chasing them, but they did not see the patrol that appeared unexpectedly in front of them until it was too late.

Staring straight ahead as they neared the camp, Iron Hawk heard the first keening cries of Black Snake's wife. The sound alerted Yellow Dog to their impending arrival. He attempted to sit upright when his young son appeared at the edge of the waiting crowd, but he could not.

Lifting Yellow Dog down when their horses stopped, Iron Hawk looked at White Horn where he appeared at the edge of the crowd, then carried his friend to the aged shaman's tepee. No conversation was necessary. White Horn would care for Yellow Dog's wounds and raise the healing spirits.

Confident he had left his friend in good hands, Iron Hawk stepped outside the tepee— his blood running suddenly cold when he saw three women with wooden clubs running toward the edge of the clearing where Eden stood bound.

Fear rose in Eden's throat as the squaws rushed angrily toward her. She saw White Calf, Woman Lying Down, Spotted Deer—all Kiowa women who had previously kept their distance from her with scorn. She had seen Iron Hawk's party return to camp. She knew what had happened, and she knew what the women intended.

Frantic to escape as the women neared, Eden jerked at the leather thongs binding her wrists to the tree, but to no avail. Her eyes widening as the women reached her, she ducked and bobbed to avoid their blows. Struck painfully on the shoulder, she turned in time to see another club descending toward her head. She gasped as it was struck aside by Iron Hawk's heavy hand. She breathed a sob of relief when he stepped in front of her, shielding her with his body as he ordered, "Step back from here! This woman belongs to me!"

"Iron Hawk is a fool!" White Calf's eyes were blazing. "He uses this woman well, and he forgets that she is our enemy!"

"She is my prisoner! I will do with her as I please!"

Spotted Deer sneered, "The thing between your legs speaks for you—as it does for most men. But it betrays you! It makes you forget the Kiowa blood this woman caused to be spilled many moons ago—and the Kiowa blood she caused to be spilled today!"

"This woman caused no Kiowa blood to be spilled today."

"Iron Hawk thinks we are children! Iron Hawk believes we do not know that because of her, soldiers now patrol farther into our land."

"The soldiers patrol because of the new fort."

"Because of her!"

Iron Hawk's voice deepened with threat as he commanded, "Go back to the camp."

"No! We will not!"

Gasping when Iron Hawk drew his knife, Eden heard true menace in his voice as he rasped, "Leave here now, or more Kiowa blood will be shed needlessly this day."

The women took a backward step. They turned to see Standing Man and Gray Fox angrily approaching them. Cringing at the sight of the warriors' ire, they ran back toward the camp.

Trembling, Eden watched as the Kiowa warriors followed the women back to camp without speaking a word. She looked back at Iron Hawk to find his gaze heated as he spat, "The rage of that day long ago still lives."

Iron Hawk raised his knife, and Eden gasped. He slashed the ties at her wrists and jerked her roughly forward, dragging her behind him as he walked rapidly toward his mount. Mounting, he pulled her up onto his horse and clamped his arm around her waist, then dug his heels into the animal's sides.

Iron Hawk clutched her painfully tight, riding fiercely. The warm air whipped Eden's face, and the ground raced past underneath their mount's hooves as the camp disappeared from sight.

"You almost did what?"

Jim McGill stared at Curt Masters, incredulous. He had arrived at Fort Worth only an hour earlier. Six days had passed and the Diamond R hadn't heard a word about Eden, from the fort or anywhere else. McGill didn't need anyone to tell him that old man Richards wouldn't live through the next few days if he didn't hear something about Eden soon.

Frustrated, he had taken it upon himself to head for the fort, a peculiar lump rising in his throat when he recalled the days he had stood watch over Eden while her pa held her prisoner at the ranch. He remembered her despair. He'd never know what made him agree to release her that last day so they could chase after her pa. His stomach still revolted at the memory of what they'd seen when they got to that Kiowa camp. He knew he'd never forget it.

He had felt partially responsible for everything that transpired afterward, but he knew that even if she were his own daughter, he could never be more proud of the way Eden worked to overcome all the bad things.

He had arrived at the fort that afternoon in time to see two patrols return in a state of elation. He heard the shouts and the laughter. He heard the troopers say they had encountered a band of Kiowas, but this time the Injuns hadn't gotten away without taking back some of the Army's lead with them.

McGill stared at Masters a silent moment longer before repeating, "You almost did what?"

"I said I almost got that Kiowa bastard." Masters gave a harsh laugh. "I told that damned lieutenant he was ridin' the wrong way. I told him I'd find them Kiowas for him if he gave me a chance—and I did! We saw them comin', but they didn't see us. They was high-tailin' it away from another patrol, and they was so busy lookin' behind them that they never saw us comin'. You should've seen their faces when we came racin' toward them." Masters laughed again. "Hell, they almost jumped out of their skins!" His face sobered abruptly. "I recognized that Iron Hawk right away. I couldn't miss him. I had him in my sights—"

"You shot at him?"

"Damned right, I did!"

"Are you crazy? What if you killed him? How'd we get Eden back then?"

"I wasn't tryin' to kill him."

"You wasn't—"

"I just wanted to hurt him, bad. I wanted to *make* him tell me where Eden is—and I wanted to see his face when I brought her back."

"What if you missed?"

"I did miss him!"

"What if you missed *wingin'* him and ended up *killin'* him, damn it?"

"Then he'd be dead."

"You stupid bastard." Grasping Masters by the shirtfront, McGill shook him roughly. "You'd better thank your lucky stars that Kiowa ain't dead . . . because if he was, and anythin' happened to Eden, I'd make sure you followed him."

Masters blinked. He took a short breath, then blinked again. When McGill released him, he fell a few steps back against the fort wall behind him. "You're right . . . I know you are. I don't know what happened. I just kept thinkin' about that Injun and Eden—"

"Thinkin' like that is makin' you act crazy. You can't do nothin' to stop whatever's goin' on if you don't find out where he's holdin' Eden first. And I'm tellin' you another thing. That old man back there ain't goin' to last long if somebody don't get her back soon. He got a letter yesterday. Jimmy will be here in two days. I don't want to be there to see what happens if that boy arrives and his mama ain't there to meet him." McGill paused. "I want that Kiowa, too, but not bad enough to sacrifice Eden."

Masters scowled. "I don't know how them Injuns got away from us today. We tried followin' the bastards, but we lost them."

"Which way was they headin'?"

"West."

Holding Masters's gaze soberly, McGill nodded. "All right . . . that's where we'll start."

Iron Hawk's horse was breathing heavily. Sweat foamed on his skin and his gait grew uneven as they continued across the sunlit terrain. Eden knew the signs. The animal could not go on much longer.

Eden did not react when Iron Hawk drew back, slowing his mount. His arm a band of steel around her waist, he pulled her more tightly against him in a silent warning that did not need to be verbally expressed. She was not surprised when Iron Hawk directed his mount over a rise toward a stream that glittered in the light of the setting sun. She made no comment when Iron Hawk halted and dismounted, then swung her down to her feet.

Unable to bear the silence any longer, Eden said.

"Thank you—for stoppin' those women."

Iron Hawk's eyes met hers coldly. He did not reply.

"They hate me. If you hadn't come, they would've killed me."

Still no response.

"You stopped them this time, but next time—"

"There won't be a next time."

"You're sayin' that now, but—"

"They won't try to attack you again unless they're provoked. They know the price they'll pay if they do."

"I don't want those women to be hurt! There's been too much bloodshed already." Eden took a spontaneous step toward him. "Iron Hawk, please . . . can't you see? Things are just gettin' worse here. Let me go, for all our sakes! Sooner or later another Kiowa is goin' to get killed, and they'll start lookin' at me again. And the truth is, if one of those women starts grievin' hard enough, she won't care what happens to her afterwards."

"It won't happen again."

"If that's true, why did you take me away from there? Why did we stop here instead of turnin' around to go back to the camp when it's goin' to be dark soon?"

"We're staying here tonight."

"Why?" Eden was suddenly angry. "Why are we stayin' here if I'm safe at the camp?"

Suddenly as angry as she, Iron Hawk grasped her arms and grated, "Because it's safe for *you* at the camp, but it might not be safe for others."

"Wh . . . what are you talkin' about?"

His jaw tight, Iron Hawk rasped, "How do you think I felt when I realized those women were going to attack you? What do you suppose I was thinking when I raced after them? And when I saw the first club hit you . . . what do you think I wanted to do then?"

"I don't know."

"If they had drawn your blood, I would have drawn theirs."

"Iron Hawk, I—"

"You belong to me. You're my property. I won't have anyone damage my property."

"Your property—"

"You are mine!"

Eden's throat tightened. Iron Hawk was breathing heavily. His eyes were sudden pinpoints of heat that seemed to bore into her soul. He whispered, "The danger in that camp tonight lies in my anger. I needed to get away from the women who tried to hurt you. I needed to let my rage cool. I felt that club when it hit you. The pain is still with me."

Iron Hawk touched her shoulder, and Eden winced at the tender spot there. He pushed her shirt aside to bare her skin.

"You're bruised."

"It's all right."

"No, it isn't." He paused. "I didn't take you captive to cause you physical pain, Eden."

Eden raised her chin. "No. You took me for revenge."

"I took you for many reasons. And I keep you . . . for many reasons." His breathing growing more rapid, Iron Hawk whispered, "Why don't you ask what those reasons are?"

Eden shook her head. She didn't want to know. She didn't want to feel the heat in Iron Hawk's eyes warming the intimate core of her. She didn't want to shiver under his touch. She didn't want to yearn for the comfort of his mouth as he held it a tantalizing distance from hers. And she didn't want to *want* as he was wanting.

Eden closed her eyes.

"Look at me, Eden."

Iron Hawk slipped his arms around her. He fit her against him, the contours of his body accommodating hers with sensuous familiarity as he whispered, "The reasons . . . because the taste of you doesn't satisfy. It only whets my appetite for more."

Iron Hawk kissed her then, his arms crushing her close as he caressed her flesh with increasing ardor. Drawing back from her, he trailed his lips against her cheek, rasping, "Because my appetite for you won't be sated. Because the hunger surpasses reason, and because when you're in my arms, the past fades into the shadows and

251

I can't think of anything but you. You're a fire in my blood, Eden."

Iron Hawk kissed her again, more deeply. His mouth drew from hers, and Eden trembled with the joy of it. His hands found her breasts, and anticipation swelled.

Iron Hawk looked down at her quivering lips, at the pulse throbbing in her throat, and he whispered, "No, I won't let you go."

Scooping her up into his arms, Iron Hawk carried her a few steps toward a nearby tree. With the hard ground beneath her back, Eden slid her arms around him as he lay full upon her. She parted her lips under his. She wanted as he wanted, gave as he gave, knowing nothing but the moment as he stripped away her clothes and joined his body to hers.

Basking in the glory, Eden clutched Iron Hawk close. Her heart filled to bursting, she indulged the passionate emotions holding them in thrall as Iron Hawk worshiped her flesh, as he brought them to rapturous climax.

Iron Hawk drew back from her at last, and Eden's pounding heart stilled. Where fire had previously glowed in his eyes, she saw ice.

Stunned, she did not move when Iron Hawk stood up abruptly and drew on his buckskin leggings. Her humiliation was complete when he commanded, "Get up."

Eden sat up and reached for her clothes as Iron Hawk turned his back and walked away.

* * *

"I'm about to turn in, boss."

Jesse Rowe's worn leather boots echoed hollowly against the board floor as he walked out onto the porch. He frowned at Tom Richards. The old man sat with his back toward him, staring into the twilight. The sun was setting, and Richards had been sitting in that same spot since morning. When Richards didn't respond, Rowe tried again.

"You might as well turn in, too. You ain't goin' to see nothin' in the dark."

"It may come as news to you, but I don't need no nursemaid to tell me when it's time to go to bed."

Annoyed, Rowe responded, "Seems to me you might. Seems to me I've had to remind you when it's time to eat, too, although you ain't been doin' much of that lately."

"That's my business."

"The hell it is! Things is goin' to pot around here! Or maybe you just forgot who the boss of this ranch is."

"I didn't forget nothin'."

"Well, I got different thoughts about that."

"I'm not interested in your thoughts."

"What *are* you interested in?" Walking around to face Richards directly, Rowe grated, "You look like hell, you know that?"

Richards sneered, "I ain't thinkin' about enterin' no beauty contest."

"No? Well, maybe you should start worryin' about what that grandson of yours will think

when he gets here and sees his grandpa lookin'
like death warmed over."

"I ain't worried about Jimmy, neither."

"You should be! What's the matter with you,
old man? Did that Kiowa take your common
sense when he took your daughter?"

"Don't you talk to me like that!"

"Somebody has to or there ain't goin' to be
nothin' left of this ranch for Eden or Jimmy! If
you'd open your eyes and look around you instead of starin' off into the distance, you'd see
that the work on this place has stopped dead.
Mullen won't be back on his feet for a while yet,
Masters might never come back, and McGill
took off without tellin' anybody when he was
comin' back. In the meantime, you got cattle
out all over the range that should be rounded
up before somebody starts thinkin' that the Diamond R brand means they're strays. And you
got paperwork to do about them steers that the
boys drove to that buyer."

"Them Injuns took half the herd, and they
took Eden, too."

"The way you're actin' ain't goin' to make anybody find her any faster."

Richards glanced away. Rowe saw the old
man's chest begin a slow heaving as he muttered, "I'm stuck in this wheelchair. There's
nothin' I can do to help get her back."

"You make me sick, you know that?"

Richards didn't answer.

"Eden's goin' to get back home, one way or
the other. Hell, you know her! There's no way

them Injuns are goin' to beat the gumption out of that woman, especially when she knows her son's goin' to be comin' back soon. The least you could do is your part."

"My part?"

"Get the boys movin' again! They're not doin' nothin' but hangin' around and mopin'—just like you. Get this ranch goin' like it should, so's Eden's work won't be doubled up when she gets back!"

"I thought you said you was goin' to turn in."

"If Eden was here right now, she'd say—"

"Eden ain't here." Richards looked back at him. "Do yourself a favor and get somethin' through your head. I'm goin' to stay right here on this porch for just as long as it suits me, and nobody's goin' to make me do nothin' different."

"All right!"

Rowe turned away, his step halting when Richards whispered in a voice betraying a world of pain, "It's been too long, Rowe. Where is she? What's happenin' to her?"

Rowe looked back at Richards briefly, seeing the wasted figure of a once vibrant man. He walked into the house without responding. What was the use? Richards wasn't listening.

Night sounds echoed in a darkness lit only by the moon as Eden lay beside Iron Hawk, pretending sleep. She watched the steady rise and fall of his chest through slitted eyes, remembering.

They had spoken little after they had lain together. Iron Hawk grew progressively colder toward her as they ate a meager meal from the remains of his day rations, but Eden had little appetite. When night fell, Iron Hawk motioned for her to lie down beside him. He covered them with a single blanket, then drew her into his arms and held her close until he slept.

You belong to me. You're my property.

Iron Hawk's words rang in her mind. He wanted her. He needed her. He was intoxicated with the emotions that flared between them when she was in his arms—but he despised her.

Eden closed her eyes briefly against the torment those thoughts raised. She knew how Iron Hawk felt, because she shared those feelings. She wanted him. She needed him. She was intoxicated by the emotions that flared between them when she lay in his arms—with a difference. Iron Hawk accepted those feelings and indulged them, looking toward the moment when he would be free of them forever.

Eden almost laughed. She had told herself she hated him for all the horrors of the past— that she had been a young fool when she declared her love for him years ago, believing they could overcome all the impediments between them. She had convinced herself that she knew better now, and would never make the same mistakes again. She had told herself she needed to think of Jimmy first, and that everything else faded into insignificance beside his welfare.

But words seldom changed reality.

Reality. She loved Iron Hawk. The brief moments when the shadows were swept aside and *Kyle* reappeared in Iron Hawk's eyes set her heart afire. She longed for those moments to linger. She ached for that man who had been expelled so violently from him. She lived for the moments when she would see him again, however briefly—and she knew she would never love another man the way she loved him.

But despite that love, Eden knew she must escape. Her future, Jimmy's future, the future of the ranch and everything her father had lived for, depended on it. No risk was too great to free herself from Iron Hawk's loving bondage—before it was too late for her ever to escape at all.

Eden scrutinized the surrounding darkness, straining to recall the terrain they had passed en route to this spot. The night was bright, with few dangers to be faced in the darkness along the way. Eden glanced at Iron Hawk's horse standing a short distance off. Once she was mounted and on her way, Iron Hawk would not be able to catch her.

Eden turned subtly toward Iron Hawk. He lay on his side facing her, his arm thrown across her breast. She could see his face clearly—his strong, even features and chiseled cheekbones. His dark hair shone like a raven's wing in the moonlight where it lay against his shoulders.

He's a Kiowa. He'll always be a Kiowa.

Yes. There was a time when she had unconsciously sought to deny those words.

Her heart beginning a slow pounding, Eden gently lifted Iron Hawk's arm from her chest.

She waited. When he did not stir, she slid herself carefully away from his side, then halted again. His broad chest continued its slow heaving, and Eden released a relieved breath. Not bothering to take her boots, she walked silently toward the place where Iron Hawk's horse stood. At his side at last, she loosened the tether and mounted.

Elation surging when she sat firmly astride, Eden dug her heels into the horse's sides. Startled when the animal reared, whinnying loudly, Eden fought to retain her seat. She held the reins firmly when the animal was under control and dug her heels into his sides—but it was too late!

Struggling fiercely against Iron Hawk as he attempted to drag her from the horse's back, Eden punched and shoved to no avail. She was panting heavily when he swung her to the ground. The horse galloped off into the darkness as he grated, "You're wasting your time. You can't get away from me."

"I will get away, you'll see!"

"No, you won't."

Her heart racing, Eden rasped, "You wanted the truth from me once, and now I'm goin' to give it to you. You're crazy if you think I'm goin' to stay here and let you use me for whatever vengeance you have in mind! I can't pretend to know what you're thinkin', but I know this. There's no way you can stop me from tryin' to get away. I'll keep tryin' and tryin' until I make it—whatever it costs!"

"If we're talking truth tonight, there's something I have to say, too." Iron Hawk's eyes were dark pools of rage as he continued. "I could stop you from trying to get away. It would be easier than you think, but I have other thoughts in mind."

Eden turned her head, refusing to succumb to his intimidation.

"Look at me, Eden."

She would not.

Gripping her chin, Iron Hawk turned her toward him and whispered, "You're mine as long as I want to keep you."

Eden could not resist a glance in the direction in which Iron Hawk's horse had vanished. His comment was casual. "I'll find him in the morning. He belongs to me. He won't go far."

That thought resounded in her mind as she resumed her place beside Iron Hawk. She closed her eyes as he dropped his arm around her. She'd get away. There was no way he could stop her.

"Are you ready, Masters?"

Mounted, Jim McGill addressed Masters as the younger man approached across the fort yard. He had slept on a blanket in the stable beside his horse, and had had a miserable night's sleep. Masters had slept in the next stall just as uncomfortably as he, but they had both been up at dawn. The sun was just rising, and he was anxious to begin.

"Come on, Masters!"

"All right, hold your horses!" Masters slid his rifle into the sheath on his saddle and mounted. He patted it, saying without a trace of a smile, "I wanted to make sure old Betsy was in good shape. I missed yesterday." He halted at the look in McGill's eyes, then continued, "I wanted to check the sights to make sure I hit what I aim at today."

"Let's get somethin' straight." McGill's bearded face twitched. "I ain't goin' out huntin' Injuns. If that's what you're thinkin' of doin', let's part company right here. There's only one person I'm interested in findin', and that's Eden."

"All right, since we're puttin' our cards on the table, I got somethin' to say, too." Masters's expression tightened. "Seems like everybody on the Diamond R knows how I feel about Eden—includin' her. Seems like everybody thinks they know what I'm thinkin'—but they don't." He shrugged. "I got off track yesterday. I missed when I shot at Iron Hawk, and it's good that I did, but I'm tellin' you now, once Eden's safe and sound, there's no way I'm goin' to let that fella ride away if I can get him in my sights."

"Seems to me you might do some thinkin' on that for a while." McGill's frown tightened. "Eden had strong feelin's for him a while back."

"That's all past—and I wouldn't give a damn if it wasn't! I'm tellin' you now, like it or not, that fella's not goin' to live a minute longer than he has to, once Eden's safe and sound."

"And I'm goin' to repeat what I said yesterday,

just in case you don't remember—if anythin' happens to Eden because your trigger finger itches, I'll make sure it happens to you, too. And I mean every word I say."

Masters did not reply.

"Just so's we understand each other."

"Oh, we understand each other, all right."

His small eyes intent, McGill followed behind as Masters swung his mount out through the fort gates.

The sun had risen on a new day, but Iron Hawk was unconscious of the bright rays that warmed his back as he rode with Eden sitting stiff and silent before him. He had slept fitfully after Eden's attempted escape. He had gone over the scene a dozen times in his mind, and each time his anger had flared hotter.

He was not sure what had awakened him, but he remembered his shock when he'd looked up to see Eden mounting his horse. He was up at a run when the animal balked and reared, and his heart still pounded at the thought that had he gotten there a moment later, it would have been too late.

The thought had haunted him through the night.

There's no way you can stop me from tryin' to escape. I'll keep tryin' and tryin' until I make it, whatever it costs!

He had told Eden that there were many ways he could stop her from attempting to escape, and there were. Eden was unaware how easy it was to control a prisoner when rawhide thongs were soaked in water before a prisoner's wrists and ankles were tied—so the bonds grew tighter as they dried, cutting the skin and circulation, and eliminating the power or the desire to run. But Eden's wrists had healed, and he had no desire to see her flesh again torn and bleeding.

He had left Eden with Woman Who Walks Lightly each day. Eden did not realize that it would be just as easy to leave her with Bow Woman, whose lack of tolerance with prisoners was undisputed, and who had none of Woman Who Walks Lightly's ways. But he had been a prisoner. He knew what it was to be tormented by guards, and he had no desire to see Eden suffer that abuse.

Iron Hawk's jaw tightened. Yet, he could not tolerate continued attempts at escape that could put the lives of his people in jeopardy. He had made his decision.

Warm rays of morning sun lit the sky as the camp came into view in the distance. Iron Hawk felt Eden tense. She remained silent as they rode, her back stiff and her chin high. He did not speak as they entered the camp and made their way toward his tepee. He saw the Kiowa women gathered in a group, and he felt Eden's instinctive shudder. Halting deliberately beside them, he lifted Eden down from the horse and dropped her onto her feet beside them. He saw her face whiten.

Addressing Woman Who Walks Lightly in

their native tongue, he said, "I leave this woman again in your care."

Woman Who Walks Lightly nodded.

He felt Eden's gaze burning into his back as he rode on toward White Horn's tepee. Dismounting beside it, he entered, relief flooding him when Yellow Dog looked up at him from the sleeping bench.

Responding to his unasked question, White Horn announced, "Yellow Dog will be well. His wound heals."

Crouching beside his friend, Iron Hawk spoke softly to him. His heart warmed when Yellow Dog's smile flashed. Noting that his friend's eyes were weary, he stood to leave.

Emerging outside, Iron Hawk scowled at the realization that the women had disappeared from view. He didn't like that. Black Snake's body had barely cooled and emotions were still heated. He had wanted to talk to Woman Who Walks Lightly first, so she would be certain that he would not tolerate unkindness to Eden from the other women.

Scrutinizing the wooded glade nearby, Iron Hawk took a few steps further. He would search the women out if necessary, and he would—

"The woman is safe. You need not concern yourself."

Iron Hawk turned toward Running Deer, who stood behind him. Her pleasant face colored as she continued, "The woman is your captive. She belongs to you in the same way as your horse and bow, and the white man's gun you carry.

But look! See yourself clearly! See what every-one else sees, that the captor has become the captive!"

Anger flaring, Iron Hawk replied coolly, "You concern yourself unnecessarily with my affairs, Running Deer. The woman is mine to do with as I choose and I need make no explanations to you."

Her eyes filling with tears at the harshness of his reply, Running Deer responded, "I did not mean to anger you, Iron Hawk. Rather, I seek to make known the thoughts of the camp so you will not suffer ridicule."

"No man in this camp would dare ridicule me."

"People whisper."

"*Cowards* whisper."

"*I* do not whisper, Iron Hawk!" Running Deer raised her chin, her eyes flashing in sudden an-ger. "I know no fear except of your displeasure, yet I come to you openly, in warning."

"I don't need your warning."

"You do!" Stepping closer, Running Deer placed her hand on Iron Hawk's arm. He felt her trembling as she continued, "So great is my esteem for you that I must continue to speak despite your disapproval. I must say what is clear to all, that the woman controls Iron Hawk's thoughts. They say that Iron Hawk, the brave warrior who takes each day in new chal-lenge, facing it bravely and with honor, is the same man who returns each night and surren-ders in the arms of a woman!"

His patience expired, Iron Hawk shook off Running Deer's hand. "If you were a man, Running Deer, my knife would speak in response to your words. But you aren't a man. If you were any other woman, I'd turn my back on you now and walk away, never to acknowledge you again, but you aren't any other woman. You despise this woman because of the past, and I won't attempt to challenge your hatred. Because your life is your own, I expect you to live it as you like." His voice deepening, Iron Hawk rasped, "Just as I'll live my life as *I* like."

"Why can you not see what this woman—"

"Stop!" Taking a firm hold on his anger, Iron Hawk slowly continued. "Standing Man is your brother and my good friend. Because of my respect for him, I'm telling you now never to speak to me again about this. This woman isn't your concern. She's not the concern of any of the other women in the camp. I made my thoughts clear to the women who tried to attack Eden yesterday, and I'm making my thoughts clear to you, too."

Moisture grew heavy in Running Deer's eyes as she asked, "You are angry with me, Iron Hawk? It was not my intention to anger you."

"I'm finished talking, Running Deer." Softening at the sight of her tears, Iron Hawk said, "Go. We'll forget this conversation took place."

Running Deer raised her chin. "If you look for the woman, she is with Woman Who Walks Lightly at the stream. Woman Who Walks Lightly bathes her child there."

Turning away abruptly, Running Deer disappeared between the nearby tepees.

"Running Deer speaks from the anger that twists inside her."

Iron Hawk turned back toward White Horn's tepee as the old man emerged. His expression grave, the shaman continued, "But Running Deer's concerns are just. There are some who whisper, as she said."

"I don't worry about whispers!"

"Whispers grow to shouts if caution is cast aside."

Iron Hawk took an aggressive step. "You've read the smoke. You know the truth. You know I won't find peace within myself until the blood of our people has been avenged."

"I have read the smoke." White Horn nodded his head. "It is as you say."

"There are many paths to vengeance."

White Horn's small eyes narrowed.

"My people will be avenged."

White Horn's gaze locked with his. "That you will avenge our people is clear. The question that remains is what price you will pay for retribution."

Not waiting for Iron Hawk's response, White Horn lifted the flap and disappeared into his tepee.

The question lingered.

Chapter Twelve

The midday sun beat warmly on John Waters's shoulders as he cautiously scrutinized the wild terrain surrounding him. Satisfied that no one had observed their meeting, he turned back to Iron Hawk as the warrior prepared to mount. He recalled the first day Kyle Webster arrived in town years earlier. Waters remembered his silent empathy for the man who came in peace, only to be greeted with contempt.

Half-breed. Waters had heard that name applied to himself too many times by ranchers and townsfolk who looked at him with that same contempt. It meant little to them that his mother's blood was as pure as theirs, that she was born and raised in that town, and that she had raised him there, too, after leaving his Comanche father. More white man than Indian, he had married the storekeeper's daughter, only to have his children suffer the same taunts of his own childhood. Kyle Webster had treated Waters's family and him with respect from the first moment of their meeting. Kyle spoke to him as a brother and they became friends; yet, when the town turned against Kyle, Waters had been helpless to aid him in any way. But he was helpless no longer.

Their meeting had been short. He had responded to Iron Hawk's signal when Iron Hawk's smoke rose from the bluff beyond town. He had given Iron Hawk the information he sought—Iron Hawk, who had suffered far more than he for the Indian blood that flowed in his veins.

Mounted, Iron Hawk offered his hand in gratitude, and Waters accepted it proudly. He watched as Iron Hawk rode away. He then mounted his own horse, knowing he had served his friendship well at last—and knowing that when Iron Hawk moved to repay his longstanding debts, Iron Hawk would move against those who had scorned his own Comanche blood as well.

John Waters smiled. The Diamond R would never be the same.

McGill looked up from scrutinizing faded tracks that were barely discernible on the dry ground. "You said the Kiowa and his band traveled west?"

Masters turned sharply when the older man

spoke. They had spent the day riding in circles as they followed those tracks, and Masters's patience was spent. He snapped, "I said they traveled west, and that's what they did!"

"There's no way they ended up travelin' west."

"I told you—"

"Look at these tracks, damn it!" McGill's bearded face reddened. "They traveled west, then they doubled back over the same trail."

"A blind man could see that! What them bluejackets and me couldn't decide was which direction they finally ended up goin' in."

Straightening up slowly, McGill replied, "Look, Masters, I ain't in no mood to take your guff. If you ain't got the stomach for this trackin', then go back to the fort and leave it to me."

"I got the stomach for it. What I ain't got the stomach for is them pictures of Eden and that Injun that keep floatin' around in my head while we're ridin' around like two jackasses."

"Call yourself a jackass if you want, but don't include me unless you're lookin' for trouble."

His anger suddenly draining, Masters rasped, "I'm startin' to think we won't find out where Eden is until that bastard's ready to let us—and the thought of that damned Kiowa laughin' at us is drivin' me crazy."

"We'll find her. It'll just take time."

"Time . . . sure. That's easy for you to say, McGill. You're thinkin' in terms of the future, but I'm thinkin' about now."

Masters looked up at the cloudless sky where

the sun had already begun a gradual descent from its apex. He shook his head. "Another day is slippin' away and I'm *still* wonderin'—what's happenin' to Eden now?"

Eden lay in a heap on the ground. She looked up at Bow Woman, who stood with a wooden club in her hand, railing at Woman Who Walks Lightly and gesturing wildly at Eden.

Her head still reeling from Bow Woman's blow, Eden was unable to draw herself upright. She did not understand a word that was being spoken in the Kiowa tongue, but the meaning of Bow Woman's words was clear.

Iron Hawk had left early that morning, leaving Eden in Woman Who Walks Lightly's care. The humiliation of the previous day had remained vivid as she worked with the women through the morning. It became a hard knot of resolve by afternoon, when she was bound while the camp slumbered. Determined to act, she had grasped the first opportunity to escape by coaxing Bright Bird into bringing her a knife so she could cut herself free from her bonds while Woman Who Walks Lightly busied herself elsewhere.

She had almost made it to the horses.

Almost.

Eden raised her hand to the painful lump on the back of her head made by Bow Woman's club. Bow Woman continued her harangue until Woman Who Walks Lightly grasped Eden by the arm and pulled her to her feet. Eden did not become aware of Iron Hawk's arrival until Bow Woman stopped abruptly and slipped away, leaving Woman Who Walks Lightly to face Iron Hawk alone.

Eden remained silent as Iron Hawk addressed Woman Who Walks Lightly in the Kiowa tongue. Irate, Woman Who Walks Lightly motioned toward Eden, speaking swiftly. Iron Hawk responded curtly to Woman Who Walks Lightly, then grasped Eden's arm.

Eden stumbled behind Iron Hawk as he pulled her into his tepee and turned toward her, his face tight with fury.

"You're a fool, Eden! All you succeeded in doing when you tried to escape was to anger Woman Who Walks Lightly and give Bow Woman the opportunity she was looking for. Bow Woman knew I couldn't rebuke her for stopping you. It's lucky for you that the women of this camp respect Woman Who Walks Lightly's authority and let her handle things from there."

Eden snapped, "And if they didn't and I had been killed, who would have been to blame then?"

"Yourself!"

"Not you?"

"Look at me, Eden!" Holding up the iron cuffs that still encircled his wrists, Iron Hawk rasped, "The man responsible for putting these bands on my wrists is the man responsible for bringing you here. The man whose order destroyed the Kiowa camp and killed so many of its people those years ago is the reason you're here."

Eden rasped, "I won't be a part of your vengeance! I told you I'd keep tryin' to escape!"

"I remember."

The throbbing in her head increased, and Eden could manage no more than an unsteady whisper as she responded, "I'll keep tryin'. I won't give up."

Eden took a staggering step, and Iron Hawk grasped her arm. She could feel him tense when he touched her head and drew back his hand to see his fingers stained with blood. He demanded, "Bow Woman did this to you?"

"Does it matter?"

The world spun briefly. When it righted, she was lying on the sleeping bench with Iron Hawk crouched beside her. The tone of his voice sent chills down her spine as he whispered, "You're wrong, you know. You said you'll keep trying to escape, but you won't. I'm going to make sure of that."

"Nothing . . . *nothing* will stop me."

Iron Hawk did not reply.

Staring up at Iron Hawk as his enigmatic gaze held hers, Eden whispered, "I loved the man you once were . . . but that man's gone now . . . without a trace."

"Is he, Eden?"

Iron Hawk lowered his mouth to hers and Eden had no power to fight him. Despising herself almost as much as she despised the man whose kiss still stirred her, Eden waited until Iron Hawk drew away from her at last. "I loved that man . . . but I hate the man he has become."

"Don't hate me now, Eden. There'll be plenty of time to hate me tomorrow."

Iron Hawk's mouth captured hers again and Eden closed her eyes.

Tomorrow. Yes, she'd hate him tomorrow.

Motionless, Major John Henry Peters read the communiqué again. Originating in the War Department, it had been delivered by courier with strict instructions that it be put directly into his hand. He read the last two lines with growing ire.

Complaints continue to arrive, stating that your command is ineffective in protecting the U.S. citizens under your care. A full report is expected.

Seething, Major Peters slapped the sheet down on his desk. Politicians—totally ignorant of the needs of the frontier! There wasn't a military man worth his salt in the entire pompous group!

Striding stiffly toward the window where the sun was setting with a glorious display of red and gold that no Easterner could ever imagine, Peters clamped his jaw tight. It was obvious that his correspondence and this letter had crossed in the mail. He wished he could be there when those pretentious fools received the "report" that they had demanded so belatedly. He hoped they read it aloud, so the full impact of his statements might be felt.

Peters smiled at the thought of it. His smile faded to a grimace when he acknowledged that his forthright report, stating that the situation had been severely underestimated and incompetently appraised before he was sent to assume his command, might mark the end of his career.

Well, if that happened, so be it! He'd be damned before he'd be held accountable for a situation that was unavoidable under the present circumstances.

Comanches and Kiowas: a savage, ignorant people who stood no chance against a civilized military force—that misconception was a joke at which few were presently laughing! He knew the truth. There was only one way U.S. Government troops could defeat the people native to this frontier, and that was by superior arms and sheer force of numbers. If he couldn't convince Washington of that, his command was doomed.

Of course, there was another course of action. He had proposed it boldly, but they would never accept it because it had failed countless times before.

Major Peters scowled. Countless times. No, they would never accept it.

The stars were out and the campfire was blazing. The smell of coffee boiling in the small pot hanging precariously above the flames raised a growling in McGill's stomach that was not mollified by the stringy dried beef he chewed.

Glancing across the fire, McGill studied Masters's somber expression. It occurred to him that in all the time he and Masters had worked side by side on the Diamond R, he hadn't realized Masters's feelings for Eden went so deep. Or maybe they didn't. Maybe Masters just couldn't stand the idea that an "ignorant savage" was making a fool of him.

McGill ventured, "There's no way them Injuns can keep on dodgin' us. We're bound to run into some fresh tracks soon. We just have to keep at it."

"Yeah."

"It's not like we've got somethin' more important to do. Hell, old man Richards ain't done nothin' but sit in his chair since Eden was took. I got the feelin' he ain't goin' to do nothin', neither, until things is settled about Eden, one way or another."

Masters's head turned toward him. "What do you mean, 'one way or another'?"

McGill paused, then frowned. "I don't really know what I mean . . . except I'm thinkin' Iron Hawk is smarter than anybody ever gave him credit for. He ain't the average Injun, just out for blood and vengeance. If he was, we'd have heard somethin' about Eden already."

His tone belligerent, Masters demanded, "We would've heard somethin'? Like what?"

"You know what I mean. There ain't no need for me to explain."

"He ain't goin' to kill her, if that's what you mean. I ain't got no doubt about that. He could've killed her anytime he wanted, if that's what he had in mind. He had a rifle, and he's a good shot, but not a one of those shots when I was hit that day came near Eden." Masters unconsciously rubbed his healing wound. "No . . . he had somethin' else in mind—and that's what's burnin' a hole in my belly."

"We'll get her back."

"Yeah."

Watching as Masters lay down on his blanket and turned his back to the fire, McGill unconsciously shook his head. Masters hated that Injun, but it was Eden who was driving him. The fella's feelings for Eden went deep, all right. He must've been blind not to see it.

Spitting his last mouthful of beef out into the bushes, McGill muttered a curse and reached for the pot on the fire. Cursing louder when he burned his hand, He noted that Masters didn't even raise his head.

Yeah, the fella had it bad.

The night sky was lit by a bright half moon as Iron Hawk strode toward his tepee, his mind intent on the sober meeting that had just concluded. Black Snake's body had been cared for, his widow had grieved, and his friends had mourned that brave warrior's death. He mourned Black Snake, too, but his was not a passive mourning.

Iron Hawk's powerful stride slowed as he reviewed the responses he had just received from the Kiowa braves he had called to council. Spotted Elk and Black Cloud had indicated immediate concurrence. Sitting Bear and Gray Fox had nodded their agreement after thoughtful speculation. Only Standing Man remained silent. Waiting until the others left their meeting place, Standing Man had approached him. Iron Hawk saw resentment in the brave warrior's eyes when Standing Man addressed him soberly.

"Running Deer has spoken her thoughts to me. She fears for you. She feels the woman has affected your judgment. She feels your life and the lives of those who ride with you are endangered."

"Running Deer and I have already spoken about that. Her fears are unfounded."

"I feared your judgment, too." Standing Man's words stunned Iron Hawk as the brave continued. "I saw a strangeness in your eyes when you looked at the woman, and it unsettled me. I remembered that Lone Bear fell from that woman's bullet, and I knew you sought vengeance, but I wondered that you could use the woman the way you do. I mourned Black Snake's death and did not wish to see my sister, who has suffered much, left without a man to care for her because I followed you. But you have spoken well this night, and the course of your vengeance is clear."

Iron Hawk waited silently as Standing Man then said, "I will follow you toward your vengeance—for your vengeance is ours."

It occurred to Iron Hawk as Standing Man walked away that he had unconsciously sought the approval as well as the aid of his fellow braves—but that if none of them had agreed to accompany him in the morning, he would not have changed his plans.

Iron Hawk considered Standing Man's words. Vengeance? Yes, that was what he sought, but a quick vengeance would not suit. He demanded full measure for the deprivations his tribe had suffered. Hardship for hardship, anguish for anguish, blood for blood—he would settle for no less—and if he indulged his weakness for Eden along the way, it would not change the end result of his pursuits.

Halting at his tepee, Iron Hawk pushed aside the flap to find Eden asleep on the sleeping bench. With those thoughts fresh in his mind, he slipped down beside her and drew her into his arms.

Eden awakened abruptly. Disoriented, she glanced around the tepee, searching the shadows as dawn silvered the darkness surrounding her. She was alone on her sleeping bench and her head ached. Iron Hawk had left and she had not even stirred.

Her mind gradually clearing, Eden recalled the sensation of Iron Hawk's tight, muscular body curved around her as she slept. She remembered the security his presence evoked in her before reality flashed, reminding her that Iron Hawk enjoyed his power over her, that he enjoyed tormenting her. She was uncertain if she would ever be sure what his plans for her included—but she was resolved. She would not waste time waiting.

Her head ached, but her determination had not weakened. She would escape. She needed to go home. She needed the familiarity of the Diamond R so she could clear her head. She needed to see Pa . . . and she wanted to be there when Jimmy returned. She wanted that with all her heart.

Eden reached up to touch the cut on her head. The swelling had lessened, and the cut was small. She had steeled herself against Iron Hawk's unexpected gentleness when he tended to it the previous evening—but she was keenly aware that her resistance to his touch was weak.

Early morning activity outside the tepee severed the stillness, but Eden ignored it. The men were walking out to get the horses grazing on the rise beside the camp. She stood no chance of avoiding being seen by them should she attempt an escape, and the price would be too high if she failed again. Her head ached. She'd plan more carefully next time and she'd rest a little longer now—until Woman Who Walks Lightly came to get her.

Eden closed her eyes.

The morning sun shed its golden glow over the landscape. Mounted, Iron Hawk scrutinized the trail from his vantage point atop a slight grade. He glanced behind him at the silent braves awaiting his signal, then looked at the others waiting on the opposite side of the road. They had started out before dawn to reach this point on the trail. Time had passed slowly since their arrival, while the morning sun baked their skins and their eyes grew weary of scanning the distance.

In a moment of humility, Iron Hawk reflected that these men followed him just as loyally as they had followed Lone Bear. It was clear in his mind that he had not truly earned their allegiance, but that these men honored Lone Bear by trusting him. He was determined he would not dishonor that trust.

His sober thoughts interrupted by the appearance of a dust cloud on the distant trail, Iron Hawk felt his heart begin a slow pounding. A stagecoach gradually materialized, swaying and rumbling along the rough road as it neared. Glancing at the waiting braves, Iron Hawk saw that their formerly stoic expressions reflected a growing excitement.

The stage drew closer. Iron Hawk watched the snorting team pull the bulky conveyance up the blind grade beside which they waited. Aware of the stage's vulnerability at the point when it would reach the top and was almost slowed to a halt, Iron Hawk jammed his heels into his mount's sides and signaled the braves forward the moment it came into view.

The stage was immediately surrounded, and Iron Hawk shouted, "Throw down your guns!"

Stunned, the heavily mustached driver hesitated momentarily, then complied. Iron Hawk glanced toward the rear of the stagecoach where Gray Fox and Spotted Elk held their weapons trained on the passengers within. He saw guns sail out the window in response to his command, and relief flooded his senses. He wanted no gunfire. He knew the danger that could bring.

Iron Hawk looked back at the driver and commanded, "Get down from there!"

Whispers sounded inside the stage as the driver complied.

A woman's voice: "He doesn't talk like an Indian."

A man replied, "I heard about him. His name's Iron Hawk."

The woman again: "Iron Hawk? He's that Indian who escaped from prison, isn't he? The soldiers are looking for him."

A second man: "It don't look like they found him."

Signaling the driver to walk ahead of him, Iron Hawk nudged his horse toward the rear of the stagecoach. Behind him, Sitting Bear climbed the coach to topple the luggage to the ground and Black Cloud loosened the team.

Iron Hawk ordered coldly, "I want everybody inside to get out—now!"

The door opened and a burly fellow in a frock coat emerged shakily. A huge woman followed, grunting when she took the last long step down onto the road. A short, bearded fellow with bowed legs squinted up at Iron Hawk as he exited the coach. Last was a short, anxious fellow who appeared to be an Easterner.

Iron Hawk demanded, "Where is the boy?"

"The boy?" The Easterner shook his head. "There's no boy on this stage."

His blood high, Iron Hawk raised his rifle.

"Tell him, you fool!" The woman's flabby bulk shuddered. She sobbed hysterically, "Tell him before he kills us all!"

Jerking the stagecoach door open wider, Iron Hawk peered inside to see a boy lying motionless on the floor of the stage. The child had sandy-colored hair, fair skin, freckles, dark eyes . . .

A slow flush suffused Iron Hawk's skin.

The Easterner stepped nervously forward. "Leave him alone, please! He . . . he's my son. We're from Chicago. We're visiting friends in Texas."

Iron Hawk stared at the petrified child. The boy's lips quivered. They were Eden's lips.

The boy came to life as Iron Hawk leaned over and snatched him up with a swoop of his arm. Kicking and screaming, he fought wildly as Iron Hawk placed him astride his horse in front of him, holding him captive with his superior strength.

The child's struggling continued, and Iron Hawk grated, "Be still, Jimmy Broker! I'm going to take you to your mother."

"Liar!" The boy struggled harder. He shouted, "You aren't takin' me to Mama! You goin' to scalp me!"

"Look at me, Jimmy!" Iron Hawk gripped the child's chin, forcing his gaze up to meet his. "Your mother is at my camp."

"No, she isn't!"

"She misses you. She wants to see you."

The boy stared back at him, then stilled. Iron Hawk turned back to the Easterner. The man shook visibly as Iron Hawk addressed him.

"I know why you tried to deceive me. I want you to see that Tom Richards gets this message. Tell him that I have his daughter, and now I have his grandson. Tell him they're my prisoners, and I have no desire to trade them for him—not yet."

"What are you going to do?" The woman's small eyes were bright with panic. "Are you going to take us prisoners, too? Are you going to kill us?"

Iron Hawk's lips curled with contempt. He ordered, "Start walking!"

Holding his rifle steady, Iron Hawk watched as the shaken group turned to obey. They were walking rapidly up the trail when he turned back toward Black Cloud and Sitting Bear to see that they had gathered their fill from the suitcases and stuffed the goods into into sacks. He then glanced at Gray Fox and Spotted Elk, who drew the horses from the team along behind them. He looked at Standing Man, who had gathered the discarded guns and ammunition and jammed them into sacks as well.

Pulling the boy back tight against him, Iron

Hawk kicked his mount into motion, leaving the abandoned stage behind him.

Her arms filled with firewood, Eden walked silently back toward the camp. She glanced at the women walking beside her. She had spent the day working among the same women who had attempted to attack her. The only one missing was Bow Woman, who had remained at camp.

A chill moved down Eden's spine. Aside from Running Deer, no other woman in the camp looked at her with such malevolence as Bow woman. If not for Iron Hawk, she was certain those two women would need no excuse to finish the job Bow Woman had started. She was also certain that if not for Woman Who Walks Lightly, her day would have been far more difficult than it had been.

Eden's conscience nagged. She had taken advantage of Woman Who Walks Lightly's fairness by using Bright Bird's innocence to aid her escape. Woman Who Walks Lightly had kept the child out of her reach since then, and Eden supposed she couldn't blame her. But she missed the child's laughter. She somehow believed that under different circumstances, Woman Who Walks Lightly and she might have been friends.

Eden halted the wayward direction of her thoughts. What was wrong with her? Woman Who Walks Lightly was her jailer. She followed Iron Hawk's orders. The woman had no affection for her. She didn't—

Her attention caught by a stirring of excitement within the camp, Eden looked up to see a party approaching in the distance. The braves sat proudly. She knew that meant they had been successful in their endeavor that day, and she wondered again how many of her own people now suffered for their success.

The party drew closer. She recognized Iron Hawk from his outstanding size. She saw horses trailing behind the warriors in the rear— large horses, the kind that were used for hauling teams. She saw . . . she saw . . .

Eden's heart leaped. Someone was seated in front of Iron Hawk on his mount. The figure was small—a child.

Oh, God!

Dropping her firewood on the spot, Eden started running toward the approaching party. She didn't hear the shouts of the women behind her as they started after her in pursuit, then halted when they realized her direction. Her gaze intent on the approaching horses, she didn't hear the murmurs of the gathering crowd as she ran out in front of them, then stopped short.

She was shaking, tears streaming down her cheeks when Iron Hawk drew near.

"Mama!"

Eden sobbed aloud as Iron Hawk's mount drew up beside her and he lifted Jimmy down to the ground. Incredulous, Eden knelt down and engulfed her son in a hungry embrace. His body was small and warm against her as he hugged her tight, then drew back abruptly.

"Mama . . ." Jimmy fought to maintain a brave facade, but his voice trembled. "Don't cry. I won't let anybody hurt you."

"I'm not afraid, Jimmy." Eden brushed away her tears. She forced a smile. "I'm just so happy to see you."

"He made me come." Jimmy glanced back at Iron Hawk, who had dismounted. "He said he was bringin' me to see you, but I didn't believe him at first."

Standing, Eden clutched Jimmy's hand. Her throat constricting, she searched Iron Hawk's eyes for a sign that he—

Jimmy stepped forward and shouted boldly, "You stay away from my mama! I'm takin' care of her now!"

Ignoring Jimmy, Iron Hawk addressed her coldly. "Are you glad to see your son, Eden?"

Eden could not respond.

"His presence here frees you. You may leave anytime you want."

Eden blinked.

"The boy stays."

"Wh . . . what?"

"I'm releasing you. You can go back to the Diamond R and no one will stop you."

"Mama . . ."

Eden squeezed Jimmy's hand to silence him. Her heart began a frantic racing. "You know I won't leave Jimmy here."

"Won't you?"

The crowd gradually dispersed. Running

Deer remained unmoving, but Eden saw only Iron Hawk as she whispered, "I go where Jimmy goes. Not you or anyone else will separate me from him."

Allowing the weight of his gaze to linger, Iron Hawk then turned and walked away.

They were coming!

Trembling, Tom Richards pulled himself upright in his chair as horses appeared in the distance. He rolled himself forward on the porch, then adjusted his shirt, frowning when it lay limply against his chest. Rowe was right. He had lost weight. He'd probably scare the boy.

Frowning, he rubbed a nervous hand against his cheek. He had shaved real close, so he'd look as good as he could. Eden wasn't there to meet the stagecoach like the boy expected, but he wanted to be sure that he was the first person his grandson saw when he reached the ranch.

Footsteps sounded behind him, and Richards glanced up at the grinning cook. His voice trembled with excitement, despite himself. "He's comin', Rowe. Remember, I don't want nobody tellin' him nothin' about Eden. I'll do the explainin', understand?"

But Rowe wasn't listening. His smile was fading as he stared at the approaching horsemen.

Richards looked back at the riders as they drew nearer. His breath caught painfully in his chest when he saw them leading Jimmy's horse. The saddle was empty.

"Don't go gettin' upset, boss." Rowe's voice

was cautious. "Maybe Jimmy's comin' on the next stage."

The horsemen drew closer. Richards scrutinized their faces, one by one. Quinn avoided his gaze. Curry's expression was somber. Hawkins looked downright riled.

Unable to bear the torment any longer, Richards called out as they dismounted, "What happened? Where's Jimmy?"

Quinn responded, "He ain't here."

"I can see that!" His face reddening, Richards demanded, "Where is he?"

Curry shook his head. "I don't know, boss."

"What are you sayin'?"

"The stage was stopped by Injuns."

"Injuns . . ."

Hawkins retorted, "Iron Hawk got Jimmy, boss! I don't know how he knew the boy was comin' home on that stage. Somebody from town must've passed him the word that we was expectin' him, because he was lookin' for the boy."

"What do you mean, 'lookin' for him'?"

"All the rest of them Injuns took everythin' they could from the stage, horses and all, but Iron Hawk didn't want nothin' but Jimmy."

"The bastard . . ." His chest heavy, Richards struggled to breathe. "He's got my grandson!"

Speaking up again, Quinn added, "The bastard had the nerve to send you a message, too. He said to tell you that he has Eden, and now he has Jimmy, and he ain't interested in exchangin' either one of them for you—not yet."

"Not yet."

His body jerking spasmodically, Richards turned toward Rowe, who stood silent behind him. He ordered, "Get me my gun."

"You don't need no gun, boss."

"Get me my gun! I'm goin' out after that bastard. I'm goin' to get him, too, and when I do, he—"

The pain that struck Richards was sudden and excruciating. It stole his breath. It blacked out the world temporarily, then sent him spiraling through a blaze of colors as he called out at the top of his lungs—without making a sound.

Still gasping, Richards opened his eyes to stare upward from the porch floor as the wranglers moved excitedly around him. But he wasn't moving. He couldn't move. He couldn't breathe. He couldn't think, except for a rage that was deep and overwhelming—when he realized he was dying.

I want to go home.

His boldness temporarily fading, Jimmy had whispered those words to her as night fell and he struggled against sleep. Eden stroked her son's hair back gently from his forehead. He was sleeping now, but there had been little she could do to allay the fears he tried to hide.

I don't like it here, Mama. Grandpa told me about these Injuns. They're bad. They just want to kill everybody and take their hair.

She had tried to convince Jimmy that they

289

wouldn't be staying long, that they'd go home soon. She told him not to worry, that Iron Hawk wouldn't let anyone hurt him.

He said I'm his prisoner. He said you're his prisoner, too. He told the men on the stage to give Grandpa a message, that he's got us, and that he doesn't want to exchange Grandpa for us.

Eden had caught her breath at that. Yes, Kyle Webster was gone forever.

Tell him to let us go, Mama. He'll listen to you. Everybody on the ranch listens to you.

Eden had almost laughed.

He said you could leave but I couldn't. Don't leave me, Mama!

She had told Jimmy she loved him. She told him she would never leave him—and in that moment, Iron Hawk's reason for kidnapping Jimmy became suddenly clear.

Iron Hawk had not shown his face since he'd walked away from her that afternoon. Uncertain what to do, she had prepared a pallet for her exhausted son, had fed him from the bowl of food that was left for them outside the tepee in the usual manner, and had then held him in her arms, the sweet, little-boy scent of him filling her heart with love until he finally slept.

Weary beyond words, Eden laid her head on the pallet beside Jimmy and closed her eyes. She was tired of the hatred and the fear. She was tired of wondering. She was tired of it all.

"He had a stroke."

"A stroke?"

Motioning Rowe away from Tom Richards's bedside, Doc Bitters faced the worried cook, his lean face grave.

"He's in bad shape. He's paralyzed on the left side, and his heart isn't doin' too well, either. I don't know if he's goin' to make it."

"Damn it, Doc, you got to do somethin'!"

"What would you like me to do, Rowe? Restore the nerves that were sliced when Lone Bear's knife hit his spine five years ago? Give him a new heart, maybe? Make his blood pump normally again? It isn't goin' to happen."

"It's that damned Injun who's to blame for this!"

Doc Bitters frowned.

"No offense, Doc. Your wife's a good woman, even if she is an Injun. She ain't nothin' like that Iron Hawk."

"I don't want to discuss it."

"You ain't tellin' me you're on that Injun's side in all this?"

"Remember who you're talkin' to, Rowe." Doc Bitters's lean face creased in a frown. "I was here while most of this was happenin'. You weren't. I know a lot more about what went on than you do."

Rowe shook his head, his whiskered face tight. "The boss was just doin' his best to keep things together, is all. He's an ornery cuss, but he don't know no other way."

"You think so? It might be good if you got some of the fellas to talk to you about how all this came about in the first place. Mullen's fee-

291

lin' well enough to talk. He could clear some things up for you, and that might be a good thing, since you'll be runnin' the place for a while."

"What're you tryin' to say, Doc?"

"I'm sayin' that fella in the bed over there might not make it through this siege—so it might be time to talk a little truth around here."

Rowe glanced back at the bed, and Doc Bitters shrugged. "Give the old man a few days. We should know what's goin' to happen by then. I'll be back tomorrow."

Still staring at Tom Richards's motionless form, Rowe mumbled, "I should talk to Mullen, huh?"

Doc Bitters was already out the door.

They were sleeping.

Iron Hawk stood over the pallet where the boy lay. Eden's head lay beside her son's, her bright gold hair lying close to his cheek. He recalled the look on Eden's face when they approached the camp and she saw the boy. He knew he'd never forget it. Even fear for her son's safety couldn't overcome her joy at being reunited with him.

Bitter feelings had stirred within him then. He had not expected the jealousy that gnawed when she stood with the boy against him.

Iron Hawk perused the boy's sleeping face. It was smooth, free of the fear he had first seen when the child looked up at him in the stagecoach. But the fear had not lasted long. The boy had fought ferociously, calming only when his mother was mentioned. He had trembled when they neared the camp, but the sight of his mother's tears had straightened his spine and turned the boy around to face him in challenge.

A rabbit facing down a hawk.

Iron Hawk's unconscious smile dimmed. He wondered if James Broker had been as brave as his son. He wondered if Eden had loved James Broker, if she had come to life in Broker's arms the way she did in his. He wondered if Eden thought of Broker when they lay together, and whether she wished—

Angry at the direction of his thoughts, Iron Hawk brought them to a sharp halt. His jaw tight, he leaned down and touched Eden's shoulder. Her eyes opening, Eden was momentarily disoriented. He saw the confusion in her gaze, and a fleeting vulnerability that raised an unexpected ache inside him. Forcing it aside, he said, "It's time to go to sleep."

Eden glanced at his sleeping bench. Frowning, she replied, "I'll sleep here."

"No, you won't."

"Do you think you can force me to sleep beside you?"

"I expect you to do what's best for your son's welfare."

Eden drew herself to her feet. "I don't want to talk here. Jimmy might hear us."

Eden strode out of the tepee without waiting for his response. Iron Hawk waited long moments before following her. She was rigid with anger when he emerged. Still refusing to speak, he drew her along with him until they were a distance from camp where their voices would not be heard.

Eden rasped, "What did you mean by that—that you expected me to do what's best for my son's welfare?"

"I meant what I said. I expect you to control your son's anger and his fear, because he'll suffer if you don't."

Hardly able to contain her shaking, Eden responded, "And if he behaves?"

"Then he'll ride with me and I'll teach him to be a good Kiowa brave."

"No!"

"What's wrong, Eden? Don't you trust me with your son?"

"He's only four years old. He needs to be with his mother."

"You'll have the freedom of the camp when he isn't with you. That's what you want, isn't it? Then you can leave anytime you wish. Of course, if you decided to ride to the fort to bring the soldiers back here, you couldn't be sure what would happen to Jimmy."

Close to tears, Eden whispered, "Why did you do this?"

"You know why, Eden."

"You want to stop me from tryin' to escape."

"I have stopped you."

"If you hurt my son . . . if you try to frighten him in any way—"

"You love him, don't you, Eden?"

Eden did not need to respond.

"You loved me, once, too."

Eden closed her eyes.

"Love and hate—sometimes the lines become unclear. Are they blurred for you now?"

"No." Eden opened her eyes. "They're very clear."

"You hate me."

Eden took a shuddering breath. "I hate you as much as I ever loved you."

Eden's words cut sharp and deep, even as the remembered smell of a burning camp returned to assault Iron Hawk's mind, bringing with it the echoing cries of the wounded and dying—a debt of blood yet to be repaid.

He could not allow his weakness for her to stop him.

Never more conscious of that truth, Iron Hawk reached for Eden. He whispered, "There are times when I feel the same, Eden, but I don't hate you right now." He drew her close and pressed his mouth to hers. The taste of her lit a familiar fire inside him. His breathing was ragged when he said, "Right now, I just want to show you how things might have been. Let me do that, Eden."

He kissed her again, his mouth separating her lips, his hands moving warmly against her back as he crushed her closer. His kiss deepened. The beauty of holding Eden in his arms . . . the wonder.

Scooping her from her feet, Iron Hawk carried Eden farther into the shadows and laid her in a leafy bower. He covered her body with his, his endless desire for her a driving need.

Bodies warmed. Lips melded. Eden slipped her arms around his neck at last. She parted her lips under his, returning his kiss with growing ardor.

The lusting ended. The loving began.

Alone in the shadows, Running Deer fought the waves of jealousy that threatened to consume her. She would not allow herself to speak the white man's language, but she understood the words that Iron Hawk had spoken to the woman before he carried into the darkness. She heard the passion in his voice. The sounds of their mating tormented her.

The woman had cast a spell on Iron Hawk. She had captured his senses and she used them at will.

Iron Hawk had said he would ride out with the boy and teach him to be a good Kiowa brave. No! She would not see Iron Hawk honor a white man's child in that way. She would see him reserve that distinction for the son that *she* would one day give him.

Standing Man had explained Iron Hawk's plan of vengeance to her. It was Iron Hawk's intention to take from the man who had burned their Kiowa camp—this woman's father—all that he esteemed most highly, before he then took that man's life.

Iron Hawk carried his plan forward relentlessly, but he did not see its flaw. He did not realize that the danger he faced with the woman was greater than any he had ever faced in battle. In bringing the boy to camp, Iron Hawk was assured that the woman would not again attempt escape, because she feared for her son's welfare. But if something happened to the boy, the woman would turn from Iron Hawk forever and Iron Hawk would be free.

Running Deer raised her chin with new resolve. The boy was the key. She would find a way to dispose of him.

Chapter Thirteen

A gentle softness brushed Eden's lips as she slept. Responding instinctively, she turned toward the warmth enveloping her, toward strong arms that drew her closer, toward a powerful body curved to hers.

Eden opened her eyes to the darkness of the tepee as Iron Hawk held her passionately close. In the shadows across the firepit, Jimmy slept, his head turned toward the entrance of the tepee. Iron Hawk followed her gaze briefly, then looked back at her, his dark eyes singeing her with growing fervor. With a rasped word of surrender, he covered her mouth with his. She felt the hard rise of his passion against her. She gasped at its probing warmth. She caught her breath as Iron Hawk sank himself deep inside her.

Eden opened her eyes when Iron Hawk remained motionless within her. Meeting his gaze, she glimpsed what had once been, and she sought to reclaim it, clutching him close.

Silent kisses, building heat—sweet, throbbing release that held them breathless in a world reserved for them alone.

In the quiet aftermath, reality flashed in Eden's mind with brief and startling clarity. She was Iron Hawk's captive—but when she was in his arms, he was as much the captive as she.

Iron Hawk spoke softly to her then. She was uncertain of the meaning of the Kiowa words, but she would not allow herself to question them. They were a secret—words precious to Iron Hawk's heart—a loving enigma shared by them alone.

The treasured moments ended when dawn pierced the darkness with silver shards of light.

The day began.

Agitated, Jesse Rowe stared at Doc Bitters as the quiet physician leaned over Tom Richards's bed. It was early morning. Doc Bitters had come to the ranch at the same time every day since Richards had suffered the stroke a week earlier, but he said little.

"How are you feelin', Tom?"

Rowe silently groaned. Doc Bitters started every visit the same way, and the result was always the same. Richards struggled to talk, with his eyes growing increasingly panicked when he failed. Then the doc always said, "Are you managin' to eat somethin', Tom?"

Rowe sniffed. He had already told the damned doc that he managed to get a few mouthfuls of food down Richards's throat at mealtimes, but even a dimwit could see that the man was wasting away.

Doc Bitters put his ear to Richards's trembling lips. He straightened up and shook his head.

"I don't know anythin' about Eden or your grandson. Sheriff Duncan's lettin' the Army take care of things."

Richards's frail body twitched.

"Now, don't go getting' yourself excited or you'll have another stroke." Doc Bitters frowned, then turned toward Rowe. "Haven't you heard anythin' from McGill and Masters?"

"Them two ain't come back yet. We ain't got no idea what they're doin' or how things are goin'."

Richards closed his eyes.

"Look at me, Tom." When Richards's eyes opened, Doc Bitters addressed him soberly. "You've got to face the facts. You're not doin' yourself any good gettin' yourself all riled up like you are. Concentrate on gettin' well so's you'll be in decent shape to welcome Eden and your grandson back. In the meantime, why don't you send Curry out to the fort to check on things?"

"We already sent him." Rowe shook his head. "They don't know nothin' at the fort. They keep sendin' out patrols, and the patrols keep comin' back with nothin'.' "

"Well, no news is good news, I guess." Doc Bitters shrugged, then addressed Richards more softly, "You've got two good men out there lookin' for your daughter and grandson. They'll find them."

Following close behind the doc when he picked up his bag and headed for the doorway, Rowe hardly waited for the door to close before he snapped, "It's time for some answers, Doc!"

Doc Bitters turned toward the beleaguered cook. "If you're talkin' about how that old man in there is doin', I haven't got any answers. I don't know how he survived that stroke. If he wasn't so ornery, he probably wouldn't have."

"So, what are you sayin'?"

"I'm sayin' that the simple fact he's lastin' this long is in his favor. He is showin' some improvement. He's managin' to say a few words."

"No, he ain't."

Doc Bitters raised his brows. "He just said a few words to me."

It was Rowe's turn to look surprised. "I thought you was just playin' along with him."

"He asked about Eden and the boy. He slurred his words, but I couldn't miss the name 'Eden.' "

Rowe paused, then asked, "Does that mean he's goin' to make it?"

"I told you, I don't know."

"Hell, you're a doc, ain't you? Don't you know nothin'?"

Holding Rowe's gaze coldly for long seconds, Bitters replied, "I'm doin' all I can for him. That's sayin' somethin', too, given what I know about the past and my personal feelin's about it. That old man's got a lot to think about, and I got the feelin' he's startin' to look at things different from the way he looked at them before. I don't think that's helpin' him rest any easier."

"Are you sayin' he's got some fault in this whole mess?"

"I'll be back tomorrow."

"Doc—"

Rowe snorted as the door banged shut behind Doc Bitters. That was the second time the doc had done that, and he didn't like it too much.

Well, he guessed he knew what he had to do.

Jimmy fidgeted. He sat back on the sleeping bench, watching as Eden filled a wooden bowl with the steaming morning meal that had been left outside the tepee in the usual manner. Dawn had become morning. Iron Hawk had ridden out alone without explanation, leaving Jimmy and her alone in the tepee. Uncertain what the day had in store, she handed the bowl to her son. He accepted it listlessly.

A week had passed since Iron Hawk had brought Jimmy to the camp, and it had been a strange week indeed. The first day had been the most difficult. Fresh from Iron Hawk's arms, she had seen the fear on Jimmy's small, pale face when Iron Hawk awakened him and ordered him up on his feet. She had seen him fight to hold back his tears when Iron Hawk told him they would ride out together, leaving her behind.

She had protested being separated from Jimmy, but the Iron Hawk who turned to face her then had borne no resemblance to the man who had whispered soft words of love to her minutes earlier. The ice in his stare had chilled her, and when Iron Hawk again ordered Jimmy to follow him, Eden had known that further protest would only make it more difficult for her son.

The day had been endless until they returned. She had waited for Woman Who Walks Lightly to come for her, and when time passed and the squaw did not appear, she walked outside the tepee to see that the women of the camp had already left for their individual chores— Woman Who Walks Lightly among them. She realized belatedly that Iron Hawk, true to his word, had given the order that she was to be allowed the freedom of the camp.

Freedom. Eden was almost amused. She had spent the day wondering where her son was . . . what he was doing . . . if he was safe, only to see him return amidst a hunting party that had obviously seen great success that day. When Iron Hawk lifted Jimmy down from his horse, her son had run directly into her arms—and he was smiling.

"When are we goin' home, Mama?"

Jimmy's unexpected question drew Eden's attention. The following day had been a repetition of the first, as was the next and the next, with Jimmy falling asleep the moment his head hit his pallet at night, to then be awakened at daybreak by Iron Hawk's firm hand. But Iron Hawk had not taken Jimmy with him this morning, and when she looked outside the tepee, she saw that Standing Man was on guard.

Standing Man—Running Deer's brother. Eden didn't like the way brother and sister whispered while looking her way. She didn't trust Running Deer and she—

"Mama."

And now Jimmy wanted to know when they were going home.

Eden attempted a smile. "I don't know, Jimmy."

Jimmy's cheeks were no longer pale. They were tinted a soft warm gold from exposure to the sun, a color that reddened unexpectedly when he said, "Grandpa was wrong. The Injuns don't want to scalp me."

Eden's smile faded. "No, Injuns don't want to scalp everybody. Grandpa meant that Injuns scalp people in battle sometimes."

"Grandpa said all Injuns want to kill people an' take their hair. Why did he say that when it isn't true?"

"It's true to Grandpa, Jimmy. He doesn't like Injuns."

Jimmy frowned. "When I go back home, I'm goin' to tell Grandpa he was wrong. I'm goin' to tell him Iron Hawk isn't like those bad Injuns he doesn't like."

305

"Jimmy . . ." Eden sat beside her son and whispered, "A lot of what Grandpa told you about the Injuns is true. There's been a lot of fightin', and Injuns have killed some of Grandpa's friends."

"Not Iron Hawk! He wouldn't kill anybody! Grandpa's just sayin' that because Iron Hawk's an Injun."

"You're right. Grandpa doesn't like Iron Hawk, especially since Iron Hawk took you and me away from him and brought us here."

"I asked Iron Hawk why he did that." Jimmy's voice became a begrudging whisper. "He said Grandpa and him were mad at each other because of somethin' that happened a long time ago. He said the Kiowa way was to pay Grandpa back for what he did, and that's why he brought me and you here—to make Grandpa mad."

Eden did not respond.

"But Iron Hawk is goin' to let us go back to the ranch."

Eden's heart leaped. "Did he say that?"

"No, but I know he will." Jimmy shrugged. "Iron Hawk's teachin' me to hunt like a Kiowa boy. He says it'll be good for me to know how."

Apprehension crawled up Eden's spine. "Things aren't always like they seem, Jimmy. I don't want you to get too attached to him."

"He likes you, Mama."

"Did he say that?"

"Yes, because I asked him. I asked him why you were sleepin' on his sleepin' bench with him, and he said it was because when he first brought you here, you were angry and he thought you would try to run away from him . . . so he kept you close, so you couldn't. He said he's comfortable that way now, and you're comfortable that way, too."

Eden remained silent.

"I told him that the people on the stagecoach said he escaped from prison, and that the Army was after him."

"What did he say about that?"

"He said it was true. He said the Army put him in prison by mistake, and he escaped because it wasn't a nice place. He said he won't go back." Jimmy paused again, then asked, "Do you think Iron Hawk's mad at me?"

"Why would he be mad at you?"

Jimmy shrugged. "He didn't take me with him today."

Eden's stomach tightened. "No, I don't think he's mad at you. I think he had someplace to go where he couldn't take a little boy."

"Is he goin' to fight with the soldiers, Mama?"

"I don't know."

"I hope he doesn't."

Eden paused. "Would you like it if I could talk Iron Hawk into takin' you back home?"

"No. I don't want to go home without you."

Suddenly unwilling to allow the conversation to progress any further, Eden stood up abruptly. "Eat your breakfast, Jimmy."

Pushing aside the flap as Jimmy dutifully picked up the bowl, Eden stepped outside. She breathed deeply of the morning air, but the knot inside her remained. Jimmy was confused. He didn't know what to think or believe. She had to get him away from the camp, before it was too late, before—

A sense of uneasiness turned Eden abruptly to see Running Deer looking malevolently in her direction.

Yes, she had to get away . . . before it was too late.

Iron Hawk lay flat on his stomach on the rise, observing. He had left his horse concealed a distance away, and had made his way cautiously to this place where he had a clear view of the fort. He had been there since sunrise, determined to continue a surveillance that had been interrupted when he brought Jimmy Broker to the camp.

Iron Hawk steeled himself against feelings he could not afford to indulge. Aware of his weakness for Eden, he had deliberately taken the child with him each morning so as to demonstrate to her his full control of the situation. He had seen the relief with which she welcomed the boy home each afternoon, and he knew he had made his point. Eden would not attempt an escape while the boy remained vulnerable.

Complications had arisen, however, that he had not anticipated. He had not expected to like the boy. He had not believed himself capable of overcoming the bitterness he felt each time he thought of the man who was this child's father— the man whom Eden had accepted so easily in his place. He had not expected to feel an affinity for the boy, or to experience pride in the boy's obvious intelligence and outspoken concern for his mother. He had not foreseen the aching sadness that would begin each time he forced himself to acknowledge that this temporary interlude would soon come to an end.

A stirring of activity within the fort interrupted Iron Hawk's thoughts. Drawing back as the gates opened and a patrol rode boldly forward, Iron Hawk could not help smiling. If the soldiers only knew that the man they sought was so close, observing their futile maneuvers.

Iron Hawk's smile faded as the patrol rode out of sight. He was well aware that he could not allow himself to become overconfident. He had heard the braves talking of couriers seen coming and going at the fort, and patrols that continued to increase in frequency. Something was happening, and he had no desire for his camp to be caught unawares as it had been once before.

Two horsemen rode into view on the trail, heading for the fort, and Iron Hawk's eyes narrowed. His lips tightened into a hard line when he recognized Masters, the wrangler who had put his hands on Eden and who had felt the weight of his anger because of that presumption. The other man was Jim McGill. Yes, he remembered that man, too.

Iron Hawk studied the two men more closely. They were alone, and from their appearance, they had been on the trail for a while. He con-

Elaine Barbieri

sidered that thought. Masters had a twofold interest in him—a desire to bring Eden home and a hunger for revenge. McGill had been deeply involved in the events five years earlier which sent him to prison. Both men would not be satisfied until he was brought to *their* justice.

Yes, they had been out tracking *him*.

Iron Hawk's expression sobered. The fact that the two men had been unsuccessful allowed him little satisfaction. Instead, their appearance confirmed a stark reality. Time was growing short, for him and his people.

Iron Hawk continued watching the wranglers as they entered the fort. He could not wait much longer to make his move.

"I ain't goin' back with you!" Dismounting amidst the morning activity of the fort, Masters turned toward McGill. His expression adamant and his disposition sour, he continued, "You can go back to old man Richards and listen to him rant and rave if you want, but I'm not goin' to waste my time there."

McGill fought to control his annoyance. "No, you ain't goin' to waste your time at the Diamond R. You'd rather waste your time here, watchin' the patrols goin' and comin' from the fort with nothin' new to report."

"Maybe. Or just maybe I'll be where I should be if somethin' new turns up. Maybe I'll be able to follow through real quick without givin' that bastard Kiowa the time he needs to get away again."

310

"You're dreamin', Masters. That Kiowa ain't about to make no foolish mistakes. He's too smart to foul things up now, when everythin's goin' his way."

His face twisting with true malevolence, Masters took an aggressive step. "You're right. That Kiowa's smart, but he ain't goin' to let this thing drag on forever. He wants revenge, and he's not goin' to be satisfied with just makin' the old man sweat. Sooner or later he's goin' to go for blood—and that's when I'll be ready."

"If you was thinkin' clear"—McGill's voice rang with criticism—"you'd realize the best place to be when that happens is the Diamond R."

"You're wrong. There's goin' to be some kind of sign when that Kiowa is about to make his move, and the only place anybody's got a chance of seein' it is here, at the fort."

"Here, where all these soldiers are so good at readin' Injun signs . . ."

"No, here, where patrols out lookin' for Injuns would have a chance of seein' a change comin' on."

"You're graspin' at straws, Masters."

"And you're just plain quittin', McGill!"

McGill's bearded face twitched. "Maybe you're right. Maybe I've had enough of wanderin' around and feelin' like that Kiowa's eyes are starin' at my back."

"I ain't had enough of it. I ain't goin' to be satisfied until I'm starin' right back at him."

"Yeah . . . well, good luck." McGill dropped

his mount's reins over the hitching post. "I'm goin' to talk to the head man here one more time before I leave."

Masters sneered, "Like you said, good luck."

Frowning as Masters started toward the stable, leading his horse, McGill called out, "What do you want me to tell Richards?"

Somehow, McGill was not surprised when Masters didn't bother to reply.

It had been a difficult day.

Standing beside the stream, Eden looked down at the hide sack gradually filling with water in the stream beside her, then glanced up at the cloudless late afternoon sky. The sun would soon set, and Iron Hawk had not yet returned. For the last hour Jimmy had been counting the minutes.

Eden's throat constricted tightly. She hadn't realized her son was developing such a strong attachment to Iron Hawk. It worried her. Iron Hawk had his own motives, and Jimmy was so young. There was no way Jimmy could understand the complications of her relationship with Iron Hawk. How could she make Jimmy comprehend that Iron Hawk's feelings for her were contradictory, driven by a desire for revenge and a conflicting physical hunger stirred by memories of a past that stood no chance of being revived? How could she explain that her emotions also fluctuated so severely in her contacts with Iron Hawk that she was never truly certain how she felt? How could she make him understand that the bitter events of the past muddied the emotion between Iron Hawk and her, that they were bound to lead to disaster, and that she needed to get Jimmy to a point of safety before that disaster occurred? And lastly, how could she explain that she ached with longing for the man who posed the greatest physical threat to Jimmy and herself, a man who she knew now existed only in her mind?

She couldn't. She wouldn't even try.

Leaning down as the sack filled to the brim, Eden picked it up and turned back toward camp. She was well aware that no one observed her wanderings around the camp. There was no need when Jimmy was being watched so carefully.

Emerging at the top of the trail, Eden glanced toward the tepee where Jimmy had been playing, but he was gone. Her step quickening, she walked to the tepee and lifted the flap. He wasn't there.

Her heart pounding, Eden hung the sack on a peg and went back outside to scan the area. Panic tightened her throat when she saw Standing Man walking alone a distance away. She raced up to him and gripped his arm.

"Where is my son?"

Standing Man shook off her hand.

Refusing to be intimidated, Eden pressed, "I know you understand what I'm sayin'. Tell me where my son is!"

Standing Man remained silent.

Panicking, Eden rasped again, "Iron Hawk

said my son would be safe! I want to know where he is!"

Standing Man's eyes narrowed. She held her breath when he raised his hand to point toward a nearby stand of trees.

Eden started off at a run. Breathless, she entered the wooded glade and halted abruptly when the change in light blinded her. Desperate, she called out, "Jimmy, where are you?" When there was no response, she called out again, "Jimmy, answer me!"

"I'm here, Mama!"

Following the sound of his voice, Eden ran toward a small clearing to see Running Deer standing beside Jimmy. Confronting the hatred in the squaw's eyes with a rabid fury of her own, Eden hissed, "What are you doin' with my son?"

"Your son is Iron Hawk's prisoner—just as you are Iron Hawk's prisoner. I do not need to answer your questions."

Surprised when Running Deer responded so clearly in the white man's tongue, Eden addressed Jimmy softly. "Can you find your way back to camp from here?"

Jimmy's fair brow wrinkled with annoyance. "Of course I can. I'm not a baby!"

"Go back and wait for me in Iron Hawk's tepee."

"But Running Deer said I could—"

"Go back to the tepee now!"

After hesitating a silent moment, Jimmy turned back toward camp. Waiting until he had disappeared from sight, Eden faced Running

Deer and spat, "Stay away from my son!"

"You cannot give orders to me!"

Eden stepped aggressively forward. "I'm tellin' you to stay away from my son or you'll be sorry!"

"So, the prisoner threatens Running Deer!" Running Deer's shrill laughter sent shivers down Eden's spine as she continued, "The prisoner believes she has twisted Iron Hawk's mind so that he can see no wrong in her . . . so that he will turn against his people for her, but she is wrong."

"I don't care about Iron Hawk! I care only about my son!"

"You seek revenge against Iron Hawk for taking you prisoner. You seek to tarnish Iron Hawk in the eyes of his people so they will turn against him, but I will not let Iron Hawk be deceived by you."

"Stay away from my son!"

Running Deer's face twisted with rage. "I will make my people see the truth, that your son is no different from the Kiowa children who were killed when your father burned our camp five years ago. They will seek justice on him—as I do, and you will have no power to protect him!"

Shuddering, Eden rasped, "I warn you, injury to my son will be injury to Iron Hawk as well!"

"Iron Hawk will accept the truth. He will feel the will of his people!"

"No, he will not!"

"Iron Hawk has promised his people vengeance. He will see what his people's vengeance includes, and he will bow to their wishes."

"He won't do that!"

"You seek to control Iron Hawk with your body, but Iron Hawk will sicken of your white skin when he is forced to remember the blood that was spilled in your name."

Desperate, Eden rasped, "You'll make a greater mistake than you could ever realize if you hurt my son."

"Blood for blood! It is the Kiowa way!"

"Blood for blood—but is it the Kiowa way to shed *Kiowa* blood for vengeance?"

"Your son—"

"If you would shed my son's blood, you would shed Kiowa blood as well! You would shed Iron Hawk's blood!"

"Iron Hawk—"

"My son is Iron Hawk's son!"

Her eyes widening, Running Deer took a spontaneous backward step. "I do not believe you!"

"You don't want to believe me, but you know it's true!" Eden took a shuddering breath. "Iron Hawk's blood runs in my son's veins. If you would spill that blood, you would spill Iron Hawk's blood, and he—"

But Running Deer wasn't listening. She was staring past Eden, at a point behind her, her eyes wide with apprehension.

Eden turned, fear striking her motionless when she saw Iron Hawk.

* * *

Hardly aware that Running Deer ran past him toward camp, Iron Hawk stared at Eden where she stood rigidly a few feet away.

"Is it true?" Slow rage replaced incredulity, and Iron Hawk pressed, "Is Jimmy my son?"

"I . . . I . . ."

Closing the distance between them in a few rapid steps, Iron Hawk grasped Eden's arms roughly, demanding, "Is Jimmy my son?"

Eden rasped, "I couldn't tell you. I was afraid you'd try to take him away from me."

Releasing Eden so abruptly that she staggered a few steps backwards, Iron Hawk felt the venom of pure hatred boil within as he grated, "You lie! You didn't tell me—you didn't tell anyone—because you didn't want anyone to know he had Kiowa blood."

"That isn't true!" Eden took a tentative step toward him. "I didn't want anyone to know Jimmy was your son—that's true—but not because I was ashamed. I knew what Jimmy would have to face if anyone found out. You killed Witt! You shot him in the back and went to prison for that! Lone Bear—your uncle—attacked my father. If I hadn't shot him, he would've killed my father. I was surrounded by hatred for all Indians. Do you think I wanted my son to grow up the object of that hatred?"

Iron Hawk rasped, "I told you I didn't shoot Witt Bradley in the back, but you believed others instead of me. You knew your father was responsible for the destruction of a peaceful Kiowa camp, but you denied it to yourself, because it was easier. And when Lone Bear struck your father in rightful vengeance, you shot to kill."

"I had no choice. He was my father!"

His fury a palpable force in the heavy evening air, Iron Hawk accused, "You gave my son to another man."

"I had to protect him any way I could!"

"You taught my son to hate his own people."

"I didn't!"

"And when I returned, you continued your deceit—even when you lay in my arms."

"I am your prisoner! You are wanted by the Army! Your life is in danger and Jimmy's life would be in danger, too, if anyone knew he was your son."

"You would've kept my son from me forever."

"You would've taken my son away from me!"

Iron Hawk stared at the woman before him. Beautiful eyes that beguiled . . . soft lips that lied . . . a warm body that deceived so well.

"Iron Hawk." Eden's voice wobbled. "What are you goin' to do?"

Contempt flushed hotly through him.

"Iron Hawk."

Repulsed, Iron Hawk walked away.

His mouth agape, Rowe stared at Mullen. The foreman's wounds had been serious, but he was getting stronger every day. He was well enough to answer some questions that needed to be asked.

But the answers were hard! Somehow unwilling to accept them, Rowe pressed, "You're tellin' me that you all burned that Kiowa camp without givin' them people a chance?"

"We did what them Injuns would've done to us if they could. And it wasn't only the men on the Diamond R. Every other spread in the area had a part in it—Jesse Walters's, Sam Hart's, Larry Neece's, Marty Lane's. Even Sheriff Duncan's deputies went along with us."

"That's when Iron Hawk was shot."

"No, that Kiowa bastard wasn't around when we got there, and Richards was damned frustrated when he wasn't. We burned the camp anyway, but the boss wasn't about to let him get away. He was sure Iron Hawk would show up, so he went back to make sure he got the bastard, and I went with him." Mullen sneered. "I never should've stopped him from puttin' the last bullet in that Injun. It all would've been over then if I hadn't."

Rowe was incredulous. "All that—because Eden was seein' Iron Hawk?"

"All that because of them murderin' Kiowas! Them Injuns was killin' and butcherin' all around these parts. There wasn't one of us in that posse who didn't have his own axe to grind. The boss just gave us the chance we was waitin' for."

Rowe shook his head. The pieces were beginning to fall into place. "That's why Sheriff Duncan didn't want no part of chasin' after Iron Hawk. He didn't want to see the same thing happen again."

319

Elaine Barbieri

Mullen's lips tightened. "That sheriff's got his reasons—and we got ours."

"And now the boss ain't got nothin' . . . no daughter, no grandson, and no life."

"It's that Kiowa's fault!"

"I ain't so sure."

"I ain't interested in whether you're sure or you ain't! Witt Bradley was a fine fella. They didn't come no better than him. He didn't want nothin' but to see that Eden got the best—and he's dead because of that Injun!"

"Iron Hawk shot him—in the back?"

Mullen paused. "He's dead, ain't he?"

"So what you're sayin' is—"

"What I'm sayin' is, this ranch was a real fine place for all of us until that Injun came back to Texas, struttin' them fine Eastern clothes and thinkin' he was goin' to fit right in between us and them heathens. Because of him, everythin' changed around here, one way or another, and there ain't a man on this ranch who's not out to make him pay."

"Seems like Iron Hawk's got the same idea."

"Yeah? Well, it ain't goin' to work. Things is goin' his way right now, but we'll get Eden and the boy back, and when we do—"

But Rowe wasn't listening anymore. He was walking back toward the house. His questions were answered and he had heard enough.

The sun had set hours earlier. The tepee was in darkness and Jimmy was sleeping.

Sitting on the ground beside Jimmy's pallet,

Eden looked down at her sleeping son, her throat tight with conflicting emotions. She knew she would never forget the look on Iron Hawk's face when he learned the truth. Jimmy . . . Iron Hawk's son. How had he not realized it from the first? Granted, the physical resemblance was limited. Jimmy's hair was light and his skin was fair, but his eyes . . .

The knot in Eden's throat tightened. She had seen Iron Hawk in Jimmy's eyes from the moment her son took his first breath. Jimmy's eyes were keen and sharp like Iron Hawk's. They were so black that they seemed fathomless, yet they were clear mirrors of his emotions. Jimmy's face had the fullness of a child, but the gradual emergence of his father's finely sculpted cheek and jaw was already becoming visible to the discerning eye.

And her eye was discerning. She had searched for those features, only to be struck with both pride and a steadily encroaching fear when she saw them gradually appearing.

But Iron Hawk had not stopped to search out his own features in his son when he strode away from her. Finally freed from her frozen immobility, she had raced after him in time to see him mount his horse and ride off into the twilight. He had not returned.

Eden glanced up through the smoke hole to see stars twinkling overhead. The camp had settled down for the night and all was quiet. Shaken by Iron Hawk's anger, she had not left Jimmy's side since returning to the tepee. She had already decided that she would not let Jimmy out of her sight until she was able to talk to Iron Hawk and explain.

Explain.

Eden closed her eyes briefly in frustration. She waited, hoping to explain to Iron Hawk things that she was not really sure she understood herself.

Eden sighed and brushed away a tear. She was sure of one thing, however. She needed to assuage Iron Hawk's anger and make it clear to him that she had meant what she said—that through all the uncertainties, she had never felt ashamed that Jimmy was his son.

Jimmy sighed and moved restlessly in his sleep. Eden stroked his smooth cheek. No, she would not move from his side until Iron Hawk returned.

Stretching out beside Jimmy, Eden laid her head beside his. Comforted by the sound of his steady breathing, she closed her eyes.

Eden awakened with a start. Disoriented, she squinted in the bright morning sunlight streaming down through the smoke hole, then turned toward Jimmy.

Jimmy's pallet was empty.

Her heart leaping to an erratic beat, Eden sat up abruptly. Iron Hawk's sleeping bench was empty. The fire was out and the tepee was silent.

"Jimmy!"

On her feet in an instant, Eden pushed aside the flap and stepped outside. Her body quaking so violently that she could barely stand, she called again, "Jimmy! Where are you?"

Suddenly realizing that the camp had gone silent around her, Eden looked at Woman Who Walks Lightly, only to see her turn away from her. She met the glances of the other women and they did the same.

Panic flushing her face hot, Eden was about to call out again when Running Deer stepped into view. Leading a horse, she approached to within a few feet of Eden and halted.

"Where's my son?" Her voice quaking, Eden rasped, "Tell me! What did you do with him?"

"I did nothing with your son. Iron Hawk has taken *his son* away."

"I don't believe you!"

"Look at Woman Who Walks Lightly!" Running Deer's anger flared. "See the truth of what I say in her eyes!"

Woman Who Walks Lightly turned toward her in confirmation, and Eden's throat choked tight. She rasped, "Where did Iron Hawk take him?"

Running Deer almost smiled. "Iron Hawk said you are free to go. No one will stop you."

"I won't go!" Eden took a backward step. "I'll wait for him to come back!"

"Iron Hawk will not return." Triumph in her eyes, Running Deer raised her chin. "He travels to another place, where he will raise his son as a true Kiowa. He leaves behind him the message that you will never see your son again."

Stunned into immobility, Eden was unable to respond.

"This horse is yours." Running Deer pulled the animal forward and forced the lead into Eden's hand. "Iron Hawk left him in fair exchange for your son."

"Fair exchange . . ."

"Take the horse and leave. You are not wanted here."

Shuddering, barely controlling her desire to strike the sneer from Running Deer's scarred face, Eden clenched the lead tightly in her hand. She glanced upward at the morning sky. It was only a few hours since dawn. Iron Hawk and Jimmy could not have gotten far, and the notched hoof on Jimmy's mare would make them easy to track. She'd find them.

Turning toward the mount Running Deer offered, Eden spared no glances for the onlookers who had observed the scene in silence. Mounted in a moment, she dug her heels into the animal's sides and spurred it forward.

A shout sounded from the fort's parapet.

"A rider approaching, Major Peters! It's a courier."

Halting in mid-stride where he was crossing the fort yard, Major Peters turned at the guard's call. His cleanly shaven cheek twitched. It was barely past noon. The couriers were beginning to arrive like clockwork! He was sick and tired of it—communications coming and going from politicians who had not a clue what was really happening on the frontier.

His temper short, Major Peters turned abruptly back toward his office. He'd be damned if he'd take the communiqué in full view of watchful eyes. To his disadvantage, he wasn't a good actor and his disgust at the drivel that passed for official orders would be too obvious in a command where morale was already at an all-time low.

"Send the courier to my office when he arrives, Corporal."

Turning on his heel, Major Peters walked back to his office with as much decorum as he could muster. He had no doubt that the missive presently racing toward him was a direct response to the report he had sent out earlier. And he had no doubt that he had stirred up a hornets' nest with his blunt assessments. Well, if he had, he was glad. Anything would be better than sitting idly by as the local tribes made fools out of him and his men on a daily basis.

Major Peters's determined step halted abruptly at the sight of the unshaven civilian leaning against the fort wall. He addressed the man directly.

"So, you're still here, Mr. Masters."

To his credit, the man pulled himself away from the wall with a semblance of respect for his office as he responded, "That's right, Major."

"You haven't been able to find any trace of Miss Richards, I presume."

"That's right."

"Nothing on the boy, either?"

"No."

"So, since no one else seems to be able to find those Indians, I guess my men aren't as ineffectual as they're made out to be."

"Oh, they're 'ineffectual,' all right." Masters's smile was little more than a sneer. "It's just that as things stand, I'm as 'ineffectual' as they are." Masters's face hardened. "I figure on changin' that, though. And I figure that this is the best place for me to be until I do."

Despite Masters's calculated insult, Major Peters could not help sympathizing with the man's plight. If he was in this fellow's shoes, with two people who were obviously dear to him kidnapped by an outlaw Kiowa while an entire Army command remained ineffective, he doubted he'd be taking it as calmly.

Major Peters studied Masters more closely. No, the man wasn't calm. He was coldly furious . . . and he was waiting. He was a man to be watched.

"I'm sorry, Mr. Masters." Major Peters continued more softly, "You may be sure that I intend to pursue this matter and see that Miss Richards and her son are returned unharmed."

"Sure, Major."

Striding away, Major Peters felt Masters's eyes burning into his back. Masters hadn't believed a word he'd said—and he supposed he didn't blame him.

Seated at his desk moments later, Major Peters raised his head at the knock on the door.

He frowned when the communiqué was placed in his hand. He opened it and read it slowly. He read it again, then placed it on the desk, his jaw tight.

"I'm gettin' hungry."

Iron Hawk glanced at the boy riding the small mare beside him. Jimmy . . . his son.

An emotion unlike any he had ever known suffused Iron Hawk when the boy met his gaze directly, with eyes so similar to Lone Bear's that he wondered how he had allowed himself to be so deceived. Or had he? He had been drawn to the boy, despite his preconceived resentment against the son Eden had supposedly conceived with another man. His efforts to remain coldly detached from the boy had failed from the first. And, strangely, when he heard Eden tell Running Deer that Jimmy was his son, it was almost as if the thought was being confirmed in his mind.

Almost.

A familiar rage flared. Eden had deliberately kept the truth from him! She had looked at him without flinching when she declared Jimmy *her* son and stood with the boy against him. She had clutched the boy with relief when they returned each day, as if she had feared for his safety. And through the long nights while he had held her in his arms, while they had lain so intimately close that he had believed their hearts beat as one, she had maintained her secret.

"When are we goin' back to camp?"

Iron Hawk did not have to glance at the sun that was rapidly slipping into the horizon to know they would have no chance to make it back to the camp before nightfall. But Jimmy didn't realize that. It was time he knew.

"We're not going back to camp."

Jimmy's smooth brow furrowed. "Mama's not goin' to like that. She'll be mad because we didn't tell her."

Iron Hawk did not reply. He wouldn't tell Jimmy that they wouldn't go back tonight, or any other night. The boy was too young to realize that they were heading in a direction they had never traveled before. Nor would he reveal that they would travel for many days before they reached their destination, and that Jimmy would never see his mother again.

"She's goin' to be alone, you know." Jimmy was frowning. "Some of the squaws don't like Mama. They might not treat her right."

Iron Hawk allowed his gaze to linger on his son's disturbed expression. He had seen the change in the boy when the day began to wane and they had not yet turned back. Jimmy was beginning to miss Eden. And he was beginning to *worry* about her.

Jimmy looked up at Iron Hawk unexpectedly. "Mama doesn't have anybody to take care of her."

Taking the opportunity the boy provided, Iron Hawk asked, "Did your mama ever tell you anything about your father?"

"My pa's dead."

Iron Hawk pressed, "She didn't tell you anything about him?"

"He was a nice man, but he got sick. My grandpa and old Rowe took care of me when my mama was out workin' with the men." Jimmy glanced away as he continued, "My grandpa doesn't like Injuns. He says they're bad, but I'm goin' to tell him you're not bad when I get home."

"What if you don't go back to the ranch, Jimmy?"

Jimmy's gaze snapped back to his. "My grandpa's old. He's goin' to die soon, so I think I shouldn't wait too long before I go back to see him."

"What if I wanted you to stay with me?" A great knot tightened in his chest as Iron Hawk added, "What if I wanted you to learn to be a good Kiowa warrior?"

"Like you?"

Iron Hawk did not reply.

Jimmy grew thoughtful. "I don't know what Mama would say."

Eden.

Iron Hawk urged his mount on. Yes, Jimmy was too young to realize what was happening— that they were traveling steadily away from the camp and from the ranch, toward a territory where few would recognize the name Iron Hawk, and where he would achieve a powerful vengeance simply by claiming his son for his own.

Nor did Jimmy know that his mother was safe from any squaws who didn't like her—*because she had been trailing them for the greater portion of the day.*

Iron Hawk allowed thoughts of Eden to linger. He had ridden out from the camp after Eden disclosed that Jimmy was his son. His anger was so overwhelming that he had not dared remain. He had pressed his mount to the limit, only stopping when the animal could travel no more. He had camped where the horse stopped and had slept fitfully through the night while images of Eden and Jimmy vied for prominence in his mind. When he awoke before dawn, his decision was made. He had known he could not defile the memory of his father and of Lone Bear by allowing his own son to grow into manhood ignorant of his heritage and despising his people. Nor could he allow his weakness for a woman to keep him from the path he was pledged to take.

He had arrived at the tepee at dawn. In a manner established since the boy came to the camp, he had called Jimmy out to ride with him, and the boy had made no protest. He had ordered that Eden be freed when she awakened, with the message that Jimmy and he would not return. He had known she would not disclose the location of the camp for fear of retribution against her son.

He did not anticipate, however, that Eden would attempt to follow them. Nor did he expect that she would be so persistent in her tracking—or that she would be so successful.

A careful eye on the distant trail behind them had disclosed her presence at midday. Taking more care to conceal his trail, he had kept Eden in sight while she fell further and further behind, and Jimmy remained ignorant of his mother's pursuit. He had wondered how long it would take for Eden to surrender to the hopelessness of her situation.

But Eden had not surrendered.

Looking again at his son, Iron Hawk saw that his head was drooping. The boy was tired. They needed to continue on until dark, when Eden would also be forced to halt for the night, but Jimmy wouldn't last much longer.

Leaning over to lift Jimmy from his horse, Iron Hawk positioned his son astride in front of him. The boy made no protest when Iron Hawk adjusted him comfortably against the wall of his chest, then gathered the mare's reins so it would follow behind.

Jimmy leaned back, his small body warm and comforting where it rested against him.

His flesh. His blood.

Jimmy's heavy eyelids drifted closed, and Iron Hawk was consoled by the thought that his son had finally surrendered all concerns for Eden to sleep.

But Eden would not surrender. And neither would he.

Her thirst almost unbearable and her stomach rumbling, Eden held her mount to a steady pace. She glanced in the direction of the setting sun, realizing it would soon be dark. She was a fool, and she knew it. She had lived in the wilderness territory of Texas all her life, yet she had allowed emotion to trap her into a situation that was rapidly becoming desperate.

Somehow, all common sense had deserted her at the realization that Iron Hawk was taking Jimmy away from her forever. She had ridden out after them in spontaneous pursuit, so certain that she could catch up with them that she had given no thought to the necessities of survival. It was only now, when the daylight hours were fading, that she realized how dire her circumstances were. She had no food or water, nor the means to obtain them—yet without them, she knew she could not maintain the strength or clarity of mind she would need to continue her pursuit.

That reality had become clear as the day progressed and Eden realized that Iron Hawk was traveling steadily northward, into territory with which she was unfamiliar. She was now faced with desperate choices—to abandon the trail temporarily, so she could get the supplies she needed and resume tracking later, or to continue on at any cost. She knew the dangers of each choice. To abandon the trail was to risk losing it forever. To continue on was to risk losing her life.

The sun dropped swiftly into the horizon, lengthening shadows which she knew would soon yield to darkness. She would have to find adequate shelter for the night and she would need to awaken the next morning ready to pursue whatever course she decided upon.

Eden raised her chin in an automatic gesture of silent defiance. Those decisions needed to be made, but for now, she could travel a little longer.

Eden urged her mount on.

"Is it true?" His palms flat on Major Peters's desk, Masters leaned belligerently toward the seated military man. The brilliant colors of the setting sun outside the window colored his tight features as he demanded sharply, "Answer me, damn it! Is it true you're goin' to talk a peace treaty with them Comanches?"

Major Peters stood up abruptly. "I don't like your tone, Mr. Masters."

"You don't like my tone, huh?" Masters faced him squarely. "Well, I don't like what I'm hearin'."

Masters glared, awaiting the commandant's response. He had entered Major Peters's office after an angry brush with the sentry outside the door and his mood was still combative. He knew it would remain that way unless the rumors he had heard only minutes earlier were denied.

Major Peters returned his stare coldly and Masters's stomach twisted tight. "It's true, ain't it?"

Major Peters hesitated a moment longer. "I'm trying to remind myself that you're upset right now, Mr. Masters. I'm trying to tell myself that's the reason you forced your way in here, but I want you to remember something as well. I don't have to abide your behavior. This is a military fort and I'm in command."

"You're here to protect the people in this part of Texas, not to preach to them!"

"I don't need you to tell me my responsibilities."

"Look, I ain't interested in arguin' with you." Masters stood his ground. "I'm here in this fort for one thing—to get Eden Richards and her boy back."

"If that's what you're really concerned about, you should be glad that Washington has authorized the negotiation of a new peace treaty."

"Well, I ain't!"

"Give yourself time to think, Mr. Masters! A new peace treaty would mean we can demand the return of the young woman and her son as proof of responsible intent."

"What makes you think you can trust them Injuns? They've signed peace treaties before, but it never meant a damned thing to them."

"This time it will."

"Why, because you're the one who's goin' to be doin' the negotiatin'?"

"That's right."

"Hell, that's a lot to say from a man who ain't even sure he'll be able to get that proposal delivered!"

"I'm not the fool that you think I am, Mr. Masters." Major Peters maintained his calm with sheer force of will. "It's as obvious to me as it is to everyone else that our scouts lead us as far as they *want* to lead us, and that any messages the Indians want to get through, *do* get through."

"What makes you think the Injuns will want to talk peace again?"

"You underestimate the Indians, Mr. Masters. I may be new to this territory, but I've seen too much since I came here to think of them as ignorant savages. They're people who are defending their homes in much the same way you are."

"They're bloodthirsty heathens!"

"They see their land being swallowed up by outsiders."

"It's not *their* land!"

"From their viewpoint, it is. Fort Worth is new and it's alone, but other forts will follow. The Indians aren't fools. They can see it coming."

"You're givin' them too much credit."

"You forget, they have a man among them now who was educated back East and who knows the capabilities of the Federal Government. He knows what's in store for this portion of the country. From what I hear, he has a voice among them."

"You ain't talkin' about Iron Hawk?"

"Yes, I am."

"What in hell's wrong with you? He's the most bloodthirsty savage of the lot! He went to jail for killin' a white man, and when he broke out, the first thing he did was to kidnap a woman and a boy to hold them hostage."

"I'm not defending him, Mr. Masters. I'm saying he's a man who's capable of recognizing the imbalance of power that the Indians will eventually be facing—a man who knows the Indians can't win in the long run."

"He ain't interested in 'the long run.' He's only interested in now."

Major Peters paused, then continued, "In answer to your question, yes, Washington has authorized me to negotiate a new peace treaty with the Indians in the portion of the country under my command. In case you're wondering, this initiative comes at my instigation."

"So this damned fool idea is yours!"

Major Peters's clean-shaven cheek flushed. "The word goes out with the scouts tomorrow morning, Mr. Masters. I don't expect it will take long to reach its destination."

"And in the meantime, you're not goin' to do nothin' about tryin' to get Eden and her boy back."

"The patrols will continue."

"Right." Masters turned toward the door.

"Stop where you are, Mr. Masters." Waiting until Masters turned back toward him, Major Peters advanced toward him. Halting close enough to him that Masters could see the controlled fury in his eyes, Major Peters hissed, "Just a warning. If you do anything to hinder Federal efforts to effect a peace treaty with the Indians, you'll go to jail—understand?"

Masters sneered. "I understand, all right."

"You won't get a second warning."

"You won't need to give one."

Major Peters remained silent as Masters slammed the office door behind him. It did not miss his notice that the wrangler's final statement had been more threat than promise.

Jimmy was sleeping. Iron Hawk lay on his blanket beside his son, his brow furrowed. Night had fallen. A campfire burned a few feet away, enveloping them in a small circle of light, and all was silent.

Jimmy had awakened when Iron Hawk halted his mount to camp for the night. The boy had remained awake barely long enough to eat before his head was again nodding. Laying his son down, he had then covered him with a blanket and assumed his place beside him, but sleep would not come.

Iron Hawk glanced up at the starlit sky. He recalled the countless times he had looked up at that sky from his prison cell, knowing a gnawing hunger to again view that brilliant expanse in freedom. He had not realized then that escaping from his prison would not mean that he was truly free.

Eden's face flashed before him and anger returned. From the first moment he again held her in his arms, he had spent hours seeking to define his conflicting feelings toward her. Experiencing hatred and a desire for vengeance one moment, then a soul-shaking hunger for her the next, he had concluded his only recourse was to approach each moment on its own merits, without deception—but Eden had not responded with equal candor. While her body spoke with love, her heart remained cold. While she clung to him in yearning, she maintained deep deceits. She had clutched him close with an earnestness that reached the intimate core of him, and all the while she had denied him his son.

Iron Hawk steeled himself against the new fury that thought evoked. But their roles were now reversed. It was *he* whose heart was cold, and it was *he* who would deny her their child.

Vengeance? Retribution?

No. Justice.

"He ain't doin' so great, is he, Rowe?"

Standing a few feet from Tom Richards's bed, McGill addressed the scowling cook in a whisper that reverberated in the silence of the sickroom with the power of a shout.

"What's the matter with you?" Rowe scowled. "He ain't deaf, you know."

"He ain't dumb, neither. He probably knows better then we do how he's doin'."

Dragging McGill out the door, Rowe pulled it closed with a snap, then stated, "You got somethin' to ask, ask it here."

"I ain't got nothin' else to ask. Hell, all my questions was answered just by lookin' at the boss. It don't look like he'll last much longer."

"The doc ain't sayin' which way it'll go."

Rowe's small-eyed gaze met McGill's with new intensity. "You might not have any questions, but I got a few."

"I don't know nothin' about where Eden and the boy are. Me and Masters tried trackin' them Injuns, but we didn't get nowhere. Truth is, they covered their trail and they was too smart for us. Masters is determined to wait at the fort and he—"

"I heard all that before. Them ain't the answers I'm interested in. Mullen told me what really happened that day when the boss ordered that Injun camp burned."

McGill was suddenly wary. "I ain't the one you should be talkin' to. I didn't get there until later, with Eden. Everythin' was over and done by then."

"That ain't what I'm askin'. Mullen told me the whole story without a hitch, about the camp bein' peaceful and all and how everybody rode in and burned it anyways—then about how him and the boss went back to make sure they got Iron Hawk. But when he told me about Witt Bradley dyin'—"

"I don't want to talk about Witt. He's dead. It's over and done."

"Is it? Mullen wouldn't talk about it, neither. What happened with Bradley? How come everybody on this ranch turns around and starts lookin' somewheres else when the way he died is mentioned?"

"Witt Bradley was a damned good fella! There

wasn't nobody on this ranch who'd say otherwise!"

"I ain't sayin' he wasn't. All I'm sayin' is—"

"Look, you got somethin' stuck in your craw about Witt, there ain't nobody who's goin' to cough it out for you except the boss."

"You said yourself, the boss is dyin'."

"Well, then, I guess the answers you're looking for are goin' to die with him."

"McGill—"

"I've said all I'm goin' to say! That man lyin' in that bed in there ain't no angel, but he treated every man on this ranch fair. He didn't ask nothin' from them that he didn't ask of himself. Whether he was wrong or right, he always did what he believed in, and there ain't nothin' more nobody can ask of a man."

"I'd say there is."

"Yeah? What would that be?"

"Well, if you don't know, tellin' you ain't goin' to make no difference."

McGill drew back abruptly. "You know somethin', Rowe? You're right. It wouldn't make no difference at all."

McGill stomped out of sight and Rowe squinted after him. Pushing the bedroom door open, he strode back into the room, not pausing until he reached Richards's bedside. The emaciated man turned weakly toward him, and Rowe's determination drained. He asked simply, "Can I get anythin' for you, boss?"

A single rasp of sound escaped Richards's lips.

"Eden." Rowe attempted a smile. "You know she ain't here. Masters is still tryin' to find out where she is."

The next words were almost indistinguishable.

"You're dyin'?"

Richards managed a scraping rush of sound.

"You need to see her?" Rowe swallowed past the lump in his throat. "We'll bring her here as soon as Masters finds her."

Richards closed his eyes, leaving Rowe silent and shaken beside him.

The night was dark despite the stars glittering overhead. The hours stretched on interminably.

Eden glanced again toward her mount where it was secured nearby, then adjusted the horse blanket over her shoulders and forced her eyes closed. She struggled to ignore her thirst and the emptiness in her stomach that had awakened her countless times as she slept.

She had traveled as long as she was able in the fading light, while a plethora of nagging doubts assailed her. When she could follow the tracks with certainty no longer, she had halted and made camp. She had slipped off into a troubled sleep the moment she closed her eyes, only to awaken what seemed minutes later to the blackness of night and the reality that the moment of decision had come.

Eden reviewed her alternatives again. She was in unfamiliar territory. Her only guide through it was the increasingly difficult trail she

341

followed. To go back meant she'd risk losing her child. To continue on meant she'd risk losing her life.

The choice was a foregone conclusion.

Eden forced her eyes closed, knowing she must be ready to resume tracking at daybreak—but sounds and images continued to invade her mind, impeding sleep. She saw Jimmy, his ready smile flashing. She saw Iron Hawk riding beside him in the brilliant sunshine. She heard Jimmy's laughter. She heard Iron Hawk speaking to him with soft words of encouragement.

But she heard Iron Hawk speak other words as well.

You're a fire in my blood, Eden.

Let me show you how it could have been.

She felt Iron Hawk's touch. She felt his breath against her cheek. She felt his strong body warming her flesh. And when she peered out through sleep-weighted eyelids, she saw him standing before her.

Unable to bear the deluge of torturous illusions, Eden closed her eyes and drew her blanket closer. She would not submit to their torment. She would sleep, because she needed to. She would persevere, because she must.

But the touch grew more real, and the voice in her ear more insistent.

"Wake up, Eden."

Eden caught her breath.

"Eden."

Eden turned to see the specter crouched beside her, his strong features illuminated by the pale glow of moonlight. Eden reached up tentatively to touch his face. It was warm. She gasped when he grasped her hand.

"Are you all right, Eden?"

Eden could not respond.

"Get up."

Pulling her to her feet, Iron Hawk supported her silently for a moment as he scanned her camp. He drew her with him toward his horse as she questioned hoarsely, "Where's Jimmy?"

Iron Hawk offered her his water pouch and she drank greedily, then drew back to gasp, "Where's Jimmy?"

Swinging her up onto her horse, Iron Hawk mounted beside her, then spurred his mount forward.

Eden's heart pounded when a campfire came into view and she saw the small figure sleeping beside it. She glanced at Iron Hawk, who was riding ahead of her. She halted at his signal and dismounted as he secured their mounts.

Walking toward the campfire on shaky legs, Eden knelt down beside her child at last. Her throat so tight that she could hardly breathe, she saw Jimmy's face peacefully composed in sleep.

Eden stood up when Iron Hawk drew her to her feet. Uncertain, she followed when he picked up his blanket, drew her with him into the shadows across from Jimmy, and spread his blanket out.

"Lie down. You're exhausted. You need to sleep."

Silently complying, Eden lay down. Her heart began an erratic beating when Iron Hawk lay beside her and drew her against him to adjust the blanket over them.

Eden stated hoarsely, "You knew all along that I was followin' you, didn't you?"

"I saw you behind us at midday."

"You kept on going and started hidin' your trail better."

"Yes."

"Jimmy didn't know I was there, did he?"

"No."

"They why did you come back for me?"

Raising his gaze to meet hers, Iron Hawk replied, "Because I had to."

"*Why* did you have to?"

Eden waited for Iron Hawk's reply.

Iron Hawk looked down at Eden. The question reverberated in his mind as he studied her face: light eyes and yellow hair that glowed like silver in the moonlight, fine skin colored with a golden hue, and full lips that were sweeter than any he had ever known.

He raised his gaze again to hers. "I told myself that you had deceived me—because you did. I told myself that my feelings for you were a weakness—which they are. I reminded myself over and again that you had chosen others over me, and that when they sent me away, you went on with your life without looking back. It is true—all true."

Iron Hawk trailed his fingertips tentatively

against her cheek. His voice dropped a husky note lower. "Then I remembered the look in your eyes when I touch you—the way you come to life in my arms. I remembered that the anger and the hatred fade when your flesh is pressed to mine, and that vengeance and retribution become words with no meaning at all."

He continued, "I thought about my father and Lone Bear, too, recalling that they were brave men who died for their beliefs and for their people—and I realized that my intentions weren't as noble. I knew that if I had truly been thinking of my people, I would've told them the truth, whether they wanted to hear it or not—that the soldiers will continue coming until our people are outnumbered, and that no amount of bravery or courage will be able to hold so great a number at bay—that nothing will ever be right again for our people until we show the greatest valor of all by turning our backs on the temporary gratification of vengeance and look instead to the future."

Iron Hawk paused briefly. His expression tightened. "Lying in the darkness beside the campfire, I suddenly realized that the bad things that happened to us all started long before we met, that I had allowed us to be overwhelmed in the maelstrom—and now that we had a second chance, I was letting the same thing happen again. I was letting hatred and vengeance control my life while I held back the words that filled my heart."

Iron Hawk continued, "I was on my feet and

mounted before I realized my intent, and when I saw you lying alone in the darkness, I knew I could never turn my back on you again."

Iron Hawk's voice became a rasping whisper. "You asked *why* I had to come back for you. I had to because I love you, Eden."

His lips only inches from hers, he rasped, "When I hated you the most, I still loved you. While I cursed you for the humiliation and the pain I suffered, I still wanted you. And when I believed I couldn't bear another agonizing moment in chains, the hope of regaining what I lost when I lost you, drove me on to take my next breath. I know now that however hard I tried, I never stopped loving you."

Iron Hawk waited for a response that did not come.

A knot of fear formed inside him as Eden held herself stiffly apart from him. The knot tightened to pain as she responded, "What do you want me to say—that I love you, too?"

Iron Hawk's declaration of love reverberated in Eden's mind.

Her voice breaking, she continued, "Do you want me to say I never stopped loving you, either. Because I didn't, not for a moment, even durin' those terrible days when everything started goin' so wrong. But lovin' you wasn't enough!"

Eden's eyes filled as images of those early days returned. "How could lovin' you be enough when I saw Witt lyin' in his own blood with your bullet in his back? I heard him gasp his last breath, because of me. I saw my pa, who never took a backward step for any man, lyin' crippled and helpless, because of me. I saw the war between the Injuns and the ranchers flarin' hot and heavy, with people dyin' on both sides, because of me—and I was ashamed! And when you went to prison, I couldn't bear to think that I was the cause of that, too!"

Eden's eyes dropped to Iron Hawk's lips. "The soldiers took you away, and you didn't see the chaos that was left behind. Pa was paralyzed and the ranch started failin'. Everyone blamed me, includin' myself. Doc Bitters thought Pa might die. He said there was only one place where they might be able to help him—a hospital back East where they could perform an operation. I did the only thing I could do. I left Mullen to take care of the ranch, and I gathered all the money I could scrape up and took Pa to that hospital."

Eden fought to control her trembling. "The doctors operated on Pa, but he didn't get better. The medical bills started mountin' and my money began runnin' out. I tried to find a job, but I got sick. I didn't want to go to a doctor because money was tight. I met James Broker in the lobby of the hospital one day when I was feelin' real bad. James was kind and sympathetic. He knew so much about the hospital, and when I finally confided in him about my problems, he started sortin' out the paperwork and the bills for me. Pa didn't get any better, and I got sicker. When I started bleedin' and I couldn't resist any longer, James took me to the doctor."

Eden's eyes linked with Iron Hawk's. "I didn't know I was pregnant with your child until the doctor told me, and if James was shocked, he didn't show it. He stayed with me while things went from bad to worse with Pa, and when things went wrong for me, James got me to the hospital just in time. He saved my life."

Eden briefly closed her eyes. "James was with me every day. No one bothered me anymore about the bills, but I didn't know it was because James had paid them. When I was finally on my feet, he took me to his house to recuperate. Then the doctors decided to operate on Pa again, and James watched over things."

Eden's voice dropped to a whisper. "Through it all, I never knew that James was seein' doctors at the hospital about his own condition. I didn't know he was goin' to die. I didn't know any of it until James asked me to marry him."

Eden felt Iron Hawk stiffen and she raised her chin defensively. "I won't make excuses for what I did. I was six months pregnant. Pa was still struggling to survive, and I didn't have enough money to take him home, even if I thought he would live through the trip. James told me that he loved me, but he explained that he was too sick to *make* love to me. He said he didn't care who the father of my baby was, that there was only one thing he'd ask. He wanted his mother to believe the child was his, because his mother was alone, and he wanted her to have something to hold on to after he died."

Eden determinedly continued, "I married James. Jimmy was already born by the time Pa was well enough to travel. Jimmy was especially small because I was so sick when I was carryin' him, so when James brought us back to the Diamond R, nobody suspected that the baby was really three months older than we said he was."

Eden's voice quavered. "I was determined to make up for everythin' that happened, and I worked hard, right alongside the men to win their confidence back. James got sicker, but that didn't stop him from straightenin' out the ranch bills that had fallen behind while we were away. He loved the ranch, and everybody liked him. He was so proud to call Jimmy his son. When James died, I took his body back East to his mother, like he wanted—and I never regretted marryin' him."

Eden swallowed, her voice growing more tremulous as she spoke from a heart that was aching. "James was good and generous. He loved Jimmy and me . . . and I loved him, too." Eden's voice dropped an earnest note lower. "But I never, *never* loved James the way I love you."

Joy flashed in Iron Hawk's dark eyes. The sight of it tore at her heart as Eden resisted his effort to draw her closer, forcing herself to add in an impassioned rush, "But loving you wasn't enough then, Iron Hawk, and it isn't enough now! If you really love Jimmy and me, you'll let us go!"

Eden felt Iron Hawk go suddenly still. Uncertain what reaction she expected to her earnest declaration, she was unprepared when he clutched the back of her head with his palm. She was not braced to resist the sudden swell of emotion within her when his mouth descended on hers with fierce intensity, or to withstand the soul-shaking need that swept her senses when he crushed her close against the rock-hard length of him, deepening his kiss. Grasping for sanity as Iron Hawk's mouth separated her lips, Eden was overwhelmed by a yearning so deep and strong that she was powerless against it.

Iron Hawk loved her. She loved him.

He wanted her. She wanted him.

He *needed* her.

The rapturous sob that escaped Eden's lips was swallowed by Iron Hawk's kiss. Yes . . . she needed him. Only together were they complete.

Frantic kisses. Loving wonder. Consummation.

Lingering words of love.

In the silent aftermath as Eden lay motionless and replete in his arms, Iron Hawk responded softly, in solemn declaration.

"No, Eden. I won't let you go."

Chapter Fourteen

Hardly aware of the semiconscious man lying in the bed behind him, Rowe stared at Curry. The slender wrangler stood in front of him, his jaw locked angrily tight. Curry had returned from another visit to the fort to report news that still rang in the silence of the sickroom. Rowe responded incredulously, "You're tellin' me that Major Peters sent out feelers two days ago to see if the Comanches would come in for a peace parley?"

"That's what I said." Curry's tightly clenched jaw twitched. "He sent scouts out to deliver the message to them Injuns as soon as the order was received from Washington, and he couldn't be happier. The whole fort's buzzin' about the way Masters went stormin' in to talk to the major. They said he was one step away from bein' thrown out of the fort for tellin' the major what he thought of makin' a peace treaty with cheatin' Injuns who probably wouldn't honor this treaty no better than they honored all the others, but the major let him off with a warnin' instead."

"What's Masters goin' to do?"

"When I talked to Masters, he said he was stayin' right where he was. He said he wants to be there when the Army gets ready to make its move."

Rowe frowned. "What did he mean by that?"

"I'll tell you what he meant!" Speaking up sharply from where he stood beside Rowe, McGill spat, "Masters is out to get Iron Hawk, one way or another, and he doesn't care how much trouble he stirs up when he does it!"

"He ain't goin' to hear an argument from nobody on this ranch if he gets Iron Hawk."

McGill sent Curry a harsh glance. "You're as bad as Masters. You ain't usin' your head, neither. If anythin' happens to Iron Hawk before we get Eden and Jimmy back, there ain't no tellin' what'll happen to them."

A choking sound from the bed behind them brought Rowe to Richard's side in a few anxious steps. He leaned toward Richards as the old man rasped, "Tell McGill . . . get Eden."

Behind Rowe, McGill responded softly, "I tried to find her, boss, but that Injun's got her hid somewheres."

His small eyes bulging with frustration, Richards rasped, "Go . . . get her. I need to—"

His breath catching in his throat, Richards gasped. His color turned gray as he struggled to breathe and Rowe turned sharply toward McGill. "You heard what the boss said! Don't argue with him. He wants you to get Eden back here—now!"

"But—"

Lowering his voice, Rowe hissed, "I don't care where you go, McGill, just get out of here before this man has another stroke." Turning to Curry, Rowe snapped, "You get out, too! The boss don't need to hear nothin' else to excite him right now."

Still leaning over Richards's bed as the door closed behind the two men, Rowe offered comfortingly, "Relax, boss. McGill will go right back to the fort to make sure nothin' goes wrong."

Richards gripped his hand with surprising strength, and Rowe leaned closer to hear him grate, ". . . have to see Eden."

The anxiety in Richards's gaze prompted Rowe to ask, "If you got somethin' I can tell her for you . . . somethin' you want me to pass along—"

Richards made another weak hiss of sound.

"You *do* want to tell me somethin'?"

Surprised, Rowe stared at Richards for a silent moment, then pulled a chair up to the bed. Richards's trembling hand clutched his tightly as he labored to speak.

Eden looked at Iron Hawk when he crouched at the stream beside her. They had left their

horses on the raised embankment behind them
and climbed down to the stream bed to refresh
themselves after a long morning of traveling.
Jimmy was attempting to catch minnows in the
shallows a distance away, allowing a few moments of privacy for Eden to ask a question that
had gone unanswered too long in her mind.

Sensing her scrutiny, Iron Hawk turned to
meet her gaze, and Eden was struck by the silent power of the man he had become. She recalled Kyle Webster as she first saw him—
fashionably clothed, his smile ready and his
step self-assured despite the odious reception
he received from the townsfolk in general. That
man no longer existed. In his place was a person
who bore him little resemblance. This man was
taller, more powerfully muscled. He wore buck-
skins that fit his broad-shouldered physique
smoothly, and he walked in Indian moccasins
with a sure, almost silent step. His hair was
long, straight, and black, worn loose against his
back. The former Eastern pallor of his skin was
darkened by the sun to a warm hue, his mouth
was soberly composed, and his eyes were cautious and assessing.

But the greatest change wasn't in his physical
appearance. Kyle Webster had come back to
Texas fresh from a world to which he wasn't
born. He had returned seeking a part of himself
that had been lost along the way. *Iron Hawk*
was the result of that pain-ridden quest, and
now the metamorphosis was complete.

Eden took a shuddering breath. She had

awakened in Iron Hawk's arms the previous morning, suddenly aware that the love she had felt for Kyle Webster did not compare in scope with the emotion she felt for this Kiowa warrior. Fed by memories, her love for Kyle had survived torment and separation, but it was in *Iron Hawk's* arms, while they both struggled to deny feelings that would not die in the face of overwhelming odds, that the full power of their love became clear.

Somehow, Jimmy recognized that force. Jumping to his feet when he awakened the previous morning, he had covered the distance between his blanket and theirs in a few racing steps. He had halted only briefly before lying down to be included in their embrace so he might join their silent circle of love. Jimmy did not question Eden's presence in the camp that morning. Nor did he question their direction when they started out again, or their more leisurely pace. He seemed content that the tense distance between Eden and Iron Hawk had been bridged at last.

But Eden wasn't a child and she knew their loving respite was rapidly coming to an end.

Unable to wait any longer, she addressed Iron Hawk softly.

"I need to know what you're goin' to do when we get back to the camp."

Silent, Iron Hawk drew her to her feet. Urging her along with him to a point of limited privacy a short distance away, he responded, "You know what I'm going to do, Eden. I wish we could've put the past behind us and ridden on until we reached another place where we could start all over again. I fooled myself into thinking I could do that for a while. I told myself that taking Jimmy away from you and your father would be a victory I could achieve no other way, but I was only deceiving myself. Too many things were left undone behind me—things I couldn't ignore."

Iron Hawk's dark eyes searched hers. "You said you never stopped loving me, but love wasn't enough after I was sent to prison and you were faced with the chaos that was left behind. You talked about images that haunted you, and a need to redeem yourself. I understand, because I faced haunting images of my own. The renewed hope that I saw in Lone Bear's eyes when I came back to Texas, and his confidence that I would someday lead my people to honorable victory, was an irony that cut deep. The memories that followed were always the same: a burned camp littered with dead; Lone Bear with the life draining from his eyes; you with a smoking gun in your hand."

An unconscious shudder shook Eden as Iron Hawk continued. "I tried to hate you, Eden, but I couldn't. When that failed, I tried to believe I could take Jimmy away and leave the past behind me, but I couldn't do that, either. And just as I know now that there was never any hope of escaping my love for you, I also know there's no way I can elude the responsibility Lone Bear bequeathed to me. I can't desert my people when they need me most."

"I know."

"And you know that I—"

Iron Hawk stiffened at the sound of his horse's whinny from the embankment above. Suddenly alert, he cautioned Eden with a motion of his hand before he climbed out of sight. Glancing at Jimmy playing in the shallows, unconscious of any danger, Eden saw Iron Hawk drawing their horses down the incline behind him, his expression tight. She watched as he secured the animals quickly, and she saw Jimmy's stunned expression when Iron Hawk swept him up with a cautioning finger to his lips and carried the boy to her side.

Iron Hawk slipped from sight again, and Jimmy whispered, "What's happenin', Mama?"

She silenced him with a glance. Her heart bursting with relief when Iron Hawk rejoined them minutes later, Eden rasped, "What was it? What did you see?"

"Soldiers."

Eden's heart went cold. She tensed when Jimmy asked, "Will the soldiers try to hurt you if they find us, Iron Hawk?"

Iron Hawk paused, then responded, "They'll try to take me back to prison."

"I won't let them do that!" Frowning, Jimmy grasped Iron Hawk's hand. "I'll tell them they made a mistake when they put you in that place!" He turned to Eden unexpectedly. "You'll tell them, too, won't you, Mama?"

"They won't listen to us, Jimmy." Eden tried to smile. "They're soldiers. They have their orders, and they have to follow them."

"Then I don't like soldiers!" Jimmy's frown darkened. "And I don't want them to find us."

"They won't find us if we're careful." Iron Hawk urged, "Come on. We have to go."

"But the soldiers will see us!"

"They're riding in the opposite direction. If we hurry, we can be back at camp before sunset."

Refusing to relinquish Iron Hawk's hand, Jimmy questioned, "The soldiers won't be able to get you at the camp, right?" When Iron Hawk did not respond, Jimmy persisted, "Right?"

"Yes, it's safe there. Come on, let's go."

Jimmy ran toward his horse. Unaware that she was trembling, Eden turned toward Iron Hawk as he whispered, "I'm sorry, Eden. I have to go back."

She knew he did. She had somehow known he would, just as she had somehow known she'd always love him.

His two scouts had made their report. Standing opposite them in the silence of his office, Major Peters barely withheld a sneer as he responded, "So you got the message to the Comanches without any trouble."

"Yes, Major."

Major Peters stared at the two half-breeds. Somehow the Comanches had always escaped them, but when a peace treaty was offered, the message was delivered without delay—just as he'd expected.

Major Peters prompted, "Well? What did they say?"

"Chief Leaning Tree does not trust the pony soldiers."

Peters scowled. "Did you explain to them that the treaty doesn't come from this fort, that it comes from the Great White Father in Washington?"

"Chief Leaning Tree says the Great White Father speaks with truth, but his children do not obey him when they are far from his sight. He says treaties have been broken many times—"

"By the Comanches!"

"By those who come to take the land and kill the buffalo so the Comanche will starve."

"Did you explain to Chief Leaning Tree that this command was sent here to see that transgressions of that sort are halted, and to make sure that the Great White Father's word is respected by all?"

"Yes."

"And?"

"Chief Leaning Tree will speak to his people."

"How long am I expected to wait for his answer?"

"The chief will send a messenger in two days."

Major Peters forcibly quelled his rising annoyance. He didn't like the integrity of the Federal Government being questioned. He didn't like his command being considered untrustworthy. He didn't like to wait for the approval of anyone, much less of a people who didn't seem to value the risk he had taken on their behalf.

Ungrateful beggars!

Major Peters paused. "All right, two days."

"The Great White Father does not consider the Comanche his children! He sheds their blood as easily as he sheds the blood of the buffalo!"

"The soldiers turn their backs on him and laugh at his word!"

"The Great White Father wishes to drive the Comanche from their lands!"

Listening silently from the perimeter of the crowd, Iron Hawk scrutinized Chief Leaning Tree's stoic expression as the protests continued. He knew the chief would allow all present to speak before a response would be made to the offer of a peace treaty.

Iron Hawk glanced at the Kiowa warriors who stood silently beside him. Black Cloud, Spotted Elk, Sitting Bear, Gray Fox, Standing Man, Yellow Dog—all had welcomed his return to the camp. All had taken special care to acknowledge Jimmy as his son despite Jimmy's ignorance of the words they spoke. Iron Hawk had been especially pleased that some of the women had welcomed Eden as well, with Woman Who Walks Lightly standing foremost in front of them. Eden's surprise had been obvious, but his personal considerations had been put aside when he learned of the council to be held that evening.

The setting sun cast a golden glow on the warriors gathered in council outside the chief's tepee. The protests continued.

"The pony soldiers seek to trap us!"

"They will kill those who go unarmed to the fort!"

"There is no honor in talking peace with our enemies!"

Responding in protest to that last comment, Iron Hawk stepped forward. "My Comanche brothers react in anger to the offer that comes from Fort Worth. They do not weigh the result of their words. Honor is not achieved by battle alone."

"So speaks Iron Hawk, who has vowed revenge against our enemies!"

"So speak I, Iron Hawk, who sees the value of what the white man offers when others do not!"

Chief Leaning Tree broke his silence, replying coolly, "Iron Hawk claims to see what his fellow braves cannot in the white man's offer—yet it is he who has suffered most heavily at the hands of our enemy. It is he who takes his name from the symbol of the white man's bondage which he still wears."

Raising his wrists high in front of him so all might see the iron cuffs encircling them, Iron Hawk responded hotly, "I wear these cuffs to remind myself that I was wrong in believing that *right alone* would bring victory to those who pursue it. I wear these bonds so I will not forget the power that the white man brings to our land, a power that I did not believe they would use so unjustly against their Indian brothers. I wear these iron bands to remind myself that my error cost the lives of many, and that I have yet to serve my debt to my people."

"Yet you claim there is value in the white man's offer of peace!"

Lowering his wrists, Iron Hawk responded, "I speak of its value because I know the price that will be paid if it is refused."

"Such are the words of a coward!"

"What man calls me coward?" Bristling, Iron Hawk took an aggressive step, his gaze searching the crowd. His anger cooling, he continued, "I would challenge that man to combat to prove my courage—but I have no desire to shed my brother's blood. Instead, I will respond by speaking truths of which others here are unaware."

Iron Hawk surveyed the faces of the warriors surrounding him. "The blood of proud and brave Kiowas flows within me. I was born to live on this land and follow in the footsteps of my father and his valiant Kiowa brothers; but, unlike them, my childhood in this land was cut short. I spent many years living in a white man's house in the white man's land far away. I was treated kindly. I learned the ways of the people who raised me and saw many things when I traveled. I returned to the land of my people to discover to my surprise that while I was treated justly when I lived in the white man's world, I was treated unfairly here, where the white man lived in ours. I learned that there, the white man showed confusion at the differences between us—but those same differences enraged him here. And I saw our people respond with rage in return."

Glancing toward Eden, who stood silently observing, Iron Hawk continued, "I sought to prove that the two worlds could come together and live as one, but I failed."

Grunts of agreement rose from the gathered warriors as Iron Hawk continued determinedly, "I suffered for my error, and my people suffered as well. My rage surpassed any that had ever been raised against me, and I escaped from the prison where I was sent to die in dishonor. I sought revenge for my people when I returned, and I worked toward that end with all my heart."

Iron Hawk lay a broad fist against his chest. "But my heart grew heavy. In all I did to avenge the wrong that had been done to my tribe, I knew I was not serving my people as I should because I had not told my people what I am about to tell them now."

Aware of the tumult he was about to start, Iron Hawk raised his voice so it might be heard clearly as he said, "In living among the white man, I saw the superior power he possesses—an endless number of men flowing from lands far away that our people cannot hope to conquer! I realized that for each white man that our people struck down, there were five more to replace him!"

Angry shouts sounded, but Iron Hawk continued.

"I saw the weapons the white man possesses. I saw great guns that kill many with a single shot; iron carriages that could carry large masses of soldiers to battle against our people; bullets that carry death over distances that our arrows and spears cannot travel; and vast stores of food and supplies that would make the soldiers invulnerable as our people are not. I learned that the white man believes that the land of our fathers is his to claim, simply by taking it and marking it for his own. I learned that for each white man who claims our lands, there are many who race to follow, and although some may die, the quest will endure!"

Iron Hawk continued in the resounding silence, "I did not speak these words to my people earlier because vengeance filled my heart. I desired only to spill blood where our people's blood had been spilled, and to see the white man's tears fall where ours had fallen. When the first fort was built on our land, I chose not to acknowledge that countless others would follow. I knew our people would win many victories before the white man's presence in this land grew to full strength, and I sought that satisfaction."

His deep voice quaking with the passion of his words, Iron Hawk continued, "But the weight in my heart grows too heavy, and I can keep silent no longer. The Great White Father offers peace because he hopes to save the many lives that he knows will be lost in his people's quest. He asks to speak to our chiefs so the terms may be set. He will ask a price to be paid, and he will pay one in return, but the sum will never exceed the price our people will pay if they refuse to accept these truths that I relay!

"I was called coward when I chose to speak these truths, but I tell you now that it took a greater courage to declare them aloud, in a voice that would be heard by all. I say now that it is only the *brave* among us who will have the courage to put aside their rage and consider what I have said. It is only the *valiant* who will have the courage to look clearly at the path that lies ahead."

Iron Hawk's voice dropped to a harsh whisper. "I speak to you now so the honorable future of our people may come to pass. I speak for our children, so they may live their lives proudly, without fear. I speak so the time will not come when the laughter fades from our tepees to be drowned by tears. I speak for *peace*."

Iron Hawk stepped back among his brothers in the hush that followed.

The council continued, but Eden had heard Iron Hawk speak. She had seen the faces of the warriors and she had heard the silence that followed. She knew Iron Hawk had spoken for peace, and she knew all had listened. She needed to hear no more.

Filled with pride, Eden turned back toward Iron Hawk's tepee, where she had left Jimmy asleep. Hope lightened her heart. The council would send a delegation to Fort Worth. A peace treaty would be signed and the soldiers would be compelled to enforce it. She would then go to speak to the commandant. She would explain that Iron Hawk had been instrumental in forging the peace, and she would ask him to help her get Iron Hawk's conviction set aside. Surely, he wouldn't be able to refuse her.

Turning at a sound beside her, Eden drew back when Running Deer stepped into her path and spat, "You think you have won, don't you?"

Stunned by the woman's open rancor, Eden did not immediately respond.

"You return with Iron Hawk and his son! He claims you for his woman and challenges his people to accept you, but your victory is incomplete! Iron Hawk has already wreaked his vengeance!"

"What are you talking about?"

"Your father *dies*!"

"Wh . . . what?"

"When the offer of a peace treaty was brought from the fort, other news was brought as well—news of the man who burned our Kiowa camp—your father!"

"My father?"

"Your father's spirit was broken when Iron Hawk took you away from him. When Iron Hawk took his grandson, your father's body suffered as well. He now lingers at the edge of life, calling your name."

"You lie!" Eden shuddered with growing fury.

"The courier would have no way of knowin' that!"

"The man Masters told him!"

"Masters!"

"Masters waits at the fort, where he tells everyone it is Iron Hawk's fault that your father will soon die!"

"No . . ."

"It is plain for all to see that Masters's heart cries out for *you*."

"You're a liar! Get away from me!"

Still blocking her path, Running Deer rasped, "Your mind seeks to deny what I say, but it cannot. The joy drains from your eyes. Iron Hawk's woman is close to tears!"

"I told you to get away from me!"

Pushing Running Deer roughly aside, Eden strode toward Iron Hawk's tepee. She entered and dropped the flap closed behind her, the memory of Running Deer's virulent glare lingering.

Iron Hawk held Eden's intent gaze. The council had continued into the night. It had ended minutes earlier with the decision to send representatives to the fort for a peace parley. He had returned to the tepee to find Eden waiting for him while Jimmy slept.

The dim light of the interior did not hide Eden's pallor when she said, "Pa's dyin'. He's callin' for me. I have to go to him."

Stunned into momentary silence, Iron Hawk replied, "Who told you this?"

"Running Deer said the messenger from the fort told her."

"Running Deer is angry. She wants vengeance, not peace. She wants to cause dissension between us."

"She was tellin' the truth. I know she was."

Iron Hawk remained silent, knowing Running Deer would not dare to lie.

Eden's gaze searched his. Her voice trembled as she rasped, "We have so many shadows between us, Iron Hawk, so many nightmares we have to put behind us if we want to go on. But this one would be too much for me to bear! He's my father! Right or wrong, everythin' he did, he did because he believed it was best for me. He lost his legs, his health—everythin' he valued most. Now he's lost Jimmy and me—and he's dyin'." Eden's eyes filled. "I can't fault you for wantin' vengeance against him for what happened, because the truth is, my pa would feel the same if he was in your place. But he loves me! He wants to see me, and I can't let him die alone!"

The council's decision swept from his mind, Iron Hawk contemplated his response. How could he explain to Eden his reaction to her words? She asked him to feel compassion for the man responsible for the slaughter of his people. She pleaded for him to show humanity to a man who had shown none to him. She wanted him to let her nullify a vengeance that he had planned for five long years of his life. Didn't she realize that her request—asking him to sacrifice the only justice that his people might ever receive for the atrocities her father had committed—was asking too much?

Eden was standing so close. Iron Hawk could feel the turmoil within her as he raised a hand to stroke a stray wisp of hair from her face. The callused, sun-darkened skin of his fingers contrasted with the light flawless color of her cheek, symbolizing the many intangible differences between them, a gulf that stretched wide and deep.

Iron Hawk spoke at last.

"Take Jimmy with you when you go."

Eden remained motionless.

"Come back to me, Eden."

Her breath catching on a sob, Eden stepped into his arms.

"They're comin'! I don't believe it, but they are!"

Leaning out the window as far as he could, Rowe stared at the approaching riders a moment longer, then jerked his head back inside Tom Richards's sickroom to see Richards staring at him.

Rowe covered the distance between window and bed in a few shaky steps. He leaned over Richards and attempted a smile.

"Don't get yourself excited, boss, but it's Eden and Jimmy. There's no mistakin' them. They're ridin' up to the house right now, as big as life."

Reacting when Richards's breathing became suddenly labored, Rowe leaned closer. "Try to control yourself, boss. You ain't goin' to be able to do nothin' if you get yourself all shook up."

Endless moments elapsed before the sound of approaching hoofbeats halted in the yard outside.

An eternity passed before footsteps sounded in the hallway beyond the bedroom door.

Time stopped when the bedroom door burst suddenly open.

Her smile freezing at her first sight of the emaciated figure in the bed, Eden stood momentarily motionless in the bedroom doorway. She had bidden Iron Hawk farewell and left the Comanche camp with Jimmy that morning. They had traveled steadily, each hour seeming longer than the last as midday came and went and the sun began a gradual descent in the cloudless sky. Her heart had thudded in her breast when they touched Diamond R land at last, and the thudding became a hammering that almost stole her breath when the ranch house finally came into view. Yet, as apprehensive as she had been about her father's condition, she had never expected this.

Jimmy stiffened at her side, and Eden slipped a trembling hand down to clasp his shoulder as she said, "We're home, Pa."

Eden advanced slowly into the room. Jimmy's hand slipped into hers as they neared the bed, and Eden's throat tightened. She forced her smile wider when she halted and said, "Jimmy's here. He grew, didn't he, Pa?"

Her father reached a bony hand toward

Jimmy, and Eden felt a surge of pride when Jimmy took it bravely and said, "You got too skinny, Grandpa. Isn't Rowe givin' you anythin' to eat?"

A snort from the corner where Rowe stood went unnoticed when Eden surrendered to the weakness in her knees and sat abruptly on the chair beside the bed. She hadn't expected to see him looking this bad—not Pa! Even crippled, he had always snorted fire and had everybody jumping to his commands. But this man—

Richards released Jimmy's hand and reached for hers, and Eden clutched it tight. She whispered, "How're you feelin', Pa? You're not lookin' too good."

Richards glanced at Rowe. He rasped, "Tell McGill . . . take Jimmy."

Beside them in a minute, Rowe reached for Jimmy's hand. He smiled down into the boy's hesitant expression. "McGill's out in the kitchen with some biscuits I made." He winked. "I bet you ain't had nothin' like my biscuits for a while."

"You got biscuits?" Jimmy took his hand. "I sure would like some."

The door closed behind them and Eden said, "We're fine, Pa. Jimmy and me. You don't have to worry about us."

"I'm dyin'."

Eden responded instinctively, "No, you're not, Pa!"

"Yes."

"You're just—"

Richards's grip on her hand tightened. ". . . have to say some things—"

Richards's breath caught in his throat with a loud gasp. His color went gray, and Eden jumped to her feet in sudden panic.

"Pa, please, you don't have to talk now! Everythin's goin' to be all right. Jimmy and I are home, and everythin's goin' to go back to normal."

Suddenly at her side, Rowe silenced her with a look, then leaned over the bed to inquire softly, "Do you want me to tell her, boss?"

Richards nodded, then reached again for Eden's hand. Eden felt his desperation. Her gaze did not leave his stricken expression as Rowe began, "Your pa talked to me about this because he was afraid he'd die before he could talk to you in person. He said there was too much to be said for it to go undone. He said it needed to be told from the beginnin'—so's you'd understand better how everythin' came about. He said that some of it might be hard for you to savvy because you never knew your mama. He wanted you to try to understand that your mama was the best part of him, and that when she was killed in that Injun raid, the best part of him died with her. He said he didn't have nothin' left to live for afterwards—except you. He felt he let your mama down by lettin' those Injuns get to her, but he promised himself that he'd do for you all the things he wanted to do for your mama, and that he'd never let them Injuns get to you like they got to her."

Richards's sunken eyes grew moist, but Rowe continued resolutely, "He said that when you took up with that Kiowa fella, he couldn't think of nothin' but your mama lyin' dead every time he saw him. He hated that Injun, and for a while he even hated you."

"Pa."

"He said he couldn't believe it was happenin'. He always figured the man for you would be that Witt Bradley."

Rowe's words were confirmed in her father's gaze, and Eden remained silent as Rowe continued, "He said everybody knew how Bradley felt, but when he approached Bradley about doin' somethin' about that Injun, Bradley wouldn't have any part of his schemin'. Your pa figured that was why Bradley went out alone after you and the Injun that last night, without callin' him in on the chase."

Eden shuddered. He meant the night Witt died.

"Your pa said he was fit to kill when he found out you'd run off with the Kiowa. He rode out after you, and he knew if he had his choice, the Injun would never make it back alive."

A chill moved down Eden's spine.

"He said that Bradley was standin' in the doorway when he got there. Bradley had a gun on the Injun, and your pa wasn't goin' to wait for him to make his move. He fired at the Injun point-blank just as everythin' started happenin' inside the cabin, and the Kiowa dived toward

373

the floor. Your pa's shot hit Bradley in the back."

"No!"

Rowe paused. "Your pa said he couldn't think for a moment when Bradley went down, and then it was too late for him to finish the Injun off because you would've known the shot was deliberate and you'd never forgive him for it. The Injun's shot went wild, but he let you believe the Injun purposely shot Bradley in the back. Your pa never asked the other wranglers to lie for him. They knew it was your pa's bullet that killed Bradley, but they blamed the Kiowa for his death anyways. When the Injun got broke out of jail by his uncle afterwards, there wasn't a man in the county that wasn't out for blood. The Kiowa wasn't there when they found his Injun camp, but they rode in and burned it anyways; and if you didn't get there when you did, your pa said he would've finished off the job he started when he shot the Kiowa afterwards."

Eden saw the pain in her father's eyes. She heard him rasp her name weakly before Rowe continued, "Your pa said he didn't really know what was goin' on after he got knifed, when you took him back East and them doctors started doin' all that operatin' on him. He said he didn't like James Broker at first. He felt there was somethin' wrong there, somehow. He said he knew what it was when Jimmy was born."

Eden's heart missed a beat when Richards's

eyes flickered. She rasped, "You knew who Jimmy's real father was!"

Richards nodded.

Eden gasped, "But you never said—"

"Your pa knew Jimmy was Iron Hawk's son. He said that for the longest time he tried to hold himself back from the boy by makin' believe he was too sick to pay him much attention, but he couldn't hold out against him."

"Oh, Pa."

"He said there wasn't no contest after that. He loved Jimmy more than he ever thought he could, and he got to thinkin' that although your ma wasn't there to see it, she'd be happy that everythin' was goin' to be able to go on like they always planned."

Rowe paused for a breath, his voice deepening. "Your pa said it wasn't until he was lyin' in this bed, knowin' that he was dyin', that he realized the strange way things had worked out— that them Kiowa had taken the person he loved most in the world from him—your mama—but it was one of that same breed who gave him Jimmy to love and to carry on for him when he was gone. He said he got to thinkin' about that, and to realizin' that maybe that was the Maker's way of puttin' the truth in front of his eyes before he was taken."

Eden tried to speak, but Richards's hand twitched tighter on hers, silencing her as Rowe proceeded hoarsely. "Your pa wanted me to tell you that he ain't certain no more where the right or wrong was in all them bad things that happened. He said he was sure about only one thing—that he had to tell you the truth, so's you could make your own decisions. He said, whatever them decisions turned out to be, he knew they'd be the right ones."

Eden took a shuddering breath as Rowe took a backward step and said, "Your pa said that after I told you everythin', he wanted me to tell the rest of the fellas here what I told you, so's they'd be able to do whatever they felt they should without feelin' any guilt."

Rowe left the room when he finished speaking. Hardly aware of his departure, Eden stared at her father in stunned disbelief. Everything Iron Hawk—Kyle—had said was true! Years of torment and separation . . . years lost, never to be regained . . .

What was there left to say?

"Eden." Her father's hoarse whisper broke the silence between them. "Eden . . . I'm sorry."

The answer to her unspoken question was suddenly clear. Responding in a wobbling voice, in the only way she could, Eden whispered, "Oh, Pa, so am I."

Chapter Fifteen

Major Peters waited, his military posture rigid as the Comanche messenger rode his horse slowly toward the fort, a white flag of truce held high. He glanced at the sun that was rapidly dropping into the horizon. The two days he had spent waiting for a response to his peace initiative had been more difficult than he had anticipated. The first had crawled past. As the present day dawned, then drew to a gradual close, he had almost convinced himself that the Indians had decided against a formal response to his proposal. But then the Comanche was spotted approaching. Major Peters had summoned his scouts immediately to translate and had then come into the fort yard to wait.

He glanced at his scouts, who stood a few feet away. Their expressions were impossible to decipher. He called out to the guards as the Comanche neared.

"Open the gates!"

The heavy gates swung open and the rider entered. The Comanche's stoic expression was no more readable than the scouts' when he passed a folded sheet into his hand. Major Peters read it, frowning to conceal his surprise at the well-written response it contained.

Turning to the scouts beside him, Major Peters directed, "Tell this man that we accept the conditions Chief Leaning Tree specifies. Tell him that we will await his arrival tomorrow."

His stance rigid, Major Peters waited as his response was translated. He saw the Comanche's brief glance in his direction before the fellow left the fort without speaking a word.

Another day had dawned at the Diamond R. The room was silent as Eden sat at her father's bedside. She had encouraged Jimmy to keep his visits short, knowing her father's energy was limited, but she had awakened the previous day and gone immediately to his room to spend as much time as possible with him. Her father had slept most of the time, awakening briefly with an expression of pure panic before seeing her beside the bed. When another morning dawned and her father awoke a little weaker than the last, Eden accepted the truth she had struggled to deny. Pa was dying.

Eden stared at her father as he slept. Strangely, after Rowe's solemn recitation that first afternoon, Pa and she had exchanged little conversation. She had not spoken to him about Iron Hawk, except to say that she and Jimmy had left the camp with his consent. He had chosen not to question that comment, and she had not elaborated, finally realizing that her father had made his peace with the present and was leaving the future in her hands.

But the weight of it all was growing rapidly more than she could bear. Looming larger in the back of her mind with every hour was the reality that the direction of her future would soon be decided. She had left the Indian camp knowing that Chief Leaning Tree would dispatch a favorable reply to Major Peters's communication, and that he would propose a meeting the following day. The chief and his party were probably riding toward the fort at that moment. She wanted desperately to be at the camp with Iron Hawk when they returned, so that she could be standing beside him when he learned the result of the parley. She wanted to be sure he knew that whatever happened, she would never let anyone separate them again. She needed to tell him—

The sound of approaching hoofbeats interrupted Eden's thoughts. She heard the horses draw up outside, but paid little attention until the outer door of the house slammed and she heard agitated voices in the kitchen. The voices grew louder, and Eden stood up and walked to the window. She saw Curry's lathered horse at the hitching post, and her heart jumped a beat.

Curry had been sent to the fort to speak to Masters just prior to her return.

With a glance at her father, Eden walked into the hallway and pulled the bedroom door closed behind her. She had almost reached the kitchen when she heard Curry exclaim, "You should've seen Major Peters's face when he read that message. Hell, whoever would've thought that bastard would have the nerve to—"

Curry halted abruptly when Eden stepped into view. He blinked, his expression stunned when Eden demanded, "What happened at the fort?"

Curry stammered, "H . . . how'd you get back?"

Eden demanded, "Tell me what happened at the fort, damn it!"

Curry looked at McGill, who stood near the door. He glanced at Rowe, who was uncharacteristically silent, then at Quinn and Hawkins, who entered from the yard.

Eden grated, "Curry . . ."

"That Comanche Chief, Leanin' Tree, is comin' to the fort to talk a peace treaty with Major Peters."

"I know that. What else? What message were you talkin' about?"

"That chief sent him a letter—written as clear as could be—sayin' that Iron Hawk was comin' with him to negotiate the peace."

Eden gasped. "He can't! They'll arrest him if he does!"

"No, they won't. That was one of the conditions the chief set, that Iron Hawk wouldn't be arrested if he did. The major agreed to it."

McGill took a spontaneous step forward. "What did Masters say?"

Curry shook his head. "What *didn't* he say? He was wild when he heard Iron Hawk was goin' to ride into that fort and then leave again, free as a bird!"

McGill pressed, "When are them Injuns supposed to arrive at the fort?"

"The chief said they'd be comin' at noon today."

The burly wrangler cursed, and Eden demanded, "What's the matter, McGill?"

McGill's full face flushed. "Masters and me tried trackin' you when Iron Hawk grabbed you, but it didn't work out. I came back here, but he's been hauntin' that fort for anythin' he could find out ever since. You know how Masters feels about you. And you know how he feels about Iron Hawk. He hates him! He told me he didn't care what it took, he'd get that Kiowa if it was the last thing he ever did."

Eden's blood ran cold. "What're you sayin'? He wouldn't try to kill Iron Hawk in front of the whole fort!"

McGill's expression said it all.

Eden raced toward the door.

Iron Hawk rode silently at Chief Leaning Tree's right. Yellow Dog and Gray Fox rode behind him, with White Horn, Running Antelope, and Swift Wolf at the chief's rear. Between them they represented the warriors of the camp who stood for peace, as well as those who had doubts.

The importance of the meeting weighed heavily on Iron Hawk's shoulders as they rode steadily forward. Lone Bear's image returned to mind, and Iron Hawk held it briefly there. He had once believed that he could fulfill his uncle's confidence in him only by spilling blood for blood, but he had come to a gradual awareness that he was wrong. Time had moved relentlessly forward, and with its passage had come a new wisdom that challenged the old. He knew, somehow, that if Lone Bear were there to observe all that had come to pass, he would be riding with them now.

Eden replaced Lone Bear's image unexpectedly in his mind, and Iron Hawk felt a surge of emotion only she could stir. Eden, whom he had been unable to cast from his heart. Eden, who made his life complete. She would return to him. She had promised she would. She would lie in his arms, forever his, and together they would go on.

The fort came into view and Eden's image faded. The iron bands on Iron Hawk's wrists seared his skin in solemn reminder as he urged his horse forward.

There he was!

Concealed behind carefully piled wooden crates, Masters peered out through a small breech in the fort wall. The bastard was there, riding as big and bold as life, right beside the Injun chief!

Rage shivered through Masters. Damn the bastard for his gall! He thought he was safe, because the weak-kneed major was so anxious to avoid conflict with the Injuns that he'd consent to anything.

Well, he was wrong.

Glancing around to make certain his concealed presence still went unnoticed, Masters picked up the rifle that lay beside him. His hands shaking, he caressed the barrel. He had tried everything to discover where that Kiowa bastard had hidden Eden. He had finally accepted that he would not find her unless Iron Hawk wanted her to be found. There was no telling what that savage had done to her and the boy. He had heard the stories of Injuns selling off their prisoners to other tribes so they would never be found. Some of them eventually were returned, but none of them were ever the same again.

Iron Hawk had drawn his blood. He had stolen Eden away from him. Now it was Iron Hawk's turn to pay!

Masters breathed deeply to brace himself, then raised his rifle to the slit in the wall. He focused.

A little closer. A few more minutes and it would be done.

Riding wildly, Eden pushed her mount to a faster pace. She glanced upward as the hot after-

noon sun reached its zenith. Hardly aware of
the men accompanying her—McGill, who had
not spoken a word when he mounted beside
her, and Quinn, who had followed silently in
their wake—she felt a rapid panic rising.

Time was growing short. Chief Leaning Tree
would arrive at the fort on time. It was a point
of honor that he would not ignore. They would
be riding into sight of the fort walls at any minute, and she—

Eden gasped as the fort came into view on the
horizon. She scanned the distance as her horse
pounded steadily closer. She saw several riders
advancing toward the fort from the opposite direction. She recognized Iron Hawk riding beside Chief Leaning Tree, with several others
behind them. She restrained the urge to shout—
to call out Iron Hawk's name, knowing he could
not hear her.

Digging her heels into her mount's sides, she
spurred him to a breakneck pace. Her heart
cried out to Iron Hawk. Stop! Don't ride any
closer!

But her silent cry went unheard as Iron Hawk
continued his steady advance.

He was getting closer. Another few yards . . .
Masters steadied his focus.
He took another deep breath.
He squeezed the trigger.

Eden heard a shot! Then another!
The sharp cracks of sound echoed in the still-

ness of the terrain as Iron Hawk's broad frame jerked with the impact of the bullets that struck him!

He swayed—

The first bullet thudded into Iron Hawk's chest with a fiery burst of pain. The second rocked him. It spun the world into a bright kaleidoscope of colors that formed Eden's face before he dropped heavily to the ground.

The bark of a rifle rang out from behind the fort walls. Incredulous when Iron Hawk swayed with the impact of the bullets, then fell to the ground, Major Peters looked at the far wall where two of his men dragged Masters out into the open, the gun still in his hand.

Peters glanced back to see chaos within the Indian delegation. They were preparing to flee!

Reacting spontaneously, Major Peters charged out through the fort gates on foot. With no thought of personal safety, he halted outside the gates in full view. He saw the chief turn back toward him. He saw rage in the man's eyes. Remaining steadfast, he raised his hand in a sign of peace.

Her mount laboring, Eden slid to a halt beside Iron Hawk's motionless frame. Sparing not a glance for the Indian warriors who had halted their rush to escape and remained staring at the fort gates in confusion, she jumped down from her horse and ran to Iron Hawk's side.

Iron Hawk was motionless, his eyes closed. Blood streamed from his chest.

Eden called out to McGill when he drew up behind her.

"Get a doctor! Get someone to help him!"

Leaning over Iron Hawk, Eden saw his lifeless color. She felt his shallow breaths against her lips as she rasped, "Iron Hawk, it's Eden! Open your eyes! Look at me!"

Laying her cheek against his when there was no response, Eden whispered into his ear, "Iron Hawk . . . please! You said we'd never be parted again. You *promised* me!"

Iron Hawk's eyelids flickered weakly. Eden held her breath as the lids parted to allow a glimpse of dark eyes beneath. She saw recognition there. She saw love.

And she saw pained regret in the moment before Iron Hawk went suddenly still.

Chapter Sixteen

The peace parley concluded.

Seated on opposite sides of a table carefully prepared in the fort mess hall, Chief Leaning Tree faced Major Peters, his expression sober. Equally solemn, Major Peters looked back at him, his hand resting on the paper in front of him on which the signatures had not yet dried.

Observing silently from a seat in the far corner, Eden was aware that Major Peters had turned the tide of a potentially disastrous situation with his spontaneous act of bravery two weeks earlier. By running out into the open alone to signal his dismay at the shooting and then promising that Masters would not go unpunished, he had brought the chief back to the fort to negotiate a truer, more confident peace.

Silent, Eden looked at the uniformed officers

on Major Peters's side of the table as Chief Leaning Tree prepared to speak. She saw respect in their gaze. She sensed those men had seen in Chief Leaning Tree's obvious devotion to his people—expressed so eloquently through the interpreter he had chosen—a nobility that they had not believed existed in their former adversaries. She saw that their attention did not waver as Chief Leaning Tree stood to speak a farewell in his native tongue.

"I, Chief Leaning Tree of the Comanche people, have signed my name to this certificate of peace. I will hold my people, and those of the Kiowa tribe who live among us, to all that has been agreed upon there. I look to the future when our people will live as one."

Major Peters looked at the interpreter who stood beside Chief Leaning Tree. Pride flushed Eden's skin with color as Iron Hawk translated the Comanche words in a voice deep with promise. She heard Major Peters's ardent response as the parley prepared to disperse.

Eden looked at Iron Hawk where he stood proud and strong again after his near brush with death. She remembered the endless hours she had spent at his bedside, breathing life back into him with the sheer power of her love. She allowed her gaze to linger on strong features that glowed again with health, although his wounds had not yet fully healed. Iron Hawk had an intrinsic nobility of bearing which could not be denied—one that had come to full fruition under circumstances that would have broken a lesser man. She joined him in the silent realization that they had taken a first step toward the dream they both shared, on a journey they would make with patience and love.

Eden remembered the moment when Iron Hawk signed the treaty in the name of his Kiowa brothers. She still trembled with joy, knowing that with the pardon that would soon be his, he would walk freely again where once he had feared chains.

The men filed from the room into the fort yard and Eden followed. She watched as Chief Leaning Tree's party mounted, Iron Hawk beside them. She was unprepared when Iron Hawk leaned down to swing her up onto his horse with a strength that belied the seriousness of his recent wounds. Her protest dwindled when she saw that Iron Hawk had ordered her mount secured so it would trail behind as they rode out through the fort gates.

Leaning back against the warm wall of Iron Hawk's chest, Eden looked up as they rode on, gradually separating from Chief Leaning Tree's party to turn in a familiar direction. She read in his eyes the answer to her unspoken question.

Eden shivered at the heat in his gaze as Iron Hawk brushed her mouth with his and whispered, "I've hungered for this moment, Eden. I yearned to claim you openly at last. That's what brought me back when my life was draining away—the sound of your voice and the realization that in losing my life, I'd lose you. I couldn't—I *wouldn't* let that happen, not again."

Pressing his smooth cheek against hers as their mount continued its steady forward pace, Iron Hawk said, "But I know it's not over. There's still your father."

A tremor shook Eden. She hadn't returned to the ranch since Iron Hawk was shot. She knew from McGill's report that Pa wouldn't last much longer, but she consoled herself that he was at peace with himself at last.

She responded simply, "My father's put his hatred to rest."

Eden felt Iron Hawk's brief hesitation before he said, "I need to tell Jimmy the truth."

Tell Jimmy the truth? How could she explain to Iron Hawk that their young son was not as much of a child as he believed him to be—that she sensed Jimmy had somehow known the truth all along?

Iron Hawk drew her closer. His strength enveloped her. His warmth filled her heart, and it was suddenly clear that however difficult the journey that had delivered them into each other's arms, it had been worth every step.

That truth glowed in Iron Hawk's eyes. It quavered in his voice as he rasped, "I love you, Eden."

His dark eyes singed her.

His tender words touched her heart.

Yes . . . they were forever hers.

TEXAS STAR
ELAINE BARBIERI

Buck Star is a handsome cad with a love-'em-and-leave-'em at-titude that broke more than one heart. But when he walks out on a beautiful New Orleans socialite, he sets into motion a chain of treachery and deceit that threatens to destroy the ranching empire he'd built and even the children he'd once hoped would inherit it. . . .

A mysterious message compells Caldwell Star to return to Lowell, Texas, after a nine-year absence. Back in Lowell, he meets a stubborn young widow who refuses his help, but needs it more than she can know. Her gentle touch and proud spirit give Cal strength to face the demons of the past, to reach out for a love that would heal his wounded soul.

RENEGADE MOON
ELAINE BARBIERI

Somewhere in the lush grasslands of the Texas hill country, three brothers and a sister fight to hold their family together, struggle to keep their ranch solvent, while they await the return of the one person who can shed light on the secrets of the past.

No sooner has he rescued spitfire Glory Townsend from deadly quicksand than Quince finds himself trapped in a quagmire of emotions far more difficult to escape. Every time he looks into her flashing green eyes he feels himself sinking deeper. Maybe it is time to stop struggling and admit that only her love can save him.

BRAZEN
BOBBI SMITH

Casey Turner can rope and ride like any man, but when she strides down the streets of Hard Luck, Texas, nobody takes her for anything but a beautiful woman. Working alongside her Pa to keep the bank from foreclosing on the Bar T, she has no time for romance. But all that is about to change....

Michael Donovan has had a burr under his saddle about Casey for years. The last thing he wants is to be forced into marrying the little hoyden, but it looks like he has no choice if he wants to safeguard the future of the Donovan ranch. He'll do his darndest, but he can never let on that underneath her pretty new dresses Casey is as wild as ever, and in his arms she is positively...*BRAZEN.*

Tall, Dark & Hungry
Lynsay Sands

It bites: New York hotels cost an arm and a leg, and Terri has flown from England to help plan her cousin's wedding. The new in-laws offered lodging. But they're a weird bunch! There is the sometimes-chipper-sometimes-silent Lucern, and the wacky stage-actor Vincent: she can't imagine Broadway casting a hungrier singing-and-dancing Dracula. And then there is Bastien. Just looking into his eyes, Terri has to admit she's falling for someone even taller, darker, and hungrier. She's feeling a mite peckish herself. And if she stays with him, those blood-sucking hotel owners won't get her!

CONNIE MASON

The Last Rogue

All London is stunned by Lucas, Viscount Westmore's vow to give up the fair sex and exile himself to St. Ives. The infamous rake is known for his love of luxury and his way with the ladies, just as the rugged Cornish coast is known for its savagery, its fearsome gales and its smugglers.

But Luc is determined to turn away from the seduction of white thighs and perfumed flesh that had once ended in tragedy. He never guessed the stormy nights of Cornwall would bring unlooked-for danger, the thrill of the chase, and a long-legged beauty who tempts him like no other. As illicit cargo changes hands, as her flashing green eyes challenge his very masculinity, he longs for nothing so much as to lose himself in . . . *Bliss.*

Crosswinds
CINDY HOLBY

Ty – He is honor-bound to defend the land of his fathers, even if battle takes him from the arms of the woman he pledged himself to protect.

Cole – A Texas Ranger, he thinks the conflict will pass him by until he has the chance to capture the fugitive who'd sold so many innocent girls into prostitution.

Jenny – She vows she will no longer run from the demons of the past, and if that means confronting Wade Bishop in a New York prisoner-of-war camp, so be it. No matter how far she must travel from those she holds dear, she will draw courage from the legacy of love her parents had begun so long ago.

Sandra Hill

A Tale of
Two Vikings

Toste and Vagn Ivarsson are identical Viking twins. They came squalling into this world together, rode their first horses at the age of seven, their first maids during their thirteenth summer, and rode off on longships as untried fourteen-year-old warriors. And now they are about to face Valhalla together. Or maybe something even more tragic: being separated. For even the most virile Viking must eventually leave his best buddy behind and do battle with that most fearsome of all opponents—the love of his life.

SNOW FIRE

NORAH HESS

She is lost. Blinded by the swirling storm, Flame knows that she cannot give up if she is to survive. Her memory gone, the lovely firebrand awakes to find that the strong arms encircling her belong to a devilishly handsome stranger. And one look at his blazing eyes tells her that the haven she has found promises a passion that will burn for a lifetime. She is the most lovely thing he has ever seen. From the moment he takes Flame in his arms and gazes into her sparkling eyes, Stone knows that the red-headed virgin has captured his heart. The very sight of her smile stokes fiery desires in him that only her touch can extinguish. To protect her he'll claim her as his wife, and pray that he can win her heart before she discovers the truth.

___4691-1 $5.99 US/$6.99 CAN

WHITE
SHADOWS
SUSAN EDWARDS

For years after his family was massacred, the half-breed Night Shadow harbored black dreams of vengeance—and the hope of someday finding his kidnapped younger sister. Now is the chance. His enemy shows himself and is to be wed. It should be a simple maneuver to steal the man's bride-to-be, to ride off with the beautiful Winona and reveal the monster she is supposed to marry.

But it is *not* simple. Winona is not convinced. Even the burgeoning desire Night Shadow sees in her eyes has not convinced the Sioux beauty of her betrothed's evil. Can love be born of revenge? There seems but one way to find out: Take Winona into the darkness and pray that, somehow, he and she can find their way to the light.